RAJA AND THE TRUNK OF ANTOM

VOLUME II

Wings of Strength !!

Avah Broc

AVAH BROC

Suite 300 - 990 Fort St
Victoria, BC, V8V 3K2
Canada

www.friesenpress.com

First Edition — 2020

ISBN
978-1-5255-6006-4 (Hardcover)
978-1-5255-6007-1 (Paperback)
978-1-5255-6008-8 (eBook)

1. *Fiction, Fantasy, Historical*

Distributed to the trade by The Ingram Book Company

LAND OF ROUSSE
WSYRUT
SKYEP SEA
STRAIT OF THE GOLDEN SUN
YURX ISLAND
PORT SOLIS
LARCHWOOD TRIBUTARY
SAP TRIBUTARY
NORTH VEL SACA
VOLGA RIVER
THRUMB
ODYHUN
PAVEL'S ESTATE
YURPHYN RIVER
KAZANKA RIVER
ZURKIA (PLOTRIA REGION)
BOLGER
ZURKIA (MONTIA REGION)
PORT ALEXANDRA
DESERT
VICTORY MANOR
KAZAN
VOLGA RIVER
ZURKIA (TRUMIA REGION)
VOZANE RIVER
DEMARCUS
MARSH
DRACON
VALETTA
SUBTRADE
PORT TUCKIN
SOUTH VEL SACA
YURPHYN RIVER
FETHERLAND
DESERT
PORT CAPHANNE
DESERT
KULALY ISLAND
BAKU
KHVALYN SEA
N
W
E
S

Table of Contents

Part I

Three Thrones

Chapter I

The Intruder

"I'm worried about your father trying to retake this castle," said Hannah's lady-in-waiting, who was braiding Hannah's hair for the night. The two of them were alone inside Hannah's large chamber of Bolger Castle, discussing the events surrounding the reign of the Zurkian throne.

"And rightly so," said Hannah. "My father's actions of putting his sister in the Kazan dungeon shows his insatiable lust for power and it is very possible that he will continue to pursue the possession of her throne."

"An unthinkable action of your father against his sister."

Although unintended, the remark was as good as a battle-weary knife scraping the surface of her skin. She wanted a father who was thought of as honorable, not unjust. But this was not on the horizon. She hoped he would stay away from southern Zurkia now that Viktor had defeated him in the *Battle of Orsus*.

"I don't think Viktor's threats will be enough to deter him," said the lady-in-waiting, who was known as Savy. "He has more than once spoken to me about how nothing will stop him from taking the throne."

That was true. Hannah knew her father to be very determined. There was something that continually drove him to that evil. "I do agree it is probable that my father will try and regain the throne, but there is a chance he may not want to come back to Bolger Castle."

But Hannah's lady-in-waiting did not want to rule out the possibility of the Dark Prince's return. "I think having this castle along the Kazanka River was very convenient for him. It is close to Kazan and an easy route to travel north along the river. I also know that he spent many hours looking down onto the river from his chamber—a pleasure that he might not want to give up."

"Yes, the castle is very unique and the view from on top of the plateau is magnificent."

Savy nodded. "And the natural pillar the castle stands on is an excellent defense."

Hannah agreed. The castle was naturally defended by the chasm between the pillar and the land. "True, no one could ever attack from the east side. But on the other hand, he may feel the benefits are greater with his present location in the northern part of Zurkia. He would not have to travel as much to carry out his project and it would save him a lot of time."

"Do you know anything about his project?" asked the lady-in-waiting, who was now working at the end of the long braid.

"No, that is one thing he had never discussed with me, although he kept saying that the time to reveal his intentions to me were soon. But I know for sure it was to do with gaining power and control over Zurkia."

Savy quickly worked her fingers to finish the last part of the braid, which had gradually narrowed to three thin strands of hair. "Your father also employed a good deal of legionnaires from Odyhun to help him in those efforts."

Hannah handed Savy the ties for her hair. "Yes, he also talked of one day ruling the whole of the Land of Rousse."

"A devious plan indeed. And we must remember any legionnaires that remained here may still have alliances with him. This could pose a danger for us at this castle."

Hannah knew that Savy's reasoning seemed very plausible. All of the Tyhets had followed her father's retreat to the north, but only a few legionnaires had gone. And even though the tzarina had made every legionnaire in Bolger Castle swear allegiance to her, there could be those who had chosen to be traitors to the throne and agents of her father.

"I can see that we have no way of really knowing where the legionnaires stand," said Hannah. "Do you have any suggestions?"

"I think it's important for you to have more protection," said the lady-in-waiting. "Even if your father decides to leave Bolger alone, he may still come after you."

"But do you think my father would still want me to rule with him after I betrayed him in the battle?"

"It is very possible. He has a strong will and he may not give up on convincing you, as his daughter, to join him. And there is no telling how he might do that."

"I am not so sure he would actually do that. He was very angry with my actions."

Halfway through a second braid, Hannah's maid replied in a more serious tone. "Yes, he was, but remember, you are still his flesh and blood. He will not want to let that go."

Hannah thought about the feelings her father might have toward her. "What sort of protection are you suggesting?"

Savy stopped working with Hannah's hair and looked at the princess's reflection in the mirror. "Spies from the tzarina."

The two women's eyes met.

"How else will we know the deceptions of the legionnaires?" asked Savy.

"I can see that may be the only way to know the truth of their hearts. Tomorrow we will draw up a letter and seal it. The letter will be sent by . . ."

Hannah did not have time to finish her sentence. She froze as she stared at the reflection of a person in the mirror. A man with a head covering that hid most of his face had suddenly burst into the room. His dark red robe was held in place by a black sash with a sword by his side.

Savy gasped and the two women turned to face the intruder. He looked straight into Hannah's face.

"Come with me," he said.

"Who are you?" asked Hannah.

"I am your father's ambassador."

"I will not come with you! Leave at once! You are not allowed in my chamber!"

"My orders are to bring you to your father!"

The man walked toward Hannah. Savy rose to confront him. The intruder pushed her aside and she fell to the floor.

Hannah ran behind a wall curtain. She quickly escaped through a narrow passageway that led behind the wall. The intruder would never be able to follow her, as only a person her size was able to fit into the passageway. It had been built solely for the protection of female royalty and Hannah knew every other secret access in the castle.

The passageway led Hannah into a narrow corridor. She began to run down the corridor and thought she was free to make her escape, but she was stopped by the sound of hurried footsteps coming towards her from the other end of the long corridor. A dim light bounced back and forth with each hurried step. A man's voice trailed down the hallway.

"Show yourself at once! We must talk!"

Hannah quickly squeezed into a nearby alcove inside the wall, hoping the intruder wouldn't see her in the dark. She wondered how her pursuer could have found her so quickly. The footsteps slowed to a walk.

"I know you are there. I'm not here to harm you."

A few moments of silence passed, except for the approaching footsteps. Hannah's heart beat wildly. The man began speaking in a stern, deep voice.

"Your father wants you to come rule with him."

Hannah shuddered at that thought. She would never rule with him. What he really wanted was the throne of Zurkia and he was using evil to get it.

"Your father is setting up his own kingdom in the north. He will be a great ruler and you can sit upon the throne beside him. Everything will be yours."

Hannah wanted to stop breathing as the voice came closer. The voice sounded familiar.

"You cannot stay here. His army will eventually take back Bolger Castle. It is rightfully his."

Her father may have once lived in Bolger Castle, but the evil he had done to take over Zurkia's throne and the war he had caused had pushed him out to the north with orders to never return. His life had been spared because he was her father, and for no other reason.

"And you know the repossession of Bolger will happen," said the intruder. "You cannot win. Give up. Come with me and you will be safe. Otherwise you will perish in the battle."

The intruder now stood an arm's length from where Hannah was hiding. She couldn't hold her breath any longer. But she feared if she made just the slightest sound he would hear her and then it would be all over. She would be in his clutches and forced to go with him.

Relief took hold of Hannah as the figure moved past her. This was her chance. She turned behind him and ran down the corridor to where she knew she could escape.

The intruder quickly caught up with Hannah and she knew she would be overtaken. Her only hope of escape was to face the intruder. She stopped, pulled out her sword, and screamed, "Halt—or I shall kill you."

The intruder stopped. "Ah, you are quick. But I don't think you want to kill me."

Hannah's hand trembled as she held out her sword. "I swear, move any closer and you will die."

"Come now. We can talk about this. Your father wants you back."

"Never! I will never go back to him!"

"Don't you love him?"

Hannah didn't know how to answer.

"If you love your father you'll go back to him."

"No!" shouted Hannah. "It doesn't mean that!"

"You love him, don't you?"

"Yes, but what he has done is wrong. I'm not a part of that anymore."

The man stepped closer. Hannah backed away. "I mean it! Stay away. Come any closer and I will kill you!"

The man stopped. "He only wants the best for you. He was meant to rule. He is a good ruler."

"He is not!" said Hannah with authority. "Leave now! Get out of this castle!"

The man made no indication that he would leave. He kept on talking in a low convincing voice.

"And he wants you to rule. Don't you want that? You can rule with him."

"No!" shouted Hannah.

"It would be just what you want, riches, power, everything you could imagine."

"That is not what I want!"

"Look at me," said the intruder. "You know me."

The intruder's hand brought the light closer to his face. His eyes were dark and scary. Their familiarity rattled her nerves.

"You can never escape me and I will fulfill your father's orders."

He took another step closer to her.

"Stop!" shouted Hannah.

The intruder came closer. He spoke in a slow, controlled voice. "Put your sword down, Hannah. If you don't, you will regret your actions."

Hannah did not listen to the intruder. In an instant she raised her sword to his face and swiped. She knew she had cut his skin.

The man let out a low guttural cry as he raised his hand to his bloody wound.

For a moment she stood still, feeling paralyzed. Her mind screamed, telling her to run. She turned and escaped down the corridor and through an arched doorway.

The surprise attack stunned the man and Hannah gained a good distance ahead of him. She ran down a flight of stairs and down two more corridors. She reached a secret escape route that went underneath the wall of the castle. She took away some stones in the floor and climbed down into the tunnel. She hurried along the underground tunnel with her hands tracing the side of the cold rough walls. She came to the end of a passageway near the stables and climbed out of the wet and slippery incline. She had to get far away. She knew she couldn't stay in the castle. It wouldn't be safe for her.

Other horses were kept in the distant stables, but her horse was always kept in the castle stables and ready to ride at any time. Just that day it had been let out to graze in the pastures around the castle, and so now it would be full of energy. She grabbed her bow and quiver along with a bag of dried food. The items were always kept in the stall in case she ever needed to escape the castle. Hannah mounted and rode out onto the winding path, over the chasm that led away from the castle. She rode past the stables and then the sleeping village. The full moon cast enough light that she could still see where she was going.

She questioned whether she was doing the right thing. Was she just overreacting? Should she have stayed until the guards captured the intruder? But if he was who she thought he was, then yes, she had done the right thing. The guards would never have captured him and she knew why.

Hannah kept looking over her shoulder to see if she was being followed. Once she thought there was a rider chasing her, but it had only been the shadows. She kept going along the Fedoran Trail towards Kazan. She galloped off and on throughout the next day, past Port Alexandra and on down the Volga River. She only slept a bit during the nights. She would do that for the next few days and finally she would be there.

Chapter 2

Disappearances

The manor had become quite a bit larger than it once was and everyone was now used to calling it Victory Manor, a name that Raja had chosen. In a way, Raja missed the more relaxed way of life she had known when it was smaller. There had been fewer guards, and the rules hadn't seemed so strict. But, nonetheless, she had been living here for three years now, and she tried very hard to accept that living in a large manor went along with being a princess. It was part of her duty. But she couldn't shake some of the better memories of being a peasant for the first thirteen years of her life, like sitting around the bonfires or playing games while picking berries.

Raja hadn't remembered she had been abducted as a very young child. Her peasant parents had just been real parents to her. And still were. They would always be that way to her. But she had also grown to love her birth mother, the Tzarina of Zurkia.

It had been hard to say farewell to her after spending the winter at Kazan Castle, although she looked forward to seeing everyone at the manor. But she also knew that in time she would not have the opportunity to leave again and would have to stay in Kazan to rule with her mother. Raja fully accepted this and was grateful for the present leniencies as they were.

Knowing that she wasn't supposed to, once in a while Raja still snuck down to the village, now called the Manor Village, to give the peasants gifts of food. And now was one of those times. She steadied herself as she lowered herself down the side of the manor with a rope. Being very sure of her footing came with the numerous times she had scaled the side of the wall.

From her window, Raja had seen the huge bonfire rising from within the village. The flames seemed extra tall with large swirling tips shooting into the air, surely kissing the stars. On this evening in particular, the sight conjured feelings from the past of how she had enjoyed sitting by the fire's warmth, staring into its brightness and taking in the festivities surrounding it. Back then she was just a peasant, with no extraordinary expectations and threats on her life. Even though her life had been hard in different ways, she missed its carefree simplicity. She couldn't help herself from wanting to know what that felt like once more. Her plan was to find Alma and sit with her by the fire.

Raja reached the end of her decline down the side of the castle, grateful she didn't have to swim across the moat. She had made sure there was a raft situated under the hanging rope. Lowering herself, her feet barely touched the top of the raft. She let go of the rope and quickly knelt down. Using a flat piece of wood, she paddled across the gully. Lifting her skirts, she slid off the raft and stood on the edge of the moat, knee deep in water. She secured the raft and climbed up the bank.

Hurrying towards the village, Raja heard only the soft padding of her feet along the path and the crickets chirping, which seemed to cheer her on. She kept looking around to see if anyone had followed her. This was precisely the reason why her going out at night was not allowed. But, there was no one. Instead of guilt, she felt proud she was managing to make this quest once again, and, as always, she justified it with bringing food gifts. Of course, gifts were allowed for the peasants, but Viktor said going out at night was dangerous. Not because of wolves, but because of unwanted human intruders. She had spent a good two years escaping from kidnappers and so Viktor was right. But Raja was as much a risk taker as ever. Maybe her daring spirit was kept alive by the thought that if she were to be the tzarina one day, then somehow she would be protected from evil, even though others who wanted the throne would do anything to get it.

Raja felt a little more justified in making this particular trip because she also had another very special gift. It was made by the hands of her peasant mother. She could hardly wait to give it to Alma Kedves, whom she had developed a good friendship with. Alma lived by herself in the village and Raja was sure that tonight she would be by the fire with everyone else.

Coming to the outskirts of the village, she pulled her dark hood further down. She didn't want anyone to recognize her, as attention was not what she wanted this evening. The bonfire grew bigger with each step as she neared the festivities. Finally, reaching the gathering, she looked at the place where Alma usually sat. Someone else was sitting there instead. Raja looked around for the woman but couldn't see her. Alma was not hard to recognize, as she was the only woman who was constantly mending something for someone else. But she was not at the bonfire.

Raja hurried towards Alma's hut, hoping she would find her there. Standing at the door, she pushed it open a bit.

"Alma, are you here?"

The middle-aged woman came to the door.

"Shhh," she said.

"What's going on?" asked Raja.

"Nothing."

Raja looked over her head and saw that there was someone else in the hut. "Who's that person?"

"Shhh," said Alma. "She's sleeping. She came a long distance and was very tired."

"From where?"

"I don't know. She could hardly speak when she arrived and fell asleep instantly."

The girl's face was hidden, so Raja had no idea who she was. She didn't want to wake the person and so left her alone.

"I brought you some cheese," said Raja.

"Thank you, but you shouldn't have."

"Yes, I should have."

Raja took off her own cloak. Alma's eyes widened. Underneath, Raja was wearing a beautifully made, red woolen garment with red stitched roses outlined in black stitching. It even had a large pocket, an invention by Yana. "Oh, that's beautiful. Wherever did you get that?"

"Yana made it from sheep's wool purchased at the Kazan bazaar."

Raja undid the clasp by her neck and took off the red cloak. She put it over the shoulders of Alma. The red brought out the bit of pink in Alma's face.

"It's yours," said Raja.

"Mine! No, that can't be!"

"Yes, please accept it. It's a gift for you. You do so many things for others it's time you received something for yourself."

Alma's eyes grew wet with tears. "I don't know what to say. I'm so very grateful."

"That is all you need to say. You are welcome."

Alma turned around in a circle with her arms out.

"It fits you perfectly," said Raja.

"My other one is torn, so it has come at just the right time."

"Wear it with pride then."

"I shall," said Alma with a smile that showed nothing but genuine love.

Becoming more serious, Raja asked, "How is everything in the village?"

Alma's face darkened. She held back answering the question. Recently rumors had made their way to the castle that something was dreadfully wrong in the village. So far, the rumors of missing peasants had not been taken seriously. Not that Viktor was uncaring, but reports of such were not an uncommon thing. Later, the missing people would be found in another village, having left on their own, usually because they had gotten into some sort of trouble with the other villagers or they were just trying to find a better life as a free peasant with no obligations to anyone but themselves. However, Raja wanted to hear the reports for herself.

"Please Alma, tell me what's wrong. You can trust me."

Alma knew she could trust Raja, but she was still afraid to say anything.

"I can't help if I don't know," said Raja. "Please say what you know."

Raja reached out and held Alma's hand. It seemed to quiet Alma's fears and she began to confess what she knew. But she couldn't look into Raja's eyes for shame. "Two more peasants have gone missing during the night. And some of the free peasants who usually come and go from the village haven't been seen either."

Raja held her hand to her mouth. "That's terrible."

The fact that the free peasants were also missing made the situation sound more serious.

Alma managed to look into Raja's face with humiliation. "Yes, it is."

Raja understood Alma's humiliation over her type of people being exploited. It made her angry to know that this was happening. "Alma, I will get to the bottom of this."

Alma's eyes were pleading and her face fearful. "No! You mustn't tell anyone else."

"For heaven's sake, why not?"

"I can't tell you."

"But you must."

"Please, I'm afraid to tell you. You don't understand."

"You've come this far. Go all the way," said Raja.

Alma was silent.

"Alma, you have to do this so that I can understand or more peasants will disappear."

Raja could see that she was convincing her friend.

"Someone was threatened," said Alma.

"And," said Raja, trying to coax more information from her.

In a whisper, Alma continued. "The person said if anyone reported the abductions they would be taken next."

"Do you believe that?"

"I don't know."

"It is only meant to scare people into being silent. The only way to stop this is for you to tell me," said Raja.

The girl lying on the ground stirred. Raja and Alma lowered their voices.

"I will tell Pavel about this and we will stop these abductions," whispered Raja.

"Please, don't say who told you this," said Alma with a quiver in her voice.

"I won't, but don't worry, the intruders have no way of knowing. The threatening words were only said to intimidate you."

Alma's body relaxed. "Okay, I trust you," she whispered, putting her hand on Raja's shoulder.

Raja put her hand on Alma's hand and said in a serious manner, "I will see to it that no harm comes to you."

Alma nodded and then gave the princess a few more details about the abductions.

Finally, Raja looked at the sleeping girl. "How long has she been sleeping there?"

"Since noon. She may wake soon."

The girl stirred again and rolled over, facing Raja. The two girls' eyes met.

"Hannah?" said Raja.

"You know this girl?" asked Alma.

"Yes, she's my—"

Hannah interrupted. "Shhh."

"It's okay," said Raja. "Alma already knows about us."

"Is this your cousin you've told me about?" asked Alma.

"Yes," said Raja.

Hannah sat up and took the hood from off her head.

Alma smiled. "Well I wouldn't have had to ask about you being cousins, now that I can see her face properly. You two really look alike."

"Yes, we do, but Hannah's hair has gotten a bit darker than mine and I've grown a bit taller than she has."

"And I see that Hannah's eyes are a darker hazel than yours," said Alma, who was inspecting the both of them.

Hannah stood up to look at Raja's eyes to see how true the statement was. "Yes, I think you're right," she said.

Raja gave Hannah a questioning look. "Why in all the land are you here, Hannah? Not that I don't want to see you, but this is a surprise. Aren't you now the Princess of Bolger, and supposed to rule the castle?"

"Yes of course, but something dreadful happened and I had to escape."

"Tell us," said Raja.

The three of them sat down on a straw mat, but before Hannah said anything she looked again at Alma and then at Raja.

"Don't worry. She's safe," said Raja. "You can trust her."

Hannah began to cxplain her horrifying experience of how someone invaded her chamber and how she escaped through the secret corridors.

Raja eyes widened. "Did the guards capture the intruder?"

"I don't know," said Hannah. "My lady-in-waiting thinks that the legionnaires are still in alliance with my father, so that would have made it easier for him to escape. But if the intruder is who I suspect, then any of the trustworthy guards would have had very little chance of capturing him."

"Who do you think he is?" asked Raja.

"The Grand Padesha."

"No!" said Raja. "That means he survived your arrow in the battle."

Hannah nodded slowly with a serious look in her eyes. "And as far as I know, he and my father are the only other people right now who know every escape route and hideaway inside the castle."

"I see," said Raja. "So not even the guards know about the hidden routes."

"That's right. The escape routes have always been kept secret. The family of the tzarina's stepmother once ruled the castle. Its secrets have been passed on to only the royalty of the castle, which was my father. But I know he entrusted the secrets to the padesha on account of their alliances with their evil practices."

Raja stared at Hannah while she talked, beginning to put the pieces together. Her cousin's next sentence proved her assumptions correct.

"My father wants me back."

But that was the last thing Raja wanted to happen to her cousin. A tight knot sat in Raja's stomach at the thought of Hannah back with her father. "You've made the right decision to come here."

"But I can't stay here forever," said Hannah.

Raja's voice was firm. "Of course not, but something will have to be done first."

Alma looked into Hannah's face with furrowed brows.

"What about your father?" asked Alma.

Hannah sighed. "My father is not a good man. He is in pursuit of the Zurkian throne and wants me to rule with him. He's known as the Dark Prince."

"I'm sorry to hear that," said Alma.

Indeed, Hannah missed having a father she would consider honorable. She wanted things back the way they used to be, when she was a young child. Hannah didn't know exactly when it had all changed. Slowly, she guessed, over time. He just became more and more obsessed with evil practices. He didn't even seem like her father any more.

Wanting to be sympathetic with Hannah, Alma spoke in a tender tone. "It must be difficult to have a father with such a name."

Hannah rubbed her forehead. Although Alma meant well, the words were like a handful of pebbles hitting her head. Raja could see the stress on her face and wanted to change the topic. "So what is it like being the Princess of Bolger Castle?"

Hannah took her hand away from her face and looked at Raja. "Splendid, except for this last occurrence. And how do you like being a princess in a manor?"

"Fine, very fine," said Raja.

"I'm taking it that you chose the name of the manor," said Hannah, becoming more interested in this new topic.

"Yes, in honor of Viktor."

Hannah smiled at Raja. "I'm impressed with the name Victory Manor, but I thought it would have been Pavel Manor."

"A nice idea," said Raja, returning the smile, "but his name is being used for his own estate."

"So Pavel Castle?"

"No, it's called Levap Castle by my suggestion."

"Levap? What kind of a name is that?"

"It's Pavel spelled backwards."

"Ah, I see. I think you're in love!"

"I am not!"

"Are you sure?" asked Hannah with a teasing smile.

"No, it's just a good name, that's all."

"Levap Castle—the name does sound nice," said Hannah.

Alma smiled and then started to laugh with Raja and Hannah joining in.

"Excuse me for laughing," said Alma. "It is a good name. It is just funny how Hannah accused you of being in love because of the backwards spelling."

"Can I say?" asked Hannah.

"She already knows about the backwards code," said Raja. "But it's only a word, and not based on feelings."

Hannah wanted to argue the point but Alma cut in. "Raja, don't you think you should be getting back to the manor?"

"Yes, time has run out." Raja looked at Hannah. "I'm glad no harm came to you and you made it here safely. Pavel will come by tomorrow morning to get you."

Hannah nodded. Raja stood to say goodbye to Alma and Hannah.

"Wait," said Hannah.

"What is it?"

"We haven't seen each other in a long time. Now that we are together, let's practice our secret code, the one we used after you were rescued from Dracon."

"That's a good idea," said Raja, looking at Alma for support. "Do you think I have a little more time?"

"I can't say," said Alma. "But I'm sure what you're doing will be for a good cause."

Alma set out more candles and lit them, saying that they needed more light for the practice session. Alma then sat next to the girls and watched in fascination as the two girls practiced their code.

Hannah held up a number of fingers. "What time does this mean?" she asked.

Raja counted and responded.

"Right!"

Alma was given a turn to practice and she also proved to be very successful in giving the correct answers.

Raja noticed the number of candles lit in the hut.

"It looks like your candle business is going well," said Raja.

"Yes, thanks to Antom's help in building me a lot of bee houses for the wax. He showed me how to harvest the honey and I sell both products at the Kazan bazaar."

"That's very ambitious," said Raja.

"Thank you. I enjoy it. The other peasants enjoy working for me as well. Everyone who helps profits from the business."

"I wish you the best," said Raja. Alma politely acknowledged her blessing.

After a bit more conversation, Raja made her way back to the manor.

Chapter 3

The Tzarina's Disclosure

Hannah covered her face with a niqab and galloped alongside Pavel up to Victory Manor. She wanted no one to know of her whereabouts. The servants lowered the drawbridge and Hannah and Pavel rode into the large courtyard. Their horses were quickly taken away to the outer court and Hannah and Pavel entered the agreed upon meeting place. Once inside Yana and Antom's small house, which was situated in the courtyard, they saw that Raja and her parents were already sitting around the small fireplace in the middle of the room drinking tea. Pavel and Hannah joined them while Yana offered a cup of tea to both of them.

Now that everyone was present, Raja spoke first to her peasant parents. "Swear that you tell no one about our meeting. No one must know about Hannah, as her father is looking for her."

"You can count on us to keep it secret," said Yana.

Antom nodded in agreement.

"Last night, Alma told me that two more peasants were taken," said Raja.

"Did Alma say anything else about it?" asked Pavel.

"It happens at night and the kidnappers wear peasant clothing."

"Anything else?"

"Tracks were discovered heading north."

"Hannah, do you have any suspicions on this?" asked Pavel.

"Only that the same thing has happened at Bolger Castle."

"How long has this been going on?" asked Pavel.

"Not that long. At first I thought the peasants were leaving on their own accord, but now that doesn't seem to be the case."

"Do you think the Tyhets of the north are responsible?" asked Raja. "The same group who kidnapped me?"

"Who else would it be?" said Pavel. "We've got to put a stop to this."

"But we don't know that for sure," said Hannah. "We should find out first."

"How?" asked Pavel.

Staring at the fire, everyone was silent. Antom and Yana were solemn during the conversation. They were not going to be the ones to suggest a plan for Hannah's idea.

Finally, Hannah spoke up. "I'm wondering if anyone is thinking the same thing I am."

"Which is what?" asked Pavel.

"We go north ourselves."

"That's a dangerous idea," said Antom, getting up from the fire. "They've probably got spies posted everywhere."

"It's not dangerous if we're smart about it," said Hannah.

"I agree with Hannah. The only way to stop this is to first find out what's going on," said Raja. "Don't you agree, Pavel?"

Raja, Hannah, and Yana all stared at Pavel. Their actions seemed to put the right amount of pressure on him. "Me? Ah . . . of course I agree. What do you think? I'm the man."

"What's that supposed to mean?" asked Raja.

"Oh, nothing more than you might need a bit of protection."

"Well now, don't you think Hannah and I can protect ourselves?" said Raja with a bit of an air.

"Hey, I didn't mean that you couldn't. It's just that three are better than two," said Pavel, trying to get out of his blunder. "Don't get me wrong. You two are very self-reliant."

"Thanks," said Raja. "I knew you would see it our way."

"I can see that you two are determined to go north and I definitely wouldn't stay behind to miss the excitement."

Pavel pulled out a rolled scroll from his pouch. "This came from the bailiff yesterday and it's for you, Raja. Would you like me to read it?"

"Please."

Pavel unrolled the scroll and read the contents.

To the Kind and Generous Princess Raja,

I am writing to disclose some important findings. It has been discovered that Shamra is your cousin. I never got to know Shamra's aunt because they lived with my stepmother in Marsh Castle along the shores of the Khualyn Sea. Shamra's aunt is my stepmother's daughter.

I found out that the Tyhets had abducted Shamra's mother, but her children were previously hidden at the home of their mother's sister, which is Shamra and Fedor's aunt. The aunt had previously left the lineage and lived in the village to conceal her identity because of trouble in the family.

Upon discovering this news and in light of the fact that Shamra displays great ability, I have decided to make Shamra Princess of Levap Castle. I realize that Pavel owns the estate, but the castle needs to be occupied and protected. I am sure Pavel will not only understand this, but will be grateful for the servants and military I am providing for him. All profits from making clay pottery at the castle will still go to Pavel. For safety, Shamra will reside in the castle of the estate, instead of the manor. This ruling shall commence in short order.

And just as a further note, Shamra has had training in swordsmanship and has progressed very well. Please visit her and practice this skill with her. But please do not go to the castle without sending a letter beforehand stating your intentions.

Your loving Tzarina Mother Valentina, who reminds you to always persist in all circumstances

"Amazing and dreadful at the same time," said Raja.

"I should say," said Hannah.

"I certainly didn't know my mother had stepsisters. Did you know this, Hannah?"

"Not precisely, and from the letter it appears that Shamra's aunt is your mother's stepsister."

"Yes, I should think you are right," said Raja. "Very amazing news."

"Having Shamra as our cousin will work out very well," said Hannah. "Especially now that she has been made a princess."

"Exactly, and on our way north we can stop at her castle and at the same time celebrate her being a princess," said Raja. "What do you think of this, Pavel?"

"Very generous of the tzarina to take interest in my castle. I would be delighted to meet Shamra there."

"Good," said Hannah. "And while we are there we can brush up on our sword fighting skills. Imagine us three cousins playing swords."

"What fun!" said Raja.

"I suddenly feel outnumbered," said Pavel.

"Come now, you like that, don't you?" asked Raja with a twinkle in her eye. "Three girls?"

"Well, yes, I do like it. I couldn't think of better company, but with swords?" Pavel crossed his arms and smiled.

"We play safe," said Hannah. "And we'll be keeping you on your toes with our jokes."

"You're not worried, are you?" asked Raja.

"A little," said Pavel, who tried to look worried.

"You're a good actor," said Raja. "Relax. We won't be too hard on you."

Antom and Yana finally managed a little smile.

"You be good, Raja, and don't give Pavel a hard time," said Antom.

"Of course not, Father," said Raja with a respectful smile.

"Are you sure you want to go through with this, Pavel? You know Raja always seems to get into trouble," said Yana, who felt a bit uneasy about the whole thing.

"That's exactly why I have to go," said Pavel. "She'll need me to keep an eye on her so she won't get kidnapped again."

"And how was that my fault?" asked Raja.

"Only joking," said Pavel.

"It's good you can joke about it," said Hannah, trying to lighten the conversation again.

"Joking is good," said Pavel.

"Well, in that case, I've got one," said Hannah. "Who is strong enough to pick up a castle and move it?"

No one said anything and they shrugged their shoulders.

"Give up?"

Everyone nodded.

"A chess player."

"Oh, you are smart," said Raja and laughed with the others at the witty joke.

Still thinking about the previous conversation, Antom spoke again.

"I think you may want to hear this," he said. "Yana, Raja, and I used to live with the Tyhets."

"What!" said Raja.

"It's true. When you were given to us at the age of three, we lived in Lord Lythym's village, but then we were forced to move to a Tyhet village, called Thrumb Village. But wc only stayed there for a short while and then came here."

"What was it like?" asked Pavel.

"Isolated. There wasn't any contact from anywhere else and the Tyhets were cruel. They made us work harder than in our other village. And the peasants did not trust each other."

"Why was that?"

"The Tyhets encouraged the peasants to report anything they saw that was out of the ordinary in the village. If they reported something they were rewarded with extra food. There were even a few chosen people that would routinely check each hut."

"What types of things did they report?"

"It could have been anything. Someone not working, paper and ink, stealing, or a stranger."

"I imagine you felt glad when you left the Tyhet village," said Pavel.

"Very relieved. The curfews were stifling. No men were ever allowed to walk around during the evening for fear of them starting any sort of rebellion. Occasionally there were women seen who might be helping with someone sick, bringing someone food, or helping in childbirth."

"Do you know why you were moved to Manor Village?" Pavel could see that was a difficult question for Antom to answer.

"I only know that one day I was sold and ordered to move here. Otherwise we would still be there. For some reason I don't think the Tyhets wanted us in their village anymore."

"It seems then, my father consented to buying your family," said Pavel. "I know that he has enjoyed the pieces of crafted furniture you have made for him."

"Yes, very true," said Antom. "And your father has treated me well. I feel like a free man in his manor."

"I'm glad to hear it," said Pavel. "Essentially, you are now."

Antom's eyes lit up with that comment. But even with freedom he would never leave the manor.

Raja wanted an explanation from Antom that she had often wondered about. "But if Manor Village was better than Thrumb Village, why did you treat me so harshly?" Raja still held some bitter memories that were relatively fresh in her mind.

"Because, I heard rumors from other peasants who had just come from the Thrumb Village. They said the Tyhets wanted you back. I couldn't stand that thought. It made shivers run up and down my spine and I had nightmares about it. So I worked extra hard and long to make more money so that I could offer a good dowry for you to be married in the neighboring village of Lord Leo Lythym. I was afraid and made you work for me as well. I wanted to do everything I could to prevent you from going back to the Tyhets."

"I can understand how that would be frightening for you," said Raja. "But why didn't you tell me before?"

"Because when you were given to us, we were forbidden to say anything about how we got you or anything about you. And if we ever did, we would be killed. We, ourselves, didn't know where you came from."

"Do you know anything else about the Tyhets?" asked Pavel.

"They have a castle that they took over years ago from Zurkia."

"How long ago?"

"Perhaps about fifty years. It's called Thrumb Castle."

Antom got up and went over to a dresser. He pulled out a scroll and unrolled it in front of the fire. Pavel, Raja, and Hannah huddled around the map to look at it.

"After I came here to Victory Manor I drew what I remembered of the Tyhet estate. Viktor thought any information about the estate could one day prove to be useful for the throne."

The map had a detailed layout of the huts in Thrumb Village and the location of Thrumb Castle. Even some of the inside of the castle was drawn. Antom indeed had a talent for artwork.

"This is the hut that we lived in," said Antom pointing to the map.

"Interesting," said Pavel. He noticed that there was a mark on his hut.

"When the Tyhets took us away from Thrumb Village, everything happened very quickly. We weren't allowed to bring anything else with us—only the clothes on our backs."

"That must have been difficult," said Pavel.

"It was, but I was glad to be moving away from the Tyhet village."

"How did you get to know the castle's floor plan?" asked Pavel.

"Yana made dried tea leaves and I delivered them to the leader of the castle in exchange for a loaf of rye bread"

Yana bowed her head, wanting to be humble, while Antom continued. "Their leader, who they call the chieftain, had a strong liking for the tea. He said it was the finest in the land."

Everyone took another sip of the tea and heartily agreed while smiling at Yana.

"I also handcrafted furniture for the chieftain," said Antom.

"You are talented," said Pavel, who looked around the hut at the other furniture he had made. "Your work is impressive."

"Thank you," said Antom, who stood up to throw another piece of wood on the fire. He then pushed an ember back into the fire pit.

"You should know that when I delivered the tea, the chieftain would be in conversation with another man. I always felt an evil presence when I was around him."

"What did he look like?" asked Hannah.

"Tall and slender, with long dark hair. And, may I add, handsome deep-set eyes—not ones you would forget."

"That sounds like my father," said Hannah.

The others looked at Hannah. Raja felt sorry that Hannah always had to face the horrible comments said about him.

"The man was very strange in his ways," said Antom. "Always muttering about something to do with an orb. When that happened, he seemed to go into some sort of trance."

No one in the room knew anything more about the orb except that Hannah had heard these mutterings in the past from her father as well. It seemed like the man with the chieftain had indeed been her father.

Hannah decided to go back to the previous conversation. "It's strange to believe that the Tyhets would want to steal peasants from other places. I would think they would have enough people of their own after some fifty years."

"That's true," said Pavel, "but that's what we are going to find out."

"Are you saying we should go to Thrumb Castle?" asked Hannah.

"That's right," said, Pavel who had now passionately taken hold of the idea of going north. "Are you agreed, Raja?"

"I am, but I have an idea."

All eyes were on Raja, waiting for what she would say next.

"On our way to Thrumb Castle, let's make our visit with Shamra a surprise."

"You haven't changed, have you, Raja?" said Yana.

"Well, don't you think that would be fun?" asked Raja, looking from Pavel to Hannah.

"I'm not sure," said Pavel. "Your mother said to send a letter first, before we arrived at the estate."

"Where's your sense of adventure," said Raja. "Everyone knows I'm the Princess of Kazan."

"I'm for it," said Hannah.

"Oh, all right," said Pavel. "I'm for it too."

Pavel rolled up the map and tucked it into his cloak. "Anyone for a game of chess?"

"I," said Antom.

"Okay, let's play."

Antom pulled out the chessboard and game pieces from a trunk—a gift from Raja, who had purchased the items from the Kazan bazaar. The wooden pieces were elegantly carved and had been made at the monastery in Kazan by one of the monks. Antom was very proud of the chess set and showed it off at every opportunity.

The girls stayed on to watch the chess game, rooting back and forth for Pavel and Antom. The game went on for a long time and in the end, Pavel won, but it was a well-fought battle.

Chapter 4

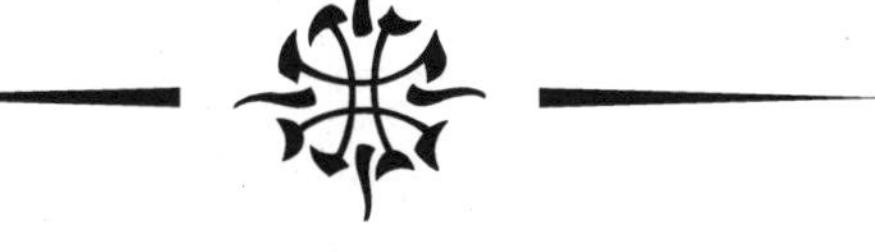

The Basket

Pavel and Raja were given permission by Viktor to ride north to Levap Castle to visit Shamra. But of course, no one knew of their plans to make an additional trip to Thrumb Castle or that Hannah was with them. The fact that Hannah was at Victory Manor had been kept secret as a precaution against her father finding her. Maya was worried about the trek, but Viktor assured his wife that travel during the day would be okay and that during the first night they would hide themselves at the base of the hillocks. They gave Raja and Pavel three weeks to visit Shamra and to help her get the castle in order.

The day came when they were finally ready for their journey. It would only be two nights before they reached Levap Castle, so they didn't have to pack too many things. Their horses were well fed and rested and anxious to start their ride. The three started off early in the morning at a trot, riding along the Hillock Trail and then into the flat terrain of the Hemencurcle Valley.

They each wore minimal armor for ease of movement and comfort. Raja wore a tight long-sleeved black tunic under a chain mail garment. Her leggings were black with brown knee-high leather boots that matched laced-up leather tubes over her lower arms. Hannah was also given a similar outfit, but instead wore a long leather vest with wide flaps at the bottom. Her arms were dressed with long leather gloves that were open at the fingertips so she could quickly get her arrows in place. Pavel wore a short chain mail vest with leather wrapped around his legs and arms. His knee-high black leather boots were made with wide flaps folded over at the top, which were more for looks than for protection. The edges of the flaps had a swirly, artistic design and had been imported by a southern country.

After a time of trotting, they slowed their horses to a walk.

"What's your plan, Raja?" asked Pavel.

"Ah . . . I don't have one."

"What? Don't have a plan?"

"Well I don't exactly know the layout of the castle estate so it's hard to say right now. And I'm also expecting that my mother has reinforced the castle with her knights since Shamra's arrival. Somehow we are going to have to avoid them in order for our arrival to be a surprise."

"There's an old tower that is part of a ruined castle. We could climb to the top of it and use it as a lookout to take inventory of the grounds," said Pavel.

"I like that idea," said Hannah.

The three agreed together and they continued to talk about their plans and the celebrations they would have during the visit.

Later that day, they made it to their first destination at the Western Hillocks. All three helped to get a fire going and they continued to talk late into the night. Everything was peaceful except for the cries of the wolves.

The fact that they slept late the next morning wasn't a problem because they didn't want to arrive at the castle in daylight. The beginning of the next part of the journey brought them through the hillock range and into the Trough Valley while still keeping on the Hillock Trail. The trail was not difficult to ride but, wanting to reserve the horses' energy, they went at a slower pace. All three kept a vigilant eye on the adjacent hills for Tyhets. So far, their journey appeared to be unknown and all was quiet.

However, the group had not been riding through the valley for very long when Raja suddenly spotted three horsemen galloping toward them. They all felt an immediate sense of danger. Hannah took out one of her arrows and readied it with her bow. As the riders neared it was now clear that they were enemies. Long swords waved above their heads as the riders held on to their reins with their other hands, a show of skilled and menacing behavior meant to intimidate and overpower.

"Tyhets!" said Pavel. "And full of rage."

The riders were quickly approaching and not slowing down. Billows of dust escaped through the air behind the horses as their hoofs pounded on the ground.

"A raid!" said Raja as she turned her horse around. "Let's get out of here!"

"Wait," said Hannah as she arched her bow. Taking careful aim, she let go of her arrow.

Raja turned her head just in time to see one of the riders fall. Hannah shot another arrow and the second rider was hit. The third rider stopped his onslaught and fled in the other direction.

"Now!" shouted Hannah. "Let's get out of here!"

The three urged their horses on and they continued up the valley as fast as they could. Eventually the terrain became more rugged with a sloped landscape and they were forced to slow their pace.

"I'm impressed," said Raja.

"Thanks to my father," said Hannah. "He always insisted that I practice."

"I have some catching up to do," said Raja.

Raja looked at Pavel for approval. "Yes, I agree," he said. "Archery would be a valuable asset to add to your skills of swordsmanship. This will be our next goal."

"Thank you," said Raja. "I shall look forward to that."

"I wonder if that was a planned attack or just an opportunist raid," said Pavel.

"It could be either, according to what's been happening in the villages," said Raja.

"But if it was planned, it could happen again. We need to really keep our eyes open," said Pavel.

The two girls agreed to that.

As the day wore on, the group finally decided to spend one of the nights beside a small trickling stream. The refreshing water was most welcoming and quenched the dry taste in their mouths. All three were still very thankful for Hannah's perfect aim and the group continued with their discussion about the raid, but in the end, it could only be speculated as to why it had happened. However, they concluded that the most logical assumption was that Hannah's father still wanted her. Upon that conclusion they decided not to make a fire.

The next morning, they continued riding through the valley and then headed west in the direction of the Volga River along the Iris Trail. Their horses walked through the long green grasses dispersed with colorful mountain flowers of wood lily, tower larkspur, and viola incisa.

Upon coming to a stream, the girls suggested that they have a rest. They enjoyed the warm sun of the late afternoon while working to make flower wreaths for their hair. They even made one for Pavel. He had the girls roaring in laughter over his silly antics of fluttering eyes.

Once on their trek again, after the sun had set, it didn't take too long for them to arrive at the castle plateau. Pavel spotted the tower. "Do you see the top of the old castle tower? It's right over there."

Both girls looked in that direction. The sun had set an hour ago and the tower was silhouetted mysteriously against the evening sky.

"Yes, I see it," they both said.

"There's a path that goes around to the back of the tower that we can take to get there."

"Are you sure the tower is abandoned?" asked Raja.

"I'm sure of it."

The three took the back path and rode their horses through a mountain stream that flowed past the castle. The stream flowed over the edge of the plateau and into the Volga River, creating a very long and beautiful waterfall, named Long Waterfall.

After riding through the stream, Raja and Hannah saw the full length of the tower. They were very surprised that it was still standing after the rest of the castle had been destroyed. The girls commented on how the tower appeared to be leaning a fair bit, and hoped it would be safe. Pavel said he had been up in the tower before so there was no need to worry. The moon was now visible and was just showing above the tower and cast an extraordinary amount of light on this particular night. They dismounted and their horses were let loose to graze.

"Let's investigate," said Raja.

"Allow me to go first," said Pavel. "It's going to be dark so we need to hang on to each other."

Pavel opened the creaky door to the spiral steps.

"Scary," said Raja.

"Why do dragons sleep all day?" asked Hannah.

"What?" asked Raja.

"It's a joke."

"Why are you telling a joke now?"

"To lighten up the mood. This is supposed to be fun."

"Okay, well I give up."

"So they can fly at knights."

"Ha, ha, ha," said Raja.

"Very witty, Hannah," said Pavel.

"Thanks."

The three kept going up the steps and came to the window that was situated midway up.

"I can't see much," said Raja.

"Wait until we're at the top," said Pavel.

"Okay, lead the way."

Taking each step steadily and carefully, they reached the top of the tower. Then, standing at the window, they could see the entire estate. Hannah began counting the guards. "There are four guards holding torches," she said.

Watching intently, they waited to see what the guards would do.

"They're in pairs circling the estate, staying opposite one another," said Hannah.

"Okay, here's the plan then," said Pavel. "You two girls go down and hide in the bushes."

"Wait a minute. Why us?" asked Raja.

"It was your idea to come here in secrecy," said Pavel.

"I guess you're right about that. There's nothing to be scared about anyway. We're not real intruders."

"Right," said Pavel. "So when I give a wolf call that means that it is all clear and that's when you make a dash for it."

"A dash for where?" asked Hannah.

"Ah . . . well, I haven't thought that far yet. Let's see . . . yes, oh, now I know!" Pavel acted like he knew what he was talking about. "First, we know that Shamra is in the castle and there is only one way in."

"I don't see the door," said Raja.

"Just hold on," said Pavel. "Do you see that bartizan on the top of the left side of the castle? That is where the guards are hoisted up to get into the castle, or anyone for that matter."

"Do you mean there is no door to the inside of the castle?" asked Raja.

"That's right, it's for absolute protection."

"Can the guards see whose coming up?"

"No, I don't think so. But they could if they look down through the holes of the bartizan. Keep your hoods over your heads."

"Now when you go there, tug on the rope and someone will throw over a basket to lift you up. But the trick is that both of you will have to go at the same time, otherwise whoever is lifting you won't believe it's a guard."

Raja and Hannah listened intently.

"Then what?"

"When you get to the top you say hello to the guard and that you are friends of Shamra. Then you can say that you are here to surprise her."

"It's that easy, is it?"

"I should think so," said Pavel.

"Okay, let's go," said Raja.

"Wait, before we go, let's practice the wolf cry. I want to learn how to do it as well," said Hannah. "You never know when it might be needed."

"Okay," said Pavel. "Take a deep, slow breath and begin with a low mournful pitch. Raise your pitch and get louder at the same time. When you're out of breath, gradually lower your voice and soften the howl."

"That sounds easy," said Hannah.

"No, it doesn't," said Raja. "It sounds complicated."

"I'll show you how it's done," said Pavel.

Cupping his hands over his mouth Pavel showed the girls how to do it. Both girls agreed Pavel was an expert and commenced to each take a turn. They surprised themselves and Pavel at how real they sounded.

"I think we're ready now," said Hannah.

Raja and Hannah held on to each other and climbed back down the stairs. When they reached the bottom they hid behind the bushes just outside the castle and waited for Pavel's wolf cry.

"Arh-woooooooo, arh-woooooooo."

"Let's go," said Hannah and the two girls took off like lightening toward the left side of the castle.

"Do you see the rope?" asked Raja.

"Found it." Hannah tugged on the rope. "Stand clear of the basket."

They looked up in anticipation of the basket being lowered. But it didn't appear.

"Tug it again," said Raja, starting to feel a bit desperate.

Hannah tugged on the rope, but there was no response.

"Let me try," said Raja, as she grabbed the rope and started tugging.

"Halt, who goes there?"

"It's the guards," whispered Raja.

"That's okay, remember we are not real intruders," said Hannah.

"Right, I keep on forgetting that."

However, instead of a civilized greeting, the guards rushed towards them and unexpectedly pushed them to the ground. The girls were pinned in their places with spears. Raja felt helpless and bewildered. There was nothing she could do but hope they could explain the perceived intrusion.

"Who are you?" asked one of the guards.

Feeling completely out of breath, Raja tried to explain. "We are not intruders," said Raja. "I am the Princess of Kazan."

"That's a good joke," said the guard. "Why would a princess be trying to break into a castle?"

"Shamra's our cousin," said Raja.

"Who's Shamra?" asked the guard.

Raja took a moment to answer that question. "Princess of Zurkia."

"There is no one here by that name."

"Yes, there has to be," said Raja.

"Enough speaking," said the guard, who then turned to yell out a command. "Take their weapons and tie their hands!"

With a sword poking into the girls' backs, two other guards confiscated their weapons and tied thick scratchy rope around their wrists.

"Get up and come with us," said the guard, who was giving the orders.

The girls struggled to stand on their feet.

"Get going," said the same guard. "And don't talk."

The group of guards forced them around to the side of the castle.

"Where are you taking us?" asked Raja.

"Silence!"

Shoving the girls through an open entrance, they were forced down some stone stairs.

"Please," said Raja. "You are making a mistake."

"The only mistake is the one you made. I said don't speak."

Raja obeyed as she felt the tip of a spear on her back push a little harder. They walked along a narrow corridor. The air was unpleasantly musty. Her body shuddered when a rat scampered just in front of them. The guards opened the bars of a cell that had one small barred window and pushed the girls onto the floor. The door was locked behind them and the guards left.

"I think we're in the dungeon," said Hannah.

"You think?" said Raja. She felt like crying. This certainly hadn't gone as planned.

Chapter 5

A Good Aim

"This wasn't my idea of a surprise for Shamra," said Raja, who was feeling quite upset at sitting in the Levap Castle dungeon, no less Pavel's castle.

"I think we are the ones who got surprised," said Hannah as she held her hand to her nose. "And it smells in here."

"Where's Pavel when we need him?" asked Raja.

"We may have to wait until morning, until Shamra awakes," said Hannah as she tilted her head back against the wall with a sigh.

"I'm having a hard time staying awake. Can I lean on you?"

"Sure," said Hannah.

The girls felt exhausted and despite their dismal state, they fell asleep leaning against each other.

* * *

Pavel didn't know whether to go down and try to rescue the girls or wait until the situation sorted itself out. Surely Shamra would eventually find out what happened. In a way, he felt it was somewhat amusing, but on the other hand he thought the situation could be quite frightening for the girls if it didn't get sorted out right away. How long it would take for them to get free was something he couldn't predict. But if it did turn out badly, he certainly couldn't leave them there.

He finally decided he would do something about it in the morning. He would present himself as a guest visiting the castle, even though he was actually the owner. He had no choice but to do this, as without papers his word would mean nothing. However, coming as a guest might not even work without a previously sent notification by a bailiff. But, nonetheless, he didn't want to leave the girls there either so he thought he would take the chance.

As soon as the sun rose, Pavel got his horse and rode to the castle. He was confronted by a guard and asked a series of questions.

"Who are you?"

"Pavel Ramazon."

"Why have you come?"

"To pay Princess Shamra a visit."

"There is no Princess Shamra here. This castle is run by Zolf."

The news was shocking to Pavel. Princes Shamra was not at the castle? And who was Zolf?

"You must be mistaken. The Zurkian tzarina has ordered Princess Shamra to rule this castle."

"There is no princess here. Do you have a paper from the tzarina stating this?"

"Ah . . . no I don't."

"Why have you come in the morning? Should you not be traveling by day and arriving here in the evening? I think you are part of the two people who tried to break into the castle last night."

"What are you talking about? I know nothing about a break in."

"Your actions are very suspicious."

Just then Zolf appeared on the castle balcony. He appeared to be not much older than Pavel, but very tall for his age. He looked down at Pavel briefly and then shouted an order.

"Guards, take this man to the dungeon."

Pavel drew his sword but he was outnumbered. Three guards captured him and forced him down the steps underneath the castle. They threw him into the cell next to the girls' cell and locked the gate. Raja waited until the guards left.

"Pavel?"

"Yes, it's me."

"What are you doing here?" asked Raja.

"Ah, just passing through. What are doing here?" asked Pavel.

"Well, it certainly wasn't my intention. Let me guess, this is your attempt to rescue us."

Pavel's eyes rolled up to the ceiling. "Ah . . . well . . . not exactly."

Despite the dire circumstances Raja thought it was rather amusing that Pavel had also been thrown into the dungeon and she laughed.

"It's not that funny," said Pavel.

"Better to laugh than cry," said Raja. "And how do you suggest we get out of this mess?"

"Me? Suggest something? Come now, this was your idea in the first place."

"Yes, but you said we needed extra protection, remember?"

"Ah, yes, just give me a moment to think," said Pavel.

"Okay, but be quick. I'm thirsty and hungry."

"I'll do my best," replied Pavel, feeling a bit irritated.

Pavel didn't know how he could have agreed to this plan in the first place. And now he was expected to get them out of here, the nerve of Raja to suggest it. On the other hand, he would be getting himself out as well so he thought he might as well put his mind to it.

"By the way," said Pavel, "Shamra isn't at this castle."

"As we found out," said Raja.

"The castle is run by Zolf."

"Who's that?"

"I have no idea."

"That's not so good. Do you think the letter from the tzarina was fake?" asked Hannah.

"I don't think so, but you never know," said Pavel. "There have been a lot of strange things happening with all of the disappearances." Pavel looked at his surroundings. "I don't have a window in my cell."

"We have a window but it's barred. I think that rules out escaping from a window," said Raja.

"Right, logically speaking, the only way out is with the key."

"And where might that be?" asked Raja with a bit of sarcasm.

"I can see it from here," said Pavel.

"You're joking," said Raja.

"No, I'm not."

"Can you reach it?" asked Hannah.

"No, but maybe we could somehow knock it down."

"I think I've got an idea," said Raja feeling somewhat excited.

Raja untied the scarf from her head and then took her doll from under her sash. She tied the end of the scarf around her doll. Then, hanging onto the doll, she put her arms through the cell bars.

"Can you reach this?"

"Yes, thank you. You still carry this doll on you?"

"Yes, always."

"Good thing!"

Pavel tested his idea with the doll inside his cell. He thought there was a good chance of succeeding. Then, hanging onto the end of the scarf, he carefully aimed at the key ring and threw the doll. He hit the key but it didn't fall off the hook. Pavel dragged the doll back through his cell bars.

The girls watched from within their own cell.

"Good aim," said Raja.

"Thanks," said Pavel, as he got ready to throw the doll again. After several tries he managed to hook the key ring with the arm of the doll and pull it off the hook.

"I did it!" shouted Pavel.

"Shhh," said Raja. "Not so loud."

"Now all I have to do is drag the key this way."

"You can do it," said Raja.

Little by little, so as not to unhook the doll's arm from the ring, Pavel dragged the key toward the bars. The girls watched while biting their lips. Finally, the key was close enough so he could reach it with his hands.

"I've got it!"

"Good job!" said Hannah and Raja.

Pavel stuck the key into the keyhole and unlocked it. Quickly, he did the same for the girls' cell.

"What about our horses?" asked Hannah.

"They still might be there, otherwise we will have to walk," said Pavel.

Groping in the dark, along the sides of the wall, they looked for the outside entrance. Pavel knew there was only one entrance to the dungeon and that was from the outside of the castle.

"We'll do the same thing as we did before. I'll go first and run to the bushes, hoping no one will see me. Then, I'll go to the top of the tower. When you hear the wolf cry that means it's okay to run."

The girls agreed to the plan.

Pavel made it safely to the top of the tower and the girls waited for the wolf cry.

"Arh-woooooooo, arh-woooooooo."

The two of them ran as fast as they could. They arrived safely at the foot of the tower where Pavel was waiting. The three of them searched for their horses but unfortunately couldn't find them. Their only choice was to walk. Luckily, they had the stream to follow.

"I think we should make it home in three nights," said Pavel.

"I'm starved," said Raja.

"We'll have to survive on berries until then," said Hannah.

For two days, they walked along the trails never eating so many berries as on this journey.

Despite the hot weather they made quite good progress. They finally arrived at their usual resting place at the hillocks. It was berries again for supper.

"I don't think I want to eat another berry in my life," said Raja.

"On the other hand, it's good that we have them," said Hannah, trying to be positive.

"If we didn't have the berries to eat I think your stomach would be complaining more," said Pavel.

"Okay, you're right, I shouldn't complain."

Raja turned her attention to the horizon.

"Pavel, do you see movement out there?" asked Raja.

"Yes, I do."

"Let's get behind the bushes," said Hannah. "There's too much going wrong to know whether it's safe or not."

The group hid behind the bushes and a large rock. They waited until they could see the movement more clearly.

"It's definitely a group of horses and people walking," said Pavel. "And there's something else there too."

"I think it's a litter," said Hannah.

As the group of riders and packhorses approached, Hannah was proved right. Right in the middle of the group of horses was a litter with red curtains being carried by four servants.

"This is very strange," said Hannah.

"Do you think we should approach them?" asked Raja.

"Let's keep out of view until they are closer. They may stop here," said Pavel.

Just as Pavel had predicted, the group of riders, packhorses, and people stopped not too far from where the three friends hid. Before the litter was set down, a girl was helped out of the carrier, and a very beautiful girl at that.

"Who is that?" asked Raja.

The three kept watching the young girl. She sat on a stone with her face turned away.

"I can't tell who she is," said Hannah.

"Throw a pebble, Pavel, so she turns around," said Raja.

"What if I hit her?"

"Don't be silly. You're a good aim," said Raja.

Pavel found a small pebble and threw it. It seemed to land in the exact spot he wanted, right behind her.

The girl turned her head at the noise.

"Could that be . . .?" asked Raja.

"It might be," said Pavel

"Yes, it is. I'm sure of it."

Raja stepped out into the open. The group of knights were alarmed.

"Careful," said Hannah, but it was too late.

Immediately, swords were drawn. The guards surrounded Raja with their swords pointing in her direction.

The girl stared at Raja, completely surprised. She immediately stood and walked over to the guards, pushing one of the swords down so she could see.

"Raja?"

"Hello, Shamra."

"We certainly do meet in odd places," said Shamra, trying to maintain her composure.

"You're befitting of your new role."

"Thank you."

"Are you here alone?" asked Shamra.

"No."

Chapter 6

The Three Thrones

Shamra continued to stare at Raja, wondering who else was with her without any horses in the middle of the desolate hillocks.

Then, right at that moment, Pavel and a familiar-looking girl emerged from behind the rock where they were hiding. They looked rather awkward, to say the least.

Shamra's mouth dropped open and then spoke in an amused voice. "An odd finding to say the least."

"Hello, Shamra," said Pavel who wasn't sure whether he should bow or not. But not wanting to appear like some court jester offered Shamra a slight nod of the head.

"And who's that?" asked Shamra, pointing to Hannah, who had covered her face with her niqab.

"Do you remember my . . .?" Raja stopped in mid-sentence, not wanting to give Hannah away.

"Oh, of course, I remember now."

"And do you think you could call off your guards now?" said Raja.

"Sorry. Guards, withdraw your swords."

Hannah and Shamra curtsied to each other, another slightly awkward moment.

"I must say, this is very unexpected," said Shamra. "What are you all doing here and where are your horses? Let me guess—this is your idea of a surprise welcoming committee."

"Sort of," said Raja, who shrugged her shoulders.

Shamra smiled at her own sense of humor. "Well you've succeeded. I just came from Victory Manor and Viktor said that you had gone to Levap Castle but I didn't expect this."

"Me neither," said Raja.

"Okay, out with the story then," said Shamra, knowing it was going to be a good one.

"We came by night to your castle and were going to surprise you but we got caught. No one believed that I was Princess of Kazan and so they threw us into the dungeon."

"The dungeon!" said Shamra, starting to laugh. "Well now I've heard it all." And with that she couldn't contain herself from going into a hysterical laugh along with everyone else. "Wait until Viktor finds out about that," she said.

"Well, who says Viktor has to find out?" said Raja with hands on her hips. "I say nobody tell him."

Raja looked around the group.

"Everyone agreed?"

No one said a word.

"Oh, come on. If I get into trouble that means the fun stops."

Pavel started to raise his eyebrows. "She's got a point there."

Everyone gave in and agreed not to say anything.

Raja looked at Shamra with a puzzled expression. "We thought you would be at the castle."

"I was detained because there was a raid on the Kazan Village and peasants were taken."

"Oh no," said Raja, "not there too."

"We've got to get to the bottom of this," said Pavel.

"What's going on? Is it happening at your village too?" asked Shamra.

"Yes," said Pavel. "It seems to be happening everywhere."

The four friends moved away from the guards and huddled together to talk about the ordeal.

"That's the reason why we came to this part of the country in the first place. We want to investigate why this is happening," said Raja.

"We think it might have something to do with the Tyhets," said Pavel. "Raja's peasant parents used to live there and her father gave us a map of the estate."

Pavel took out the map from inside of his cloak and unrolled it. "This is the castle and it was taken over from Zurkia years ago. Zurkia's never been able to get it back."

"And according to the map it's not a small castle," said Hannah.

The four friends studied the map and pointed out different parts of the estate to each other.

"Another strange thing, Shamra, was that I was almost kid-napped at Bolger Castle by an intruder who I think was the padesha," said Hannah.

"Perhaps the padesha has joined the Tyhets," said Shamra.

"Whatever it is, we need to find out why the peasants are being taken," said Pavel.

The group didn't talk for long, as Pavel, Raja, and Hannah were very hungry. A fire was made and a meal was hastily prepared from Shamra's provisions. They couldn't have been happier to have met Shamra, despite the bit of embarrassment over their failed plans. The new variety of food was very welcomed.

Everyone settled down for the night and felt much better by the next morning. After a good breakfast the four friends fit snuggly into the litter and were off to Levap Castle along the Hillock Trail. Four more servants were added to the task of carrying the litter.

"Viktor only gave us three weeks to visit," said Raja. "I don't think we are going to have time for a celebration anymore."

"And not if we want to go up to the Tyhets," said Pavel.

"Could I come?" asked Shamra.

"Don't you need to get yourself in order with the castle?" asked Raja.

"Yes, I suppose, but I'll have a lot of time for that when we get back. After all, I'd like to go with you and be a part of the adventure."

"Well, I suppose," said Raja. "What do you think, Hannah?"

"The more the merrier. I don't see why not."

"By the way, Shamra, how did you feel when you found out you were a princess?" asked Raja, who thought she could identify with her feelings.

"Very surprised, but nervous as well."

"And now?"

"After being with your tzarina mother, I feel very wonderful about it."

"Glad to hear it. My mother will always want the best for you. And you're in good company with Hannah and me."

"I am? I'm not so sure after hearing the dungeon story!"

The girls giggled and Raja added, "Just giving the guards a little practice with their duties. That's all it was."

"A good way to look at it," said Shamra. "At least I know they are protective."

"By the way, why wasn't the basket lowered?" asked Raja.

"Oh, the basket," said Shamra. "The tzarina told me there's a secret code for the tugs. It's three short tugs, count to three, and then one more short tug."

"Pavel, you didn't know that?" asked Raja eyeing him with a bit of annoyance. "After all, it is your castle."

"Sorry, no I didn't. Very clever set up though."

Raja settled down again, remembering that it had been her idea to surprise Shamra in the first place.

"Who is Zolf?" asked Pavel.

"He is one of the tzarina's knights. He is young, but very talented and dutiful. He was given strict orders to get rid of anyone who wasn't announced and so I guess that's why you ended up in the dungeon," said Shamra.

"I see, well, he was only doing his job then," said Pavel. "But quit confusing as he said he didn't know you."

"I was told that Zolf is very cunning in his ways to protect," said Shamra.

Pavel rubbed his hand on his chin. "Yes, quite."

Chatter continued during most of the journey. When they arrived at the start of the Iris Trail, the group settled down for the night. The next day, Pavel, Raja, and Hannah walked up the inclines to make it less stressful for the carriers. Shamra, of course, stayed in the litter, as she was wearing a very flamboyant dress that was entirely unsuitable for walking on the rugged terrain. When the group was on flatter ground the three got back into the litter.

The group finally arrived at the Levap Castle estate and was led onto the small arched bridge that crossed the stream. To calm her three friends, Shamra said a letter had been sent ahead of time and must have arrived after Raja, Pavel, and Hannah had escaped the dungeon. Obviously, Shamra was right, as the guards made preparations for their arrival, rushing to the litter to relieve the present carriers. Raja thought that coming this way to begin with, in an announced fashion, would have been a much better idea.

After crossing the bridge, Pavel got out of the litter first and then helped Shamra out of the box structure. Raja and Hannah followed with courteous help from a guard. Not that they needed help, but it was a polite thing to do. The four were then ushered to the corner of the castle with Shamra taking the lead. Raja had to admit Shamra was beautiful in her full-gown dress with layers of lace and silk. Her exquisite jewelry, no doubt given to her by the tzarina, sparkled in the sun. Even the way she walked was like a princess. Raja was sure her tzarina mother taught her everything about how to act like royalty. She could see that Shamra was a fast learner.

Standing beneath the bartizan, Shamra was the first to speak.

"Raja, why don't you do the honors."

Raja took the rope and gave three pulls, counted to three, and then gave another pull.

"Stay clear," yelled the basket operator.

The three girls jumped away just in time, as the basket neared the bottom.

"Okay, who goes first?" asked Pavel.

"Well, I think I should," said Shamra, "so you don't get thrown in the dungeon again."

"Good thinking," said Hannah with a smile, "and then I'll go next."

"And I'll see to it that Raja is safe," said Pavel. "I'm here to catch you if you fall."

"Well, that's very gentlemanly of you," said Raja with a little laugh.

"My duty," said Pavel trying to act serious.

The rides in the basket proved to be very fun with the girls' constant waves and giggles.

"I'm falling," said Raja jokingly when it was her turn. "Catch me."

"I've got you," said Pavel in a playful voice.

As Raja reached the top of the castle, the guard helped her out of the basket. The basket was lowered for Pavel and when he was finally hoisted up the guard immediately called for the servants to escort them to the hall.

They were led down a set of tightly coiled spiral stairs. It was like going around and around down a giant hollow sequoia tree. Once they got down the staircase the servants were waiting in the hall and bowed to show their greatest respect.

Raja thought Shamra was taking the attention very well and keeping a balance between kindness and authority. Everyone was then immediately taken to the banqueting hall where a large feast commenced and went well into the night with joking, singing, and food served in a pantomime fashion, involving all sorts of creatures. The most entertaining act was from a man dressed as a white stallion who came galloping into the hall with another man riding on his back. Singing in perfect harmony to a lively tune accompanied by a man playing a shawm instrument, the rider served Shamra a dish of potato dumplings garnished with mint sauce. The princess took the food in a very elegant but teasing manner. Indeed, the act set the tone for a very jolly feast.

Huge baskets of fruit, cheese, and nuts were continually passed around the tables. Candles wedged in tall stands were displayed around the room reflecting their flickering light in variously shaped mirrors on the walls, adding a festive ambience to the feast.

When their time was spent, and no one could tell another joke or eat one more morsel of food, the chambermaids led the group of friends into their sleeping quarters where fresh clothes were prepared for them. But before the girls lay their heads down Raja made an intriguing suggestion.

"Shamra, don't you want to sit on your throne before we go to sleep?"

"Well, I hadn't thought about that. Is there a throne?"

"Yes, I should think so. Would you like to give it a try? After all, you are a princess now and that's what princesses do."

"Why not?" said Shamra.

"A lovely idea," said Hannah.

The three of them went down into the throne room of the castle and to their surprise there was not just one throne, but three thrones.

"Oh, look at that, just for us," said Raja.

"Interesting, I wonder what their history is?" asked Hannah.

"Three cousins on three thrones," said Shamra with melody in her voice.

The girls ran to sit in the royal chairs. Together, they made up a funny story that had them laughing and giggling for a good while. They finally retired to their chamber and fell into a soothing sleep.

Chapter 7

The Trunk

The next morning at the very long breakfast table the four friends made plans to go to Thrumb Castle. Pavel, Raja, and Hannah met Zolf and put aside any ill feelings over the rough treatment they had received and they each said they had understood the circumstances. The three were given back their weapons and the whole ordeal was a bit of a learning lesson for the young lord and the two girls. Although, Pavel thought it was a lesson for Zolf as well, seeing as how it was easy to escape the dungeon. Pavel advised him to move the key further away.

It turned out that Zolf knew the route to Thrumb Castle. The estate was northeast of Levap Castle and situated in the Tyhet region close to the shores of Kazanka River. Zolf drew a map with various landmarks and explained how to get there by following the Landmark Trail. Pavel instructed Zolf to tell no one of his plans.

Right after the dungeon ordeal, Raja and Hannah's horses had been found by the guards and had been taken into the manor's stables. So now their horses were ready to venture once again. They said their farewells to Zolf and headed out on the trail.

"Do you know how long it should take?" asked Raja, who was riding behind Pavel.

"Zolf thought it would not be more than five days and four nights," said Pavel.

"I'm glad we have more than just berries to eat this time," said Raja.

"Do you have any idea of what we should do when we get to Thrumb Castle?" asked Shamra.

"We could try and see if any of the peasants we know are there," said Pavel. "And we should wait until it is dark to approach any of them."

As the group traveled along, the first landmark that the four friends came to was a large boulder. Everyone knew about the rock because it was shaped like a bear. From there they rode a little more to the north. They eventually came to the second landmark, which was a huge hollow trunk of a tree. The top of the tree had snapped in a storm, but a rebirth of branches grew from parts of the hollow trunk. The tips of the branches reached the other nearby trees, which were laden with long green moss. Rays from the setting sun found its way through the branches and foliage, creating a halo of illuminating moss.

A stream was close by, which was a very welcoming sight to everyone after hours of riding. Raja knelt beside the stream and looked at her reflection. At times it was still hard to believe that she was the tzarina's daughter and Hannah and Shamra were her cousins—all of royal blood. She herself would do everything she could to fight the evil that invaded the country. She cupped her hand in the stream, bringing the water to her dry mouth. It was the sweetest water she had ever tasted. She splashed water on her face and neck, refreshing her spirit. The surroundings were so beautiful that the group decided to stay there for the night and they slept inside the trunk.

From there the group continued in a more easterly direction. After traveling for a day, they came to a den, which was the third landmark. They threw some rocks in the den to make sure it was abandoned. After creating a small torch, they went inside to inspect it. It seemed safe so the group decided to spend the night there. Wolf cries rang out during the night, which made everyone snuggle a little closer to each other.

The fourth landmark was a hill with a cliff on one side. A tall tree stood on top of the hill with an eagle's nest on the top branches. They stood and watched the eagle care for its young for a few minutes. Then they climbed to the top of the hill and found a good spot to spend the night at the edge of the cliff. They all lay down in the grass and faced the black sky.

"The stars are beautiful tonight, aren't they?" said Raja.

"Look, there's a falling star," said Hannah. "And another one."

"And another one," said Raja. "Isn't that supposed to be good fortune?"

"I think so," said Hannah.

"Do you hear something?" asked Raja.

Everyone was silent as they listened to a pounding in the distance.

"Hoof beats," said Pavel.

They scrambled to the edge of the cliff and lay flat on the ground. It wasn't long before they could see the riders. Most of them carried a torch.

"Warriors," said Pavel. "They look like Tyhets."

"They have captives," said Hannah.

"Probably more peasants," said Pavel.

"Should we follow them?" asked Hannah.

"No," said Pavel. "We could end up being caught. We can find their tracks in the morning."

"Do you think they're going to Thrumb Castle?" asked Raja.

"I'm sure that's exactly where they are headed," said Pavel, "but we'll find out tomorrow."

That night everyone had a little difficulty getting to sleep. Eventually, the group drifted off, with Raja falling into a very deep sleep. During the night she had a dream. At the end of her dream she woke up, but then fell asleep again. In the morning Raja told the others about her dream.

* * *

There was a high hill with tall grass and flowers of all sorts. On top of the hill were three thrones with three little princesses sitting on each throne. Three bears came along and each one ate one of the thrones. The bears fell asleep, leaving the girls very saddened. When the bears awoke they began to approach the girls. The princesses quickly brought out a glowing round sphere and showed it to the bears. The bears coughed up the thrones and ran away. The princesses saw that the thrones were more beautiful than before. They sat on the thrones, playing with the sphere and were happy again.

* * *

Pavel and Hannah thought the dream was strange but at the same time they thought it could have a powerful meaning. In their efforts to interrupt the dream, Hannah mentioned that her father had a peculiar liking for bears. Raja thought perhaps she and her cousins were the princesses in her dream. And Pavel added that he thought the sphere was a symbol of authority since it had chased away the evil.

After talking about the meaning of the dream and eating a bit of their food, the group packed up and left their camp. They found the hoof prints quite easily and followed them for a distance, but Pavel concluded that the tracks were heading in a more northern direction along a different track, which Zolf had mentioned as the Oak Trail. He had said not to take that trail as it led away from Thrumb Castle. So they decided to keep with their plan to go to the castle and backtracked to follow the Landmark Trail in the same eastern direction as before.

Then, after traveling for another day, they came to a small pond, which was the fifth landmark. They set up camp at that spot and made themselves a small fire. The evening was spent watching the ducks on the pond, and in merry conversation about all the events that had caused the three girl cousins to come together. Pavel agreed that he himself never thought he would be in the company of three beautiful royals. The girls all had a laugh at his comment.

The next day the group continued their journey and close to the evening Pavel spotted the top of a tower.

"There's the tower," said Pavel.

"What's our plan?" asked Hannah.

Pavel pointed out a hill that was mostly barren and which was relatively close to the Thrumb Estate. "I think we should go to the top of that hill so we can see what's going on."

The girls agreed and rode to the side of the hill. Still riding their horses, they were able to get to the top following a natural path. They tied their horses to a few small trees. Then, going to the crest of the hill, they lay down in the long grass to hide themselves. The view was grand, just as they had expected. The castle was huge and there were numerous huts not too far from the castle. However, when they looked about there was no one to be seen.

"Everyone is probably in for the evening," said Hannah.

"I think we should sleep up here," said Pavel.

"I agree," said Raja. "That way we won't miss anything."

Pavel got out his map and compared the estate to Antom's drawing. He was surprised at how accurate it was.

The night closed in and everyone found the most comfortable spot to sleep in that they could. They huddled close together to stay warm, as they could not start a fire for fear of being noticed. Eventually everyone fell asleep.

The next morning, feeling very tired, they forced themselves to get up as soon as it was light enough to see. They surveyed the village and Thrumb Castle, but there was no movement to be seen anywhere.

"The place seems to be abandoned," said Raja, who was feeling a little let down.

"I think I see some movement," said Shamra.

All eyes looked at where Shamra was pointing. Sure enough, something was wandering around the village.

"It's a dog," said Hannah.

"That means that the people who left this place probably didn't leave that long ago since the dog is still alive," said Pavel.

"The poor thing," said Raja.

"What do you say we do?" asked Hannah.

Pavel spoke first. "If no one is there, it should be safe to go down." He cast a serious look at each girl. "Is everyone agreed?"

The girls agreed and so the four rode down the hill and then towards the castle estate.

Arriving at the first set of huts, they tied their horses to a post and walked around the dwellings. The huts were almost completely empty. Raja stepped on a few eggshells and turned over a broken bowl with her foot.

Pavel took out the map from the pouch that Antom had given him.

"Let's try and find Antom's hut," said Pavel.

The three girls joined Pavel to look at the map.

"According to this map the hut is seven down from here," said Pavel.

The girls began to follow Pavel down a lane that was filled with ruts and small holes. By this time, the dog had found the group. Surprisingly, it appeared shy and nonaggressive. It was obvious that it wanted some food.

"It must be starving," said Raja. "I'm going to see if I can find some food."

Raja wandered back to the first hut and went into the little shack attached to the hut, which was a chicken coop. To her delight she found some eggs that had been left in a nest. She retrieved the broken piece of bowl she had found and cracked the eggs into it.

"Come," called Raja. The dog immediately came and in seconds wolfed down the eggs.

Raja stroked the dog's fur. It was white with gray and tan markings. Although the dog was a bit underweight, Raja thought it was a nice-looking dog, not too small or too big. Right away she considered the dog a new friend and decided to name it Tan.

Raja caught up to the others with the dog happily following her.

Seeing the dog with Raja, Pavel said, "Let me guess, you've just made a new friend."

"Yes, his name is Tan."

"I see you are already quite attached," said Pavel.

"Well, we can't leave the dog here," said Raja.

"No, I guess not."

The group walked a little further with Pavel counting the huts. "This seems to be the right hut. Let's look inside."

Almost reverently, they entered the hut. "Oh my goodness," said Raja. "To think that I used to live here."

"It doesn't look like anyone lives here now," said Pavel as he looked at the bare dirt floor.

"Do you remember any of this?" asked Hannah.

Raja looked around the one-room hut. "Yes, I do. I remember Yana making pottage stew at the fire pit in the middle of the floor. She always let me add the rosemary and would sing to me at the same time." Raja pointed to the side of the wall that had an etched woman's face. "And that is the spot where we slept and that is Yan's portrait. Antom carved it while she sat on the table."

Walking to a hole in the side of the mud wall that was used as a window, Raja ran her hand over the tiny tallies around the window that Antom had used to keep track of time. "And this is the place where we ate . . . on a small, round, three-legged table. We didn't have any stools so we sat on straw."

"What about that?" asked Pavel, pointing to a wooden trunk.

The trunk was skillfully made and stood on three legs, the fourth one broken. It was decorated with three intricately-carved bear heads, which reminded Raja of her dream. It was dusty and somewhat scuffed up. "Yes, I remember it," said Raja.

"It's strange that it's still here," said Hannah. "We'll have to ask Antom about it."

Raja opened the trunk. It was empty. "I remember that there was something secret about this trunk."

Pavel inspected the trunk. "It looks ordinary to me."

"It looks ordinary but Antom could make things disappear from inside the trunk. It was a game he played with me."

Raja removed her scarf from her head. It was still as beautiful as ever and one of a kind. There wasn't anything else like it in all of Zurkia. Its colors had not lost their vivid sheen or any of the tiny tassels that framed the edges. "Let me show you how the trunk works. You three sit over there and be my audience."

Waving her scarf in the air, she said, "Now you see this scarf." Raja placed the scarf in the trunk. Then she put her hand under the trunk and turned two pins, making the false bottom of the trunk cave in at the center. She pushed the scarf into the secret space underneath the panels, and turned the pins to again secure the false bottom.

Raja stood up and waved her arms toward the trunk as if she was a magician. "And now you don't see the scarf," she said.

Pavel, Shamra, and Hannah smiled and looked into the empty trunk.

"Very tricky!" said Pavel. He reached under the trunk to try the trick for himself. Turning the pins on both ends of the trunk, the false bottom collapsed. But going one step further, he pivoted the collapsed lids, pulling them upwards to reveal the whole of the hidden compartment.

All four were amazed at what they saw.

"Scrolls!" said Raja as she took her scarf out of the trunk to see everything inside. "These are Antom's scrolls!"

Raja picked up a scroll and unrolled it. It was a map of the estate.

"Why didn't Antom tell us about this?" asked Raja.

"Maybe fear," said Pavel. "If anyone found out he had drawn these maps he would be put to death. Obviously, Antom would have stolen the paper and ink from the castle."

Hannah added her own logic. "And of course, he had no idea we would be going into his hut or that the trunk was even still here."

Hannah picked up another scroll. "Look, there's writing on this map and it shows the first floor of the castle. Here it says *Kitchen Pantry*."

"Okay, that's good in case we get stranded here," said Raja.

"And there are more words, *Halls, Kitchens, Guard Room, Barbican, Store Room, Lavatory, and Keeping Room*."

Pavel leaned over and looked at the map as well. "And over here it says *Tower of Death*."

"Which is not where we want to land, considering we were just in a dungeon," said Raja.

"Yes, I think we should avoid that place," said Pavel.

"I take it that you want to go into the castle," said Raja.

"I think we should. It may give us some hints as to what is going on with the peasants," said Hannah.

"Only if no one is in there," said Pavel.

"If no one is out here, why would there be anyone in there?" asked Hannah.

"Let's hope we're right," said Pavel.

It didn't take long for everyone to agree that the castle was probably empty and it would be safe to enter. Before leaving, Pavel thought he would take a few more scrolls and tucked them inside his cloak.

Then, leaving the hut and looking at the map that Raja had found, they looked at a few more items, such as a bridge, the gallows, a tributary, and a number of paths. They also noticed a few places where an x was marked on the map but they didn't know what those were about. They then decided on the best route to take to the castle. Riding their horses, they started for the huge stone structure.

Chapter 8

Tower of Death

"I'm glad this castle has a door," said Raja, looking over to see that Tan was following them as they rode their horses toward Thrumb Castle.

"That's very logical, otherwise we may not get in," said Pavel.

"But we may not get in anyway," said Shamra. "The map shows it has a moat."

"But the drawbridge should be down if no one is in the castle," said Pavel. "Otherwise how would they have gotten across the moat? You can only close the drawbridge from the castle side."

"True," said Shamra, "but what if it's up?"

"Then we could swim over the moat."

"Maybe you will, but I don't think I will because that would mean someone is in the castle," said Shamra.

"Maybe they have a way of lifting the bridge from the other side of the moat," said Pavel.

Seeing that the conversation wasn't going anywhere, Shamra decided to stay quiet and wait to see if the drawbridge was up or down.

As they approached the castle they saw a stone fence surrounding a large area. They looked through the gate to see an empty pasture with a stream running through it. Inside the fence were various stable buildings. They were next to the castle with a bridge leading to a barred door. Pavel tried opening the gate and to their surprise it was open. They led their horses through the gate and into the pasture.

The three filled their pouches with water and took a lengthy drink. It was very refreshing after having ridden for such a long way. This would be a good place to let their horses graze while they investigated the castle.

After being refreshed by the mountain water, the group walked closer to the castle and saw that the stream formed a moat around the thick outer walls of the castle, which had a row of machicolations all along the tops for defense. The castle was very well fortified, to say the least. Everyone could see that going across the moat would have been impossible. Luckily, however, the drawbridge was down.

"Looks like no one is here," said Pavel.

The four walked across the drawbridge to stand in front of the barbican.

"Who's going first?" asked Hannah.

"I will," said Pavel as he looked up at the pointed portcullis and then added, "If the gate doesn't come down on me."

"You said no one was here," said Shamra.

"I know," said Pavel. "It's just a bit of the jitters."

Then, with three very long leaps, he made it through the barbican. The girls quickly followed. In front of them was another type of barbican with a very narrow passage.

Even though they had all convinced each other that no one was in the castle, they couldn't help but stay quiet as they felt their way along the walls of the narrow and dark passageway. The air became cooler and cooler the further they went along, making the experience all the more uncomfortable.

They nearly bumped into another large wooden door to the castle. Pavel pushed on the door. To everyone's relief, mixed with a bit of trepidation, the door opened. By now their eyes began to adjust to the dark and Pavel saw a torch hanging on the side of the wall. Examining it, he found it was ready to be lit.

After lighting the torch, Pavel carried it with him and led the way through the gatehouse. They then went across the inner courtyard and into a small hall, which joined a larger one. Walking from room to room they lit the torches hanging on the walls and, surprisingly, they could see that everything was in place, as it should be.

The keeping room, which was next to the large hall, had wood beside the hearth, ready for a fire. There was even a chaise in front of the hearth, which rested on a huge round rug. Pavel noticed that a trunk similar to Antom's was next to the fireplace. It, too, had carvings of bear heads, and the walls had tapestry hangings with bear images.

The hall had an enormously long table with a golden goblet set for every chair and six large golden spoons placed down the middle of the table. In the very center of the table was a very unusual decorative ornament. A tall golden bear stood on its hind legs surrounded by six candles.

Against the wall were numerous mirrors with carved bear heads on either side. Hannah immediately saw a striking resemblance to the table arrangements and wall decorations that were at Bolger Castle. When Hannah mentioned it to the others, they acknowledged it only in passing—except for Raja, who now feared her uncle could show up at Thrumb Castle at any time. Pavel told Raja not to worry and to enjoy the moment. He was hungry and wanted to check out the kitchen next.

So, after walking into the kitchen, they found it was perfectly arranged with a huge pantry of dried food to last at least two months. The food was very enticing, which helped make Raja forget about any sort of danger lurking in the castle. They soon found themselves taking the food out and arranging it on plates in preparation for their own little feast. In all, they had seven different bowls with an assortment of dried or pickled food, which included meat, berries, pickles, string beans, nuts, flat bread, and various rounds of aged cheese. After the table was laden with the various foods, Raja filled four goblets with apple cider. Having sipped it earlier, she thought it was an excellent addition to their meal. But, after having done all of that, Raja didn't forget to give Tan some of the bread and cheese, which the dog devoured in very short order.

Pavel and the girls were feeling quite a bit better after they had eaten some food, especially Pavel. The girls had even managed to find some comfortable dresses to put on. All in all, their little feast had taken up most of the day.

Pavel stood up. "I would like to make a toast to the three lovely Princesses of Zurkia."

The girls smiled in anticipation of what he would toast.

"I see you are in a jolly good mood," said Raja.

Pavel bowed to acknowledge the comment. He held up his goblet and shouted, "May you always do what you love and never trip on your dresses."

The girls laughed.

Raja took a sip of cider. "Very good advice," she said as she held up her own goblet to make another toast. "And may you never fall on your sword!"

"Indeed, I shall take heed of your advice, lest I end my life in a clumsy fashion."

Again, everyone laughed.

"Dancing, anyone?" asked Pavel as he strolled over to Shamra and held out his hand. "May I?"

Giggling and feeling a little shy, she said, "Of course." She stood, allowing Pavel to swirl her around the room.

Raja wasn't sure she felt jealous or just happy for them. However, jealousy seemed to be the stronger emotion, despite the fact that she knew it was only in fun.

Hannah saw that Raja wasn't smiling. "Are you jealous?" asked Hannah, leaning over towards Raja.

"Certainly not," said Raja.

"I think you are."

"Am not." Then, in an instant, Pavel swept Raja off her feet and the two of them were twirling around the room.

A radiant smile emerged across Raja's face. It was obvious she liked his attention.

Hannah didn't mind being left out and was quite happy just to observe. She picked up a balalaika that was hanging on the wall and started to play. Shamra clapped along with the music and Pavel started to sing. Pavel, being the gentleman that he was, could not leave Hannah out and offered to dance with her as well.

Accepting the offer and feeling very lighthearted, Hannah couldn't keep herself from commenting during their dance. "Are you saving the best till last?"

"Perhaps." He lifted Hannah up in the air and swirled her back down.

Hannah laughed, thinking he certainly was a nice lord. The four were managing to have a very good time with the noise escalating louder and louder. Pavel was not paying close attention to where he was dancing and happened to knock over a few bear statues that were standing in various places on the floor.

Suddenly, Tan barked. The bark was piercing and very loud.

The four immediately stopped what they were doing, their happy expressions turning to fear.

Raja spoke first, in a quiet voice. "Why is he barking?"

"There may be someone in the castle," said Pavel.

"What?" asked Shamra. "Someone is in the castle?"

"I don't know," said Pavel. "Raja, call Tan."

Raja called Tan but the dog paid no attention and it barked again. This time the bark was louder than before.

Pavel grabbed onto Raja's arm. "Raja, call Tan!"

"Tan, come," said Raja in an urgent tone.

This time Tan came.

"We need to put him on a leash," said Pavel.

The four looked around to see what they could use.

"I found some rope," said Raja as she took it from a hook. She quickly made a leash for Tan.

"Brilliant," said Pavel.

"We should get out of here," said Raja. "Whoever is here has heard us by now."

"But I think they would have barged in on us if they had," said Pavel. He stroked Tan to assure him that things were okay. "Let's see if Tan shows us anything."

The four walked silently out of the hall. Tan pulled on the rope, wanting to go ahead of everyone. The dog led the four friends to the base of some spiral stairs near the entrance of the castle, and desperately wanted to go up the stairs.

Pavel pulled out the map of the castle to find their whereabouts. "These are the stairs for the *Tower of Death*."

"That sounds eerie," said Raja, trying to hold Tan back. "I think we should get out of here."

"What is the *Tower of Death*?" asked Shamra.

"It's like a dungeon," said Hannah. "I think we should take a look."

Pavel agreed and tried to convince Shamra and Raja to go along with the idea. "I think there's life up there, otherwise Tan wouldn't be barking. We can't ignore this."

"What if it's a trick and someone locks us up there?" asked Raja.

Feeling annoyed at Raja's fear, Pavel spoke sarcastically. "Then you can sprout wings and fly away."

Thinking Pavel rude, Raja summoned her courage and quickly took the lead, holding Tan with the leash. "If you don't hurry, you'll have to eat my dust."

"Wait up," said Pavel, seeing that Raja was offended by his comment. "Sorry about my words."

"Apology accepted," said Raja as she went around the first coil.

A couple of small windows gave them just enough light to get to the top of the stairs. However, a heavily barred door stopped their investigation. Tan began barking again.

"Shhh," said Raja to Tan.

"Do you hear that noise from inside?" asked Raja as she put her ear against the door.

Pavel leaned in beside Raja and listened. "It sounds like someone is calling for help."

"We've got to get in there," said Hannah.

"Maybe it is a trick," said Shamra.

Pavel answered with a tone of urgency. "I don't think so. We've got to take our chances in case it is an innocent prisoner. And it's highly unlikely that it's a trick."

Shamra agreed and everyone worked together to unbar the door. Finally, the last piece of wood came down. Pavel pushed the heavy door open.

All eyes fell upon a man sitting on the floor and chained to the wall. He could no longer hold his head up and he looked as if he was barely alive. His body was thin, not emaciated, but more than likely severely dehydrated.

"Let's get him unchained and out of here," said Pavel. "He doesn't look like he has much longer to live."

"Do we have any water?" asked Hannah.

"I'll go get some," said Raja.

"All right," said Pavel, "hurry."

Raja took Tan with her and stepping as quickly as she could, went down the stairs. Reaching the bottom, she found a water bowl by the entrance of the gatehouse. She proceeded through the inner passage and into the narrow barbican. It was almost completely dark but there was only one way to go and that was straight ahead. She tried to keep from imagining the torture enemies had endured by trying to enter the castle using this same passageway.

Raja finally reached the drawbridge. There was just enough light left in the day that she could safely cross the moat and find her way to the pasture to the stream. She filled her bowl and retraced her steps back to the castle. When she reached the inner passage, it wouldn't have made a difference if her eyes were open or closed—that's how dark it was. She was glad Tan was with her to help lead the way.

Raja hurried across the inner courtyard trying not to spill the water. She stumbled on a stone. Fortunately, she saved herself from falling and only some of the water spilled. Oddly, at that moment she remembered the toast Pavel had given about not tripping. It helped to urge her on in the desperation of the situation.

Coming now to the bottom of the stairs, she carefully placed each foot on the steps as she ascended, Tan still in the lead.

"Good boy, Tan," said Raja. "We're almost there."

Tan barked as if to notify the others of their arrival. Even though it appeared no one else was in the castle, the loud barking still made Raja nervous. Relief came as she heard voices up ahead.

Pavel, Hannah, and Shamra had already taken the chains off the prisoner with a key they had found and were carrying the man downstairs.

"Is that you, Raja?" asked Pavel.

"No."

"Ha, ha, very funny. Did you get the water?"

"Yes."

"Good," said Pavel. "You were very brave to do that."

"Thank you."

Everyone continued their way down to the bottom of the stairs.

"What should we do with him?" asked Pavel.

"Let's lay him beside the hearth in the keeping room," said Hannah.

"Good idea," said Pavel.

The man was carried to the chaise beside the hearth and immediately Raja lifted his head while Shamra tried giving the man some water. Thankfully, the man was able to sip some of the liquid. Raja laid the man's head back down. Pavel worked at getting a fire going to warm the room.

Intermittently, Raja lifted the man's head to allow him more water. The two girls kept this up for another hour and then the man fell asleep.

"What do we do now?" asked Raja.

"Let's go to sleep. I'm tired," said Shamra.

"But we don't know this man. What if he awakes while we are all asleep? There's no telling what he would do," said Raja.

"You have a point there," said Hannah.

"Let's chain him to the chaise," said Pavel.

Everyone agreed to the idea. Pavel went back to the tower to retrieve the chains. After returning to the keeping room he secured the man to the leg of the chaise. Then everyone found a spot to get some sleep, including Tan, who lay down beside the prisoner.

Chapter 9

From the North

Morning came and Pavel suggested that everyone take a turn standing at the top of Thrumb Castle tower to see if anyone would return to check on the prisoner, and most likely to check to see if he was dead. Pavel took the first watch, leaving the girls with the prisoner in the hearth room.

The prisoner slowly awoke and drank more of the water that was offered. Tan nudged the man and licked his hand.

Looking at each of the girls, he asked, "Why am I here?"

"We rescued you," said Raja. "Who are you?"

"I'm a peasant under the Tyhets."

"What did you do to deserve a death penalty by starvation?"

"Not much really."

"Tell us," said Hannah.

"There was another peasant among us who we were warned to leave alone. It was death if we disobeyed."

Listening intently, the girls gave the man bits of food to eat while he talked.

"It was hard for me to watch how the peasant was always alone. I thought it was emotional torture for him to not be allowed to talk with others. I felt sorry for him and thought it wouldn't matter if I spoke a few words to him."

Giving the prisoner more food, the girls nodded as he told his story.

"However, the man turned his face down to hide it when I approached him. When I got close to him he pushed me away, telling me to go. Then a warrior, who had seen me talking with this peasant, took me away and I was left in the *Tower of Death* to die."

"How awful," said Shamra.

"The warrior told me that I was another example of what happens when orders weren't followed, and it was a pity that I couldn't obey."

"So there are others that have died?" asked Shamra, feeling terrible about the situation.

"I'm afraid so."

"Did you get a look at the peasant?" asked Raja.

"No, I didn't."

"That is very strange," said Hannah. "Why did they want to keep this peasant alive and alienate him at the same time?"

"None of the peasants ever knew why," said the prisoner.

Raising his arms, the prisoner asked, "Can I get these off?"

Deciding that the man was telling the truth, Raja removed the chains.

Rubbing his arms, the prisoner said, "I'm a lucky man." He reached over to pet the dog. "This is my dog. His name is Tan."

Raja laughed. "I can't believe that," she said. "That's the name I gave him."

"That is funny," said the prisoner.

"I'm glad you have your dog back," said Raja, who also felt a bit disappointed that she had just lost ownership of the dog.

The prisoner saw the disappointment in Raja's face. "I never thought I would have lived to see my dog or anyone else again, and because you have rescued both me and Tan, my dog is your dog as well."

A smile came over Raja's face as she petted the dog. "Thank you. I have gotten very attached to Tan in only this short time."

"I can see that," said the prisoner.

Hannah reached over to pet the dog as well. But she didn't put off asking the prisoner more questions. "Can you tell us why this place is abandoned?"

"The Tyhet chieftain ordered everyone up north. In the past, only some of the peasants left. However, this time everyone left."

"Do they come back to the village?" asked Raja.

"Yes. After leaving Thrumb Village for some time the peasants always came back. And then a different group would leave for the north. But rumor has it that after one more journey south most of the peasants will be going back to the north and staying there."

"What do they do up north?"

"Hard labor. They look even more exhausted after they come back from their forced toil."

"Have you ever been up north?" asked Raja.

"No, I haven't. I was always part of a group that stayed to work in the fields."

Then, just as the peasant finished his sentence, Pavel came running into the keeping room.

"A group of warriors and peasants are headed this way, coming from the north. We've got to leave immediately. Unchain the prisoner and let's go."

"Already done," said Raja.

"No doubt to celebrate my death," said the peasant.

"By the way," said Pavel, "nice to meet you."

"Likewise," said the peasant.

The group hurried to gather their things and then left the castle. Raja had hoped to stop in at the hut, as she remembered that she had left her scarf there, but now she wouldn't be able to retrieve it. She felt dreadfully disappointed.

Pavel helped the peasant walk, as he did not have much of his strength. They quickly got their horses from the field and mounted. The peasant rode double with Shamra, who was the shortest of the girls.

"Once the warriors get to the castle, they will see that people were there and that the prisoner has escaped, so we need to ride as fast as possible," said Pavel.

With that command the four rode with good speed along the Landmark Trail with the peasant hanging on for his life and Tan running behind. They decided not to stop for the night and instead had a short rest. Pavel had taken a torch just as they were leaving the castle and it provided enough light for them to continue their journey throughout the night. Raja carried Tan in her arms part of the way, as the dog became extremely exhausted.

After riding a few days, Pavel eventually heard the same story from the peasant that he had told the girls. Pavel agreed it was very cruel treatment to alienate a peasant.

"By the way, what's your name?" asked Pavel.

"Bogdan Netter."

"Do you have family?"

"I have a young wife."

"One day, God willing, she is going to be happy to see you again. I can imagine that right now she is mourning for you."

"Yes, she will be," said Bogdan, feeling sad that his wife had to suffer, but happy he was alive.

With much relief, the group made it to Levap Castle mid-afternoon five days later. They put their horses in the stables and walked around to the balcony of the basket lift. For some reason Raja thought it was unusually quiet and she wondered why there weren't any guards around. She tried to toss the thought away, as perhaps the guards were attending to something very important.

But eventually she decided to comment. "Pavel, did you see other horses in the stables?"

"No."

"Don't you think that is strange?"

"Yes, but maybe something important came up and they had to leave."

Pavel tugged on the rope and waited for the basket. The basket was not let down. Pavel tugged again, but still no basket.

"Are you doing it right?" asked Shamra.

"Yes, three tugs, count to three, and then two tugs."

"No, it is one tug at the end."

"Oh, right. I'll try it again." Pavel tugged on the rope again, this time doing it right. They all waited for the basket, but it was not thrown down.

"Obviously someone's off duty," said Pavel. "Shamra, you'll have to see about that, since you are the new princess here."

"How are we going to get up?" asked Shamra.

"Have you heard of climbing walls?" asked Pavel.

"Yes, but don't sound so sarcastic."

"Sorry."

"Thankfully, only one of us has to do it," said Raja.

The girls waited for Pavel to offer.

"Okay, I'll do it. In fact, I'd be honored."

Pavel grabbed the rope and braced his feet against the wall and started his climb up. He actually had no trouble climbing the wall and quickly reached the top. He hoisted himself onto the wall of the bartizan and sat on the ledge looking down at Raja.

"I can do that," said Raja and she grabbed the rope and began climbing the wall herself. She made it to the top, not quite as fast as Pavel, but she did it.

"I think I'll pass on climbing the wall," said Shamra. "Lower the basket."

Pavel lowered the basket and pulled Shamra up to the top of the castle. She graciously got out of the basket, feeling happy to be at her new home. The peasant was next and after he was lifted up, he immediately went down into the hall to find something to eat. Raja and Pavel called after him, giving him a few instructions as to where the kitchen was.

"Let down the basket!" shouted Hannah, feeling a little impatient.

"You won't be needing that," said a deep voice behind her.

Hannah whirled around to face a man who was sitting on a horse and pointing a sword right in her direction.

Chapter 10

Back to the Beginning

"Father?" said Hannah.

"That's right, you're coming with me!"

"I am not going with you!"

"You will come or I shall take you by force."

Standing on the ledge of the bartizan of Levap Castle, Pavel turned his head and spoke to Raja. "I think that's Hannah's father."

The prince's dark hair blew in the wind and contrasted with his pale face and deep-set eyes. "Yes, I'm sure of it," said Raja, who was also standing beside Pavel on the ledge of the bartizan.

Pavel called out. "Leave her alone!"

"Who are you to tell me what to do with my daughter?"

"Why do you want her?" asked Pavel.

"She belongs with me. I see that my fatherly teachings have become very useful and I do not want to put them to waste." The prince held up an arrow. "But I never meant for her to use her talents against me!"

Hannah knew the arrow belonged to her, a sure sign that her father must have sent the Tyhets after them while they were passing through the Trough Valley.

Pavel shouted back at the prince. "She's grown now and can make up her own mind. You cannot force her to go with you."

"Ah yes, grown into a princess and must mind her duties. She is to rule with me. We are a family."

Hannah didn't know whether to draw her own sword or not. But then she saw that fighting would be futile, as there were a number of legionnaires behind her father.

"Hannah is part of our family now," said Raja. "You have had your chance, but you have done evil."

"Come now, Raja. What evil have I done? I just want what is rightfully mine."

"What's that?" asked Raja.

"Why, the throne of Zurkia, of course, and I will get it."

"The Zurkian throne is not yours."

"And how do you know that?" asked the prince.

It was true that Raja did not know the precise history, but she could not image that her mother was not legitimately the tzarina.

"And you, Raja, are supposed to be with the Dracians," said the Dark Prince.

Raja shuddered at that thought and found it hard to comprehend her uncle's wish for such evil. What right did he have to say where she should be?

"But perhaps I'll let you join Hannah in her princess duties." The Dark Prince laughed. "After all, aren't you cousins?"

Raja wondered if he knew about Shamra. She made sure to stand in front of Shamra so she couldn't be seen.

"Your schemes won't work," shouted Raja.

"Ah, but you are wrong. I will soon have an infinite source of power that you don't know about and nothing will stop me from sitting on the throne."

"What power is that?" asked Pavel.

"Once I possess it then you will know. I was defeated once, but never again."

"Where does this power come from?" asked Raja.

The prince laughed mockingly. "Do you think I would tell you—the one who steals my daughter from me?"

"I did not steal your daughter. It was you who waged war and it was her decision to go against you."

"I waged war to get what is rightfully mine."

"The throne is not yours!"

"That's where you are wrong. The only reason I was defeated was because I was without my power. But mark my word, I won't make the same mistake again. It won't be long before everyone will be bowing to me!" Thrusting his sword in the air, the Dark Prince shouted, "The power will be mine!"

Then he pointed his sword at Hannah and ordered her to mount a white horse that was beside him. "This is your horse, Hannah. Get on!"

Hannah had no choice but to obey her father.

The Dark Prince called up to Pavel and Raja. "If you follow us, I have Tyhet warriors posted ready to capture you."

Pavel shouted, "You won't get away with this!"

The prince ignored Pavel. He whipped both of the horses into action and Hannah and her father, along with the legionnaires, rode away from the castle estate.

Pavel, Raja, and Shamra stood, distraught.

"He can't get away with that," said Raja, who felt like crying.

"Pavel, what do we do?" asked Shamra.

"We'll get her back."

"Where is everyone when you need them?" asked Raja.

"Good question," said Pavel.

They started walking down the steps to the main floor of the castle, not knowing what to expect. The floor was barren, with no sign of any living person.

"No one is here," said Shamra with complete surprise.

"What's happened?" asked Raja, running into the other rooms. Shamra followed her around the castle. They even entered the throne room. To their alarm, the three thrones were gone.

"The nerve!" said Raja.

"Do you think they were stolen by the Dark Prince?"

"I'm sure of it."

"He really does want power, doesn't he?" said Shamra. "That's probably what he was talking about."

"Yes, it seems he thinks the thrones are part of it."

Pavel, having caught up with the girls, offered his calculation of the situation. "I think that either there was a surprise attack and everyone gave in to the attacker, or Zolf has betrayed the tzarina and ordered everyone to leave."

"Yes, perhaps Zolf is working for the Dark Prince," said Pavel.

"I think you are right. Look how we were treated. Rather a mean decision, to just throw some girls and a boy in the dungeon, don't you think?" asked Raja.

"Yes, and it appears that the Odyhun legionnaires are still working for the prince as well," said Pavel.

"That makes sense, considering Hannah thought the padesha was the one who was after her and doing her father's bidding," said Raja. "But, if this is all true, why did Zolf give us directions to Thrumb Castle?"

"That's easy," said Pavel. "Just to get rid of us and make it seem like he was on our side. Then while we were gone, he ordered the whole group of people to leave and who knows where they ended up."

Shamra was wide-eyed as she looked back and forth from Pavel to Raja. "Can I come?" she asked.

"Well, we haven't precisely decided where we are going, but yes, you may come, but first we have to go home. Our three weeks have just about gone by."

"Okay, and obviously I can't stay here," said Shamra.

"Of course not. You can help me be the Princess of Victory Manor. It's grown to be a very large estate and it could certainly use two princesses."

Shamra lightened up despite the horrible events of the day.

"Maya will enjoy teaching you how to run aspects of the estate," said Raja.

Shamra politely accepted that prospect.

"Let's find Bogdan," said Raja.

With no trouble they found the peasant asleep on the kitchen table with some leftover goat cheese in one hand and a half-eaten apple in the other.

"Poor fellow, he must have been extremely exhausted," said Shamra.

"Let's all go to bed now so we can leave early in the morning," said Raja.

The three agreed to the idea.

In the morning preparations were made to leave the castle. The group packed food that they could take with them, but any left-over food that would go bad was thrown out the castle windows. Bogdan had a quick lesson on how to ride the horse that had been ridden by Hannah. The lesson went very well as the horse was well trained. Then, after loading their provisions on their horses, they left for home.

On their homeward journey along the Iris Trail, Raja couldn't help but think how they were right back to the beginning with Hannah back with her father.

Part 2

The Unexpected

Chapter 11

Seven Bowls

The ride home from Levap Castle was calm, but rather sad because Hannah wasn't with them. Raja, Pavel, Shamra, and Bogdan were just coming off of the Iris Trail and into the Trough Valley.

"Raja, are you worried about Hannah?" asked Shamra.

"Sometimes, but I try not to worry because it won't change anything."

"True."

"There is power in believing things will get better."

"What exactly do you mean?"

"What your mind believes will dictate your future. If you are afraid bad things will happen, they will, so keep believing in the good."

"I haven't heard it said like that before," said Shamra.

Raja allowed her horse to stop and rub its head against its front leg. Shamra's horse did likewise as Raja continued their conversation. "You have a choice to either live in fear or in faith of good. One must keep a spirit of faith and not of fear."

Shamra pondered Raja's ideas and wanted to follow her advice. "I can see why you hold the magnitude of strength you do. I shall do well if I can even bear a small portion of it."

"A small seed turns into a great tree."

Shamra smiled at Raja's wisdom. She surveyed the distant surroundings with her thoughts wandering to the near future. "Do you think we should say anything to Viktor about Hannah?"

"What do you think, Pavel?" asked Raja.

Pavel, who had been listening to the conversation, considered the question. "My first inclination is that we should," he said. "What do you think, Raja?"

"I agree, but we need to tell him to trust us to get Hannah back. I don't want a battle over the kidnapping."

"Are you sure we can do it?" asked Pavel.

"Yes, I know how Hannah thinks and she would agree with my idea."

Pavel looked at Raja with questioning eyes. "So you really think we should rescue her ourselves?"

"Yes, I believe Hannah and I can somehow work out a plan."

"Can I be part of it?" asked Shamra.

"Yes, I'm sure we'll need your help," said Raja.

"Are you going to tell Viktor about everyone missing at Levap Castle?" asked Shamra.

"I think we should," said Raja. "But I would like to have a meeting with Antom first."

Bogdan was sitting quietly the whole time. Raja turned to speak to him.

"You must promise to keep this all secret."

"You can count on me. I won't tell a soul."

"Good, you can join us at our meeting."

"Where am I going to live?" asked Bogdan.

Raja looked to Pavel for an answer.

"You can live in one of the rooms inside the manor. The information that you could give us about the Tyhets may become very important and we wouldn't want to jeopardize that by you living in the Manor Village. If word gets out that you are in the village, the Tyhets may come after you."

"Thank you," said Bogdan. "Living in the manor will suit me very well. I've gone from near death to living like a noble!"

The three smiled at Bogdan. He continued the journey trying to imagine what his new life would be like in a manor.

The next day the group finally reached the outskirts of Victory Manor estate. Once they passed the village a messenger galloped up to Raja. He bowed his head and handed her a letter. "For you princess."

"Thank you, and could you inform Viktor that we are back."

The messenger bowed again and rode off.

"I wonder what is so urgent that I should receive this letter out here?" Raja asked, looking at the other three, but then again, she could guess the reason.

"Let's go to Antom's house and have a meeting with something to eat," said Pavel. "You can read the letter to us there."

Agreeing, the friends rode to the outer court at the back of the manor where they dismounted their horses. The servants took their horses to the stables.

Antom and Yana were both in their small dwelling inside the courtyard when the group arrived.

"So you're back safely?" asked Antom.

"Well, not quite," said Pavel.

"Who's that?" asked Antom.

"Bogdan Netter."

"And who is Bogdan Netter?"

"He's a prisoner that we rescued."

"A Tyhet prisoner?"

"Yes."

"And we can trust him?"

"We can."

"Then, welcome to our home," said Antom.

"Thank you," said Bodgan.

"Where's Hannah?" asked Yana.

"She's back with her father," said Raja.

"My word, how did that happen?" asked Antom.

"We'll tell you all about it but first I'd like to read this letter," said Raja.

"Go ahead," said Antom.

Raja read the letter out loud.

Dear Kind-Hearted Raja,

Do you know something that I don't? Hannah is missing from Bolger Castle! I've anointed Fedor as prince and he is now taking over Hannah's duties at the castle. Please tell me what has happened to Hannah. This is certainly not like her to evade her duties as princess.

Also, I have been creating a coat of arms for Zurkia since members of our royalty have been found. Please tell me your suggestion for the royal arms. But I have to say, it is difficult concentrating on this when Hannah is missing.

Your Loving Tzarina Mother

After reading the letter, Raja looked around her circle of friends. "What do we do?" she asked.

"Well, you said that we should tell no one," said Pavel.

"But I think my mother should know. I will write to her saying to tell no one what has happened as we need to keep the information secret in order to get Hannah back."

With everyone in agreement, Raja wrote her mother a letter and added at the end not to worry, as everything would be fine. When she was finished writing, she read the letter for everyone's approval.

Dear honorable and loving Tzarina Mother of the throne,

Thank you for your letter and concern. I am writing to tell you that Hannah's father appeared at Levap Castle with legionnaires and warriors. He forced Hannah to go with him to the north. She did not want to obey him, but she had no choice. Do not tell anyone of this and do not worry about the situation, as Pavel, Shamra, and I will get Hannah back. And in regard to the coat of arms I am in favor of eagles as Zurkia's symbol.

From Raja, an ever-loving and determined daughter

There were no objections to anything in the letter so Raja rolled it and handed it to Pavel, who said he would give it the bailiff tomorrow. Pavel then left to tell Galina to bring everyone, including herself, a meal to the house of Antom, with that being seven bowls.

While Pavel was out, Antom and Yana first listened to how Hannah went back to her father and how they had come back to an empty castle. They were dismayed over the news about Hannah but felt better when they saw Raja's confidence that she could rescue Hannah. Further on in their conversation, Antom and Yana found humor in the dungeon story and everyone had a good laugh over the ordeal.

Then, while petting Tan, Bodgan told his story of how he almost died in the *Tower of Death*. Antom was very interested in everything he had to say and asked a lot of questions. He said that there was something very strange about Bogdan's story and that he possibly had an important contribution.

Chapter 12

Antom's Story

Galina delivered the meals in seven bowls to Antom's hut. Everyone was given a new wooden spoon that Antom had made. Beginning to eat, they squeezed in around the fire waiting for Antom to tell his own story about Thrumb Village.

"So, you went into what used to be our hut?" asked Antom.

"Yes," said Pavel.

"What was in it?"

"A trunk. And we found maps of Thrumb Castle in the trunk," said Pavel as he took out the maps from his cloak and unrolled them.

"Those are undoubtedly my maps. So, you know about the secret panel."

"Raja helped with that one. She actually remembered you making things vanish inside the trunk."

"Why is that trunk still there? Wouldn't it have been taken with everything else?" asked Raja.

"I made that trunk," said Antom.

"I noticed that it was extremely well crafted with a lot of carved detail," said Pavel. "But one of the legs was broken."

"I broke the leg on purpose because I didn't want it taken by anyone, including the Tyhets. I started a rumor among the peasants and said that I stole it from the castle. That's why I tried to make it look like it came from there."

"Which could have been true, since you regularly went to the castle," said Pavel.

"Yes, that's right. And no one would have wanted to take a trunk that was stolen from the castle. In fact, no one ever came into my hut on account of it and eventually it became known as the cursed hut, which I'm sure was reinforced after our quick banishment from the village."

"But wouldn't the peasants have reported you for stealing?" asked Pavel.

"Yes, someone actually did. But the accusation was overthrown, because the chieftain knew it was mine, since I had made him a similar one. And in addition, the chieftain didn't want anything to happen to me because he loved Yana's tea."

Pavel responded. "I can see why not having anyone taking the trunk was so important with it having the secret bottom to hide your drawings."

"Yes, I loved to sketch and draw maps. But of course, that wasn't allowed among the peasants and if I was caught I would have been put to death."

Bodgan was quiet but agreed, nodding his head fervently.

Antom got up and went over to his chest of draws. He got out some papers that he kept there and handed them to Raja.

"These sketches are very well drawn," said Raja as she passed the drawings around for the others to look at.

"Very talented," said Shamra.

"Thank you."

"Did you sketch while you were with the Tyhets?" asked Shamra, who was looking at the drawings very carefully.

"That is a very good question and that is what I wanted to tell you most of all."

Everyone had finished their meal by now and Galina collected the seven bowls to be taken into the kitchen.

"May I come back to the meeting?" asked Galina.

"Yes," said Pavel. "We like having you here."

Antom was eager to continue but waited until Galina returned. Galina reentered the hut shortly and the meeting continued.

"The answer to Shamra's question is yes. I did sketch peasants at Thrumb Village. And there was one peasant in particular that I remember."

Everyone listened with great interest.

"I had never seen this peasant before, but he came into my hut in the middle of the night and asked if I would sketch his face. He must have somehow found out that I knew how to sketch."

"And did you?" asked Raja.

Antom looked at Raja for a few seconds before answering. "Yes, I did and that sketch should still be in the trunk. There were . . ."

At that point Pavel interrupted. "We did not see any portraits, only the scrolled maps."

"But this is what you don't know," said Antom. "There are two other secret panels in the trunk."

"You've got to be joking," said Pavel. "Where?"

"I made more secret panels in the side of the trunk. The space inside the panels is about the length of a thumb."

"Clever," said Pavel. "Is there more to your story?"

Antom took a drink of apple cider and was ready to start again. "Yes, the peasant who came in told me to never tell anyone of the sketches in Thrumb Village or my life would be in danger by the Tyhets. He said to keep them hidden in my trunk. He said when I left the village to take the trunk with me and then give the parchments to someone I could trust. I didn't think I would ever leave the village, but as I told you, I did move, though the trunk had to stay behind. I couldn't say anything about the trunk for fear of the Tyhets finding out about its secrets."

"Puzzling indeed," said Shamra.

"Yes, it is and this is why I need to tell you this story," said Antom. "The odd peasant looked at my maps and wrote words on them. Then he drew a map himself and I put it with the others." Antom held out his hand. "Let's see if you have it."

Pavel gave Antom one of the maps, which he carefully unrolled. "This is the one here. It's a map of the secret passageways underneath Thrumb Castle."

"This is astonishing," said Pavel. "I wonder if it all exists?"

"He also wrote something on another parchment and told me to keep it as well. I eventually hid that parchment in the other side panel."

"So the panels come down?" asked Pavel.

"Not exactly. I made a locking pin and fastened the pieces together so no one would ever be able to tell there was a panel."

"You're a genius," said Raja, with admiration in her voice.

"There's one more thing. Before the peasant left he told me to carve three bears on the trunk and the only reason I can think of was for identification."

"What happened to the peasant?" asked Shamra.

"The next day I saw the same peasant working in the field. There were orders to not talk to him under any circumstances. He was only there a few days and then he left Thrumb Village with a different group of peasants. That was the last I ever saw of him."

Pavel put his hand to his chin. "This sounds like the same peasant that Bodgan approached."

"I agree," said Raja. "And for some reason I think someone wants to conceal his identity and that's why no one is allowed to speak to him."

Pavel agreed. "And that's why the peasant wanted his face sketched, so there would be some evidence of his existence."

At that moment, Bodgan stood up and spoke very loudly. "One of you has to get that trunk!"

"Sit down," said Galina with a bit of irritation. "And listen to the meeting."

Not that surprised at Bodgan's sudden outburst, Pavel said in a calming voice, "Stop fretting, Bodgan. I agree that the situation sounds harsh and that we need to do something about it, but let's think this through."

Antom tugged Bodgan back down to the floor and added his conclusions. "The other parchment may also hold important information that we don't understand yet."

"Somehow we need to get those parchments from the trunk," said Raja. "And we need to know who this peasant is and why this is happening to him." Raja looked around at everyone's face. "Any suggestions?"

Yana was very quiet and so was Shamra.

"I have one," said Pavel.

"Let's hear it," said Raja.

"I think the best thing to do is to retrieve the parchments from that hut during the night."

"And who would do that?" asked Raja.

"The most unsuspecting person would be a peasant woman," said Pavel, "since men are not allowed out during the night."

"Are you suggesting that I dress as a peasant and go get the parchments in the middle of the night?"

"Yes."

"Are you joking?"

"No, how else would we do it? And didn't you say you left your scarf there?"

"Yes," said Raja, who admitted that she desperately wanted to get it.

"So, that could also be an excuse for you to go there."

Raja thought it seemed like a logical plan. "And what if someone sees me while I'm walking to the hut?"

"I know," said Shamra. "You could carry some food with you to nullify any suspensions. Giving food to anyone that is hungry is a good way to gain trust and friendship."

"And I'll prepare the food," said Galina, who wanted to help.

Raja thought the idea would probably work but she still had one question.

"What if the peasants reported the scarf?"

"If they did, the scarf won't be there, and if they didn't, the scarf will be there. And in the case that the scarf is not there, we will have to think of how we can get it back," said Pavel. "But you can still get the parchments out of the trunk."

Antom added his reasoning. "Some of the peasants are afraid to reveal anything, so there is still a chance the scarf will be in the hut."

Raja was satisfied with those answers and agreed to the plan more readily that she would have thought. Losing her scarf made by her mother was quite unbearable. It had been the first thing that brought back memories of who she really was. She would take the chance and try to retrieve her scarf and at the same time get something that could prove to be vital in their discovery of the mysterious peasant.

"Remember, you have to take out the locking pins on the side panels in order for the panels to come apart," said Antom.

"Right," said Raja.

Feeling good about the plan, Pavel added, "Now the only thing left to do is convince Viktor of another trip to the north."

Pavel ended the meeting and later it was recorded in the *Book of Records* as the *Seven Bowls Meeting.*

Chapter 13

A Peasant Again

It hadn't taken long for Viktor to realize that something was going on, as word from the maids had gotten around that Galina had delivered seven bowls to Antom's house. Furthermore, Galina had eaten in Antom's house. Galina later admitted to Viktor that things may be getting out of hand in regard to Raja's safety. Viktor called for Pavel immediately the next morning.

Viktor was a good father and wanted to make sure Pavel was making intelligent decisions, especially for Raja's sake. Even though he was handsome for being middle-aged, Viktor had somewhat stern facial features. It definitely helped to acquire respect from other people. Pavel both admired and respected his father. He always felt free to say what was on his mind. The two had quite a discussion, which had Viktor on the edge of his chair with each surprising story. Of course, the most alarming story was of Hannah going back to her father.

"So let me get this straight, when you arrived back at Levap Castle, it was empty, Hannah went missing, but you managed to come home with one peasant from Thrumb Castle," said Viktor. "And now you want me to let you go to the Tyhet region again?"

Pavel nodded his head twice. "Yes, Father, I do."

"This sounds a bit outrageous. Why should I agree to this?"

"Because Raja, being a woman, is the right one to get the parchments from the trunk."

"Why do you say that?"

"Men aren't allowed out at night and she will cause the least amount of suspicion. She also left her scarf there and she very much wants to get it back."

Viktor knew how important the scarf was to Raja but her life was more important than a scarf. "I hesitate to agree to this. There is no telling what could happen when it comes to those peasants. They are trained to betray each other for the sake of rewards."

"Raja is bringing her own food to befriend any peasants who she meets. This should substantially lower any risk of peasants reporting her," said Pavel.

Viktor rubbed his chin. "I admit bringing food is a good way to win their trust."

"What is more, Raja is extremely good at defending herself in case anything does happen," said Pavel.

"True, her capabilities are very good."

"And disguised as a peasant will substantially lower the risk of the warriors noticing her."

"I can see that point."

"And we believe that getting the parchments from the trunk is an important piece of information to solve this whole puzzle."

"Yes, I agree. The lone peasant appears to be valuable to someone but we don't know why or who the person is," said Viktor.

"And that's what we need to find out. I already have a suspicion that the Dark Prince may be involved with the lone peasant," said Pavel.

"After hearing all of the bits of information, you may be right."

"So, what is your answer?"

"Will you keep an eye on the situation?"

"Most definitely."

"Okay, you have my permission, but hurry back and be careful when you get to Levap Castle. Lord Leo Lythym, the lord from the neighboring Lythor Manor has just paid me a visit informing me of peasants that have gone missing from his own village. Until we know what is going on, the situation in Zurkia is very dangerous."

Pavel agreed to take his father's warning seriously. He then informed the others of his conversation with Viktor and they got ready to leave. Then, departing from the manor, Pavel and Raja allowed Shamra to come as promised. Bodgan stayed behind with Antom and Yana to learn how to become a baker.

The three travelers estimated that the journey would take seven nights to get to Thrumb Castle and on one of their nights they could stay at Levap Castle. They dressed in light armor and each carried a sword and a shield. Raja and Shamra both wore a light chain mail vest and leather pants. Their swords were tucked into scabbards at their sides. Raja's scabbard, which had been given to her by Viktor, had an imprint of a crown, while Shamra's had an imprint of two crossed swords.

When they reached Levap Castle it didn't seem that anyone was occupying it so they deemed it safe to enter. They again climbed the walls with the rope, including Shamra this time. They cautiously went into the main hall, and as believed, no one was in the castle. They ate whatever nonperishable food they could find in the pantry in order to save their own food.

The next morning, Pavel started a conversation about the plan to go into Thrumb Village and necessary items were added to their belongings, such as food and Raja's peasant cloak.

After a thorough discussion about the plan, they started on their trek once again and after four more nights arrived at the same hill as before. The three climbed to the top of the hill and surveyed the village.

As expected, the huts were occupied with peasants and everyone was going about their usual duties.

Getting out the map of the estate, Pavel pointed out where Antom's hut was. "Do you see it? It's in the third row and seven up from the first hut."

"The one with a cart and a horse in front of it?" asked Raja.

"Yes."

"Okay, this is a bit scary, but I should be fine. It will just be a little stroll there and back."

"Right," said Pavel. "And we'll be watching from up here."

"In the dark?"

"There's going to be a full moon tonight. It'll be fairly light."

"Okay, thanks for that encouragement."

"For saying it's a full moon or that it's going to be light?"

"Never mind," said Raja.

"You're not suspicious about full moons, are you?"

The power of the full moon was one thing her peasant parents believed in, but Raja was working at changing her own belief system, even though it was taking her a while.

"Of course not," said Raja.

"I didn't think so," said Pavel.

"This is a good time to put on the peasant cloak," said Shamra.

Raja agreed and took off her chain mail garment, but left on her leather belt holding her sword. She slipped on the peasant cloak, which covered her boots but still had an opening in the front.

"How does this look," asked Raja, looking at Shamra with a smile.

"Perfect, except for your hair."

Shamra took off Raja's chain mail headband and parted some of her hair.

"Let me mess it up a bit," said Shamra, tossing some of Raja's hair in front of her face.

Pavel looked at Raja in amusement. "Raja, you look the part very well."

"Thanks, but it is a bit hard to see."

"I agree, it would be a good thing to see," said Shamra. "We need to get some of that hair out of your face." Shamra brushed some of Raja's hair to the side and Raja imitated walking like a peasant.

"Nobody would suspect that you weren't a peasant," said Pavel. "You certainly know how to act like one."

"Well, I do have experience," said Raja.

"True," said Pavel. "I just about forgot. You've changed so much."

"How's that?" asked Raja.

"Oh, just more . . ."

"Yes?" Raja gave Pavel a little smile.

"Oh, just more, you know, confident."

"Thanks," said Raja, thinking it was the best compliment she had ever had.

The sun went behind the mountains and evening came. One by one the peasants went into their huts. And sure enough, there was a full moon. The three kept watching Antom's hut. They didn't see anyone leave or enter the hut.

"It looks like the hut is vacant," said Shamra.

"Good," said Raja. "That will make the job easier."

"Remember to unlock both of the pins of the panels," said Pavel.

"I will," said Raja.

"Here's the food," said Shamra.

Raja took the bag and slung it over her arm.

Finally, it was thought to be late enough and Raja mounted her horse and started down the hill. It was still light enough that she could find her way. She rode close to the outskirts of the village and tied her horse to a tree. Walking towards the village, she began thinking about being a peasant again. Being in the cloak quickly brought back memories and she would have no difficulty fitting into the role of a peasant who was overworked. She finally stood at the edge of the village, at the third row, trying to find courage to walk towards the seventh hut. She rubbed dirt on her hands and face to appear more authentic. Feeling satisfied she started down the rough, dirt road.

Chapter 14

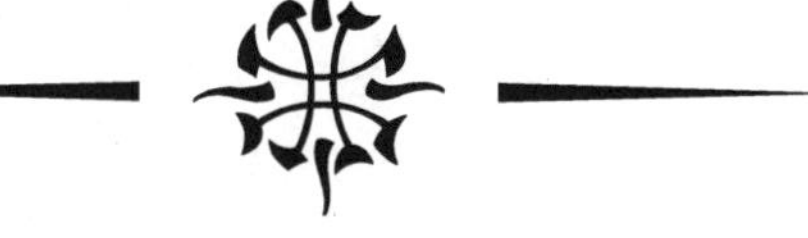

The Scarf

Raja tried walking as quickly as she could. She looked around but did not see anyone. A minute later, a woman came into the lane from behind a hut. Raja tensed and put her hand on her sword. And then two other women came out from a different hut, each carrying something in their arms. All three met and walked towards her. But, before passing her, they moved over to the far side of the lane, wanting to avoid her. Raja eased and took her hand off her sword.

Finally reaching the seventh hut, Raja stood in front of the open doorway. She quietly stepped inside, hoping to not see people sleeping on the floor. To her relief, the floor was bare. She walked along the wall where the trunk was kept.

It was gone!

She walked along the sides of the other walls. No trunk. Then her eyes fell upon a dark figure, almost right in front of her.

"Looking for this?" The voice was low and gruff. The figure held up something in his hand. It shone in the dark. Raja knew at once it was her scarf.

"Or are you looking for something else?" said the man.

Raja froze. This was not a peasant who was occupying the hut. Raja knew the man was a Tyhet by the way he spoke. She was in danger. Dropping her bag of food, her hand flew to her side and she whipped out her sword from inside her cloak. The man immediately took up her challenge and their swords clashed together in a series of clangs. The man's skills were good but so were Raja's. She felt confident that she could win this match. She told herself she had to win or she would find herself captive once again.

However, just before her next move, which she thought would have surely ended the match, something sharp jabbed into her back. A second Tyhet stopped the fight.

"Drop your sword," said the Tyhet who held his sword to her back.

Breathing heavily, Raja reluctantly dropped her sword. Then in the instant her weapon left her hand, the Tyhet behind her grabbed her and threw her on the ground. The two men tied her hands and feet and gagged her mouth with her scarf. Then, picking her up like a sack of grain, the Tyhets heaved her onto the cart that was in front of the hut. She landed with a thud as her body hit the side of the cart. A foul-smelling blanket was thrown over Raja, and the horse and cart headed toward the castle.

Raja's heart was beating wildly. She tried to calm herself so she could think. She concluded her abductors knew the scarf belonged to her and that she would come back for it. But why was Antom's trunk gone? Perhaps the trunk was left open with some of the maps still inside. She thought Antom was right and that a peasant had reported the odd findings in the hut. They would do anything for food.

But more desperately, Raja wondered where the Tyhet was taking her and what was going to happen to her. Her legs quivered and her mouth was dry. She couldn't help think that she would never see her friends or her family again.

The cart stopped moving and Raja heard other men and horses. She was handled roughly and taken from the cart. Her feet and hands were unbound, and she was forced to get onto a horse. They retied her hands in the front of her. Her horse rode alongside the others and the group of Tyhet warriors took off at a gallop. She quickly tired while trying to keep balance with her hands tied. She felt herself nearly slipping off the horse on several occasions and hung onto the mane as tightly as she could.

After having to ride with her hands tied for some time, they came to the Kazanka River at the mouth of the Sap Tributary, where a ship was waiting for them. Raja was taken to the ship and forced into the hold. Complete darkness surrounded her. She was trembling from both the cold and not knowing what was going to happen to her. Then she remembered her motto, live by faith and not by fear. She prayed for faith and felt her mind strengthening.

The groans of the ship told Raja the ship was moving. She wondered how long she would have to stay tied up. She found herself nodding off to sleep and after what seemed like a very long time her question was finally answered. The banging of the floor door up above jarred her nerves and a dim light filtered into the hold. A man entered the hold and took her scarf from around her mouth and untied her hands. If there was any small consolation to her capture, it was that she had gotten her scarf back. But deep inside of her, Raja knew her gift meant something bigger. To her, the returned scarf was a sign of strength to come. It reminded her of her mother's words to always persist.

Raja was allowed to come out onto the deck and eat with the crew in the very early morning.

Looking at the man who had untied her, she recognized him as Captain Mossovince.

"So you're back again," he said.

Raja stared at him.

"Well, it's good to see you again," said Captain Mossovince, starting the conversation a second time.

"It's good to see you too, but not in this situation."

"I understand. I have a hard time believing you actually are a princess, dressed like that."

That was true. She looked like a peasant with the clothes she was wearing. She was surprised the captain recognized her.

"It's a long story," said Raja.

"Seems your whole life is a long story."

The statement made Raja want to sigh but she instead asked, "Where are we going?"

"Port of Baku."

"Baku!" said Raja. She couldn't believe she was going back to the khan and Jafar. She felt a little lightheaded. Then she remembered Kuzma. He would get her out of this mess.

"I feel sorry for you, but I have to follow orders from the Tyhets and if I don't you know what happens to me," said Captain Mossovince.

"I can imagine," said Raja.

"The warriors who captured you said that a high price was paid for you by the khan and he should have what belongs to him."

"That is not right," said Raja. "No one should ever be bought."

"I think I agree with that, but what can be done? It's just the way it is. If I don't follow orders harm will come to my own family."

"It doesn't have to be that way. You can change things."

"I can't see that happening."

"It can."

"How?"

"By fighting for what's right. Be determined to stand up for yourself and your family."

"I hate to inform you but there just aren't any rights in this land and you aren't going to have any rights in Baku. You will only be controlled by someone higher in power."

"Well, please, let me tell you that nothing will change if you don't make an effort to change it. Think about what you are doing and the situation your family is in."

A serious look of contemplation came over the captain's face. Raja could tell he was thinking about what she said. He then returned to the duties of the ship.

Raja knew that what the captain said was true and that she would be forced to do what the royals wanted of her. At that point, she tried desperately to believe that someone would rescue her. However, it couldn't be Hannah this time. Perhaps Pavel would come. But he didn't even know where she was. She wondered how Pavel and Shamra must feel right now, horribly bad, she thought, and anxious.

Raja wanted to know if they would be sailing past Alexandra Port. She thought perhaps there would be a hope of intervention and she would be rescued.

"What direction will we be sailing?"

"North," said Captain Mossovince.

"I thought Baku was south."

"It is, but we are continuing downstream to the Strait of the Golden Sun and then heading west to Port Solis. Then we sail around Yurx Island and continue down the Yurphyn River that flows into the Khvalyn Sea. Baku is near the mouth of the Yurphyn River."

"So, I am thinking this is going to be a long trip."

"That's right, but with the boatmen towing the ship it will be faster than usual."

Raja could hear the mournful chants of the Volga rowers. She left the crew to stand by the forecastle to watch the rowers in the boats that were just ahead of the ship. In her opinion, their work was extremely laborious. They sang to the rhythm of the oars as their wooden paddles dipped in and out of the water. At first their chants sounded deeply mournful but as she continued to listen, an uplifting song replaced their sorrowful chant. There was no reason to be joyful, no reason to be hopeful, but despite their situation they sang with raised spirits. Perhaps it was the way they survived. They had to have hope or they would surely die—hope that someday they could enjoy freedom from their slavery.

The situation Raja found herself in was likewise difficult, and she was tempted to despair, but after watching the Volga boatmen she resolved to keep her spirits up during this journey away from Zurkia. She decided not to give up and was determined to somehow make it back to Zurkia. She would try to make the best out of her situation, just like the boatmen did.

As time went on Raja found that parts of the trip were interesting, as she had never traveled this far north before. They came to a bridge with ten arches, which was called the Decemarch Bridge. Raja had heard of the bridge and knew Zurkia and the country to the north had built it. Sailing along the wide shores of the country to the north, the ship was approaching another bridge, called Nexum Bridge. In the distance she saw a very large castle on top of a tall rocky hill. The ship stopped at Port Solis in the northern country, called Wsyrut. Here the ship made an exchange of Zurkian larch wood timber for gold, moss, and antlers.

The ship set sail again and as time went on, the journey became more and more tedious and hard to endure. Raja fell asleep from exhaustion on the side of the deck. When she awoke it was very early dawn and the ship was arriving at Port Tuckin along the Yurphyn River, to exchange some goods from Port Solis. The ship then made a stop at Subtrade, a small trading village just across the river in South Vel Saca. The river divided the two countries, as with all the other countries.

After trading timber from Zurkia for barrels of Jasmine rice at Subtrade Village, an exchange of boatmen slaves was also made for other goods such as wool and spindles. It made Raja sad to know the hard and unjust life the slaves had to endure.

The ship finally arrived at the Port of Baku in the country of Dracon. She was not expecting to be captured a second time. She wondered if this time it would be the end for her—never to return to Zurkia. The khan certainly would make every effort to ensure she would not escape this time.

Escorts stood ready to take Raja off the ship. However, their path was interrupted with numerous large pallets of stacked hay being loaded onto the ship. Each bale was tied with red hemp rope. The scent of the hay momentarily brought memories of the stables at Victory Manor and she remembered that some of the hay bales came from Dracon. She wondered how Viktor would react to her disappearance. He might blame the whole situation on himself for allowing them to go to Thrumb Village.

She was finally told to get into a carriage. She knew she would be at Dragomir Palace in just a short time—a princess, yet a slave. But despite her second time in captivity, she somehow felt she would still be used to free people who were caught in slavery.

Chapter 15

On Guard

Arriving at the Dragomir Palace, Raja was led by escorts to one of the courtyards and handed over to the chambermaids. There were whisperings among the maids as they looked at her thick loosely-woven clothes and her tangled hair. They even touched her red hair. Her hair color was extremely rare in this part of the lands.

Things didn't happen the way they did the first time she was at the palace. The maids promptly led her into a chamber and set about beautifying her in all the necessary ways. She was dressed with a silk robe and with layers of wide silk scarves that were wrapped around her waist, neck, and shoulders. Strands of beaded jewelry with thin strips of silk were woven into a round, braided hairstyle on each side of her head, but a thick strand of hair was let loose to hang down the front of her body. A necklace with a large opal stone was gently draped around her neck blending with her fair skin.

This took a good four hours and all Raja could do was stare at the hourglass as the sand drained four times within the conical glass tube. Then it was finally decided by the chambermaids that she was ready to meet the khan. Raja assumed she would be meeting the elderly Khan Temujunfar again. She was led through the wide corridors and thought she noticed a few more lion statues than before.

When Raja entered the throne room, the elderly Khan Temujunfar was no longer sitting on the throne. Instead, a young man was sitting in his place. He was obviously the new khan. He wore a cap with a pointed metal cone and had black eye makeup around his eyes. He had on a thick leather belt with a golden buckle in the image of a golden lion head.

She knelt before the throne with her head down.

"Welcome back," said the new khan.

She recalled hearing that voice.

"Do you know me?" asked the khan.

"Is it Jafar?"

"It is, please lift your head."

He looked different with his attire and makeup, but she still recognized his deep-set brown eyes.

"Where is your father?" asked Raja.

"My father died from an illness, and now I am the khan."

"I give you my sincere condolences."

"Thank you. I am glad to lay my eyes upon my wife again."

Raja realized that Jafar knew nothing about Hannah. "I'm not your wife," she said.

"Did I not hear you accept the marriage union in front of the sacerdos?"

"The situation is complicated and I will need time to explain myself."

"My wife will have all the time she wants. We will have dinner together and after the meal I will bring forth the subject."

"As you request."

Raja walked backwards bowing and left the room with the chambermaids. He did not seem to be the same prince she had known the last time she was at the palace. He seemed to be putting on an air that wasn't himself.

The evening came and Raja was escorted to an eating area in one of the palace's beautiful courtyards where Jafar was waiting for her. Throughout the courtyard there were large potted gardenia trees that filled the air with a lovely scent. Beside the trees on either side were large pots of flowers with purple and white amethyst flowers trailing over the edges.

Red columns wound with clematis vines were evenly spaced to form a circle in the middle of the courtyard. In the center of the circle of columns was a red bench, which was intricately designed with lion heads. The entire structure was known as the Rubra Columnaes.

Raja and Jafar sat across from each other at a round table. Bowls of different puddings, plates of exotic seafoods, and platters of desserts were already set on the table. They each had a golden bowl with a golden spoon. On one of the platters was baklava. The smell of the cinnamon, nuts, and honey immediately brought back a flood of memories. And one of those memories was Kuzma. She realized that she had not seen him in her goings and comings through the halls. She decided to ask Jafar about Kuzma.

"Does Kuzma still serve at the palace?"

"No, he was kidnapped by pirates while he was at the bazaar."

Raja knew what that was about and decided for now not to say anything. She was very sure that it had been Captain Chamomile who had kidnapped Kuzma.

"I felt sad about the loss, as I know he enjoyed entertaining my father and the children," said Jafar.

"Was there any effort to get him back?"

"No, I let him go. I didn't want to contend with the pirates. I don't know why the pirates wanted Kuzma, but I hope it turned out okay for him."

Raja wanted to tell Jafar about Kuzma, but didn't feel it was the right time.

"I hope your boat ride wasn't too bad coming over," said Jafar. "I wouldn't want my wife to suffer."

"The ordeal was terrifying."

"I'm sorry you had to endure that, but I'll assure you it won't happen again."

Raja wondered what he meant by that. It sounded like she was going to stay in Dracon forever.

"I have a gift for you," said Jafar.

"What is it?"

Jafar opened a small wooden box and gave it to Raja. Inside was a beautiful jade ring.

"Do you like it?" ask Jafar.

Raja's eyes widened. "Well yes, it is very beautiful."

"Put it on," said Jafar.

Raja put the ring on. It fit her perfectly. "I love it, but . . . but I can't keep it."

"Why not? Of course you can keep it."

"Well, because . . ." But Raja couldn't get her words out right.

Jafar lowered his head slightly, looking up at her with his dark eyes. "It is a gift I've been waiting to give to you for a long time. I haven't stopped thinking about you."

Holding her hand in front of her to look at the stone, she wanted to tell Jafar the real reason why she couldn't keep it, but instead she said, "Yes of course I'll keep it. Thank you very much."

"You're welcome. The jade comes from the mountains of Dracon."

Raja admitted it was very beautiful with its large dark green stone.

"By the way," said Jafar, "I got the ruby crown jewel back."

"By Captain Cham I'm assuming," said Raja.

"Yes, that's the name, but not directly. An old merchant carried out the trading."

"Did Cham ask for a lot of coin for the ruby?" asked Raja.

"It was a lot of coin, but the ruby came with a very expensive gold necklace."

"I see. But at least the coin went for a good cause."

"Why would you say that?"

Raja continued the conversation, telling Jafar about the details of Cham's conversion. Not listening to Raja's story all that intently, Jafar instead paid attention to her actions and her beauty, continually offering her the delicacies that were spread over the table. Despite Jafar's lack of interest in the topic, Raja felt comfortable in his presence and thought he was becoming more like the person she remembered, especially with his intermittently smiles and nods as she talked.

"I see you are wearing the opal necklace," said Jafar.

"Yes, it is very pretty."

"I had it specially made for you here in Dracon."

"Did the opal come from the mountains of Dracon as well?"

"Yes, and so does the silk. Do you like the silk scarves?"

"Yes, thank you. They are very beautifully made."

"For a beautiful girl." Jafar raised his eyebrows at her and smiled.

Raja blushed and felt a bit uncomfortable with the compliment. Jafar detected her uneasiness. He decided to bring the conversation around to something a little less personal.

"How is your sword fighting?" asked Jafar.

"Fine."

"From what I remember you were very good."

"I'm better now."

"Perhaps we should see."

"Perhaps."

"A duel?"

"A duel."

Raja took off the outer layer of her clothing. Jafar handed her a sword. The two stood in the center of the courtyard looking intensely into each other's eyes, their swords in front of their faces.

"On guard!" shouted Jafar.

The two stepped forward and locked swords, then swiftly clanged metal back and forth. Raja twirled in the air and came back to hit Jafar's sword, repeating her twirls and hits until he was forced to back down. She had him on the ground.

Jafar forced his sword up against hers and leaped to stand up. The impact forced Raja to the ground on her knees. Jafar jumped over her and turned to lock her with his sword but she was quicker and rolled over to her feet. She leaped on top of the red bench with Jafar following her. Facing each other, they dueled back and forth, coming within a hair's breadth to the end of the bench. Jafar did a backwards flip off the bench. Then, going into a single handstand, Raja flung off the bench and hid behind a pillar.

"I know which pillar you are at," said Jafar.

"Then come and challenge me."

Jafar did a flip in the air and stood in front of Raja. He challenged her with another round of fighting. Reflections of bright light bounced off the metal as the two combatants circled their swords. With tremendous speed, their swords banged together over and over. Raja held on and wouldn't let up, possessing a mindset she learned from practicing with Viktor.

Their swords locked and their chests heaved. Jafar's face grew serious. "We will show our love tonight."

"Do I have a choice?"

Piercing determination shone through Jafar's eyes as if to say no, she didn't.

Raja dealt Jafar another round of swift clashes, their swords in front of their faces.

Suddenly, Jafar's sword was knocked from his hand and Raja had the tip of her sword to his neck. She backed him against a pillar. They could feel each other's heavy breath against their faces. She looked him in the eyes.

"Give up?"

"I see you're dangerous," said Jafar.

"I can be."

"With me?"

"We'll see."

Jafar slowly pushed her sword away from his face. The tension subsided.

"You were right, you haven't lost your skills."

Jafar walked away from Raja and retrieved the robe she was wearing. He offered it to her. She took it and then at the same time Jafar turned Raja's body to face him. "I like your spirit. It's exhilarating."

"I never give up."

She always answers so intelligently, thought Jafar. If he had any doubt at all about how he felt about her, this certainly sealed his decision. "You have not lost your charm with words."

"Nor you."

Then, unable to keep it to himself, he said, "And you have not lost your beauty." He reached for her hair and let his fingers feel its soft texture.

Raja did not want to be intimate with Jafar and took a step backwards pulling her hair from his hand. Jafar's face stiffened, but then realized he may have been too quick to give such a comment. His face relaxed and he quickly suggested they move to a more relaxed environment. "Let's go for a walk in the Redvenus Garden."

Raja agreed and allowed Jafar to escort her into the garden. They slowly walked along the pathways. Jafar made sure no one was within hearing distance.

Raja spoke first. "Let me go back to Zurkia."

"Why would I let my wife depart from me?"

Instead of telling Jafar the truth about their relationship she challenged him with a question. "Why did you bring me back to Dracon? If I wanted to be your wife I would have stayed in Dracon in the first place."

Jafar refused to believe Raja's declaration. "I have a hard time believing that you went of your own free will. I could see how you wanted to marry me."

"It may have seemed like that, but I was only obeying your father."

"Perhaps to begin with, but I saw how the love between us grew. Our marriage will be strong and we will rule the country with prosperity."

Raja wanted to find out more about how Jafar was involved with the kidnapping. "So, who conspired this kidnapping?"

"The Grand Padesha was the one who approached me," said Jafar.

"And was he conspiring with the Tyhet chieftain?"

"He was, and also with the Dark Prince. But it was the chieftain who was responsible for the actual abduction."

Not a surprise to Raja.

"However, as far as I know it was the Dark Prince who was the initial instigator." Jafar didn't want to be pegged as one of the evil pursuers and hurried to say something good about his own intentions. "I agreed to the abduction not only because I wanted you back, but because I didn't want more harm coming to you from the Dark Prince."

"Was coin involved?" asked Raja.

"It was," said Jafar, who couldn't look at her at that moment.

"Why did you agree to have me captured for coin?"

"I so desperately wanted you back." Jafar stopped walking to look at Raja and spoke softly. "I love you. And I know you love me too."

Raja tried to think back to what it was like. True, she did like him and they got along very well. Really, they were so much alike. As their conversation developed he was becoming even more of the person she'd known before. He was certainly easy to talk with.

Jafar continued in his gentlemanly way. "And understand, this was my chance to have you as my wife. You know that I would do anything for you."

The word "wife" jolted Raja back to her senses. Of course, she couldn't stay in Dracon and be his wife. She decided she didn't want to hide the truth any longer. Even though Jafar was involved with her kidnapping, his intentions had been good and she felt Jafar was a trustworthy person. She would tell him what had gone on in the ceremony.

"As I said before, I am not your wife. It was my cousin who stood at the altar with you."

Jafar put his hands on Raja's shoulders and gave her an intense look. "I don't understand."

"Of course, you wouldn't, because not many people can tell us apart." Raja went on to explain how the whole plan of escape had taken place and also mentioned to keep it secret. Jafar listened the whole time with his mouth open and went from looking manly to looking incredibly disappointed and a little worried.

He finally asked in a tone that sounded a little too high pitched. "Do you mean to say that I'm married to your cousin?"

"If it helps to calm you in any way, I would say not because she gave false identity at the ceremony."

Jafar put his hand to his chest and blew out some air in relief. Then he turned to Raja with his hand on his chin. His voice returned to normal with a serious expression. "We will have to have another wedding ceremony."

Raja was not going to let the same thing happen to her twice and she decided to be firm with Jafar. "If coin was involved the answer is no."

"Please understand, it was the only way I could get you here."

"That doesn't matter. It was terrifying for me. Why did you do that?"

"Please remember, it was my father who was pressured by the Dark Prince into bringing you here to begin with. He agreed to it because of your beauty. Then when I saw you I knew I wanted to be with you forever."

"But you realize your actions are the same as your father's and you are not respecting me as a person."

Wanting to soothe Raja's wrong perception about him, he said, "Yes, I understand that now."

"Then you need to let me go back to Zurkia."

Jafar searched Raja's eyes. "But I know you love me."

Raja didn't know what to say. Did she actually have feelings for him again, now that she was here? And was she just too overwhelmed with the circumstances to admit it? Perhaps she needed some time to think about how she felt.

Jafar, seeing her hesitation, said, "I got you another horse."

"Is that so?" said Raja.

"Yes, and it is a beauty, dark red with a black mane and tail."

Feeling extremely tired, Raja wanted nothing more than to put her head against a horse and let her mind relax from all of the stress she felt.

"Show me the horse."

The two of them walked to the stalls as Jafar spoke softly to Raja. He wanted to say the right things to influence her to stay in Dracon.

"You can stay here and make a new life with me. We will be happy together and you can have whatever your heart desires. Think about that—a life of everything that is pleasurable. And you will not have to worry about the Dark Prince pursuing you."

Raja sighed. "I feel you are putting a lot of pressure on me to stay in Dracon."

"But you will be safe and protected here, and isn't that a worthwhile trade for staying?"

Jafar's offer seemed very tempting, as the thought of being sought by the Dark Prince was terrifying. She had already been kidnapped twice. Raja searched Jafar's face. Perhaps he was right. If she went back she would certainly be recaptured again or maybe even killed.

Seeing that he was influencing her to stay in Dracon, Jafar said, "Trust me, you will thank me later for this decision. By tomorrow, after you ride this horse, you will know that it is the right choice."

Approaching the horse stall, Jafar pointed to the horse. "Look, there she is—a rare beauty!"

"Ohhh, look at her," Raja whispered. "She is very striking."

"And you will have the most perfect ride with her. Hours and hours of training have gone into this horse."

"You tempt me again."

"As I want to."

Raja walked up to the horse and stroked its neck. "Such a peaceful nature."

"Yes, she's very kind."

Then, lost in her thoughts of wonderful memories with Jafar, Raja rested her head on her horse's neck. The smell of its fur was tranquilizing. She desperately wanted to ride this horse.

"Can I ride her?"

"Tomorrow."

Raja agreed and looked forward to the event.

The next day came very quickly. Raja was doted on in a hundred different ways. She was the image of a beautiful Dracian Princess, with not one thing out of place.

As a final touch, two maids braided parts of her hair with tiny beads, which took a very long time. Raja began to think of the conversation she'd had with Jafar the day before. It was true she could stay here and not have to worry about the frightful state of her country. She was sure that Jafar would make her happy, but she wondered if staying was the right thing to do. Could something wrong ever be made right? And would she later regret her decision? She started to think of her royal mother. She certainly wanted to stay loyal to her and Zurkia. She wondered if that would be possible if she stayed in Dracon. But surely the tzarina would understand how she felt about wanting to put aside the worries of the Dark Prince.

Raja was finally ready to meet Jafar and was led to the stalls. When he saw her, his face beamed with a most radiant smile. Raja wished he didn't look so happy. It made her decision all the more difficult.

Raja's horse was ready to ride. Jafar helped her up and she walked her horse quietly around the court. A most obedient horse, she thought. When Jafar saw that she was confident with her horse the two of them rode out of the city and into the country along a cliff beside the sea.

Indeed, it was turning into a most wonderful experience. Raja galloped along the path with the wind blowing in her face and lifting her hair. In those moments she felt like no life could be better. She was free from the worries of her pursuers.

Out of breath, they slowed their horses to a walk.

"Let's stop here and have something to eat," said Jafar. "I brought along a cloth and food."

"That sounds wonderful. I'm hungry."

Jafar helped Raja down from her horse. Not that she needed the help, but he wanted to show his manners, given the fact that she was dressed in a princess garment.

Raja felt taken by his actions, but quickly told herself not to be so influenced by what she may later regret.

"It is beautiful here, isn't it," said Jafar.

"Very much so," said Raja as she looked over the shimmering sea.

"We could do this every day for the rest of our lives," said Jafar.

Raja gave Jafar an innocent look. "You make it very hard for me to want to leave."

"You will stay, won't you?"

Jafar took Raja's hand. "You will be safe with me. I promise that I will never let any harm come to you ever again."

Wanting to forget her frightful experience, Raja let her hand linger in his for a few moments as she contemplated his promise.

Slowly withdrawing her hand, she didn't answer his question, but rather focused on the food. The two of them spread out the cloth. Jafar thought the silence was a positive sign because at least she wasn't saying no.

"Well?" asked Jafar as he set out rye bread and grape jelly. "What is your answer?"

"Let me have some time to think about it."

Jafar agreed and knew he could win her heart with what he had planned ahead. "Why don't we, in the next few weeks, just for old time's sake, have some practice with shooting arrows?" he asked.

Raja had not had an opportunity to practice in Zurkia, and thought that was a great idea. "Yes, I would love to, seeing as I don't even own a bow with arrows and haven't had the opportunity to practice."

Jafar smiled enthusiastically. "I have a gift for you." He got up to retrieve it from his horse and then handed it to Raja.

The gift was wrapped in burlap with a stitched design of a horse.

"What is it?" asked Raja, flattered by his generosity.

"Open it."

Raja opened the gift and immediately responded. "Wherever did you get this?"

"I had the bow and arrows made in Zurkia by a well-known craftsman."

"Thank you," said Raja. "They are beautiful."

"You are welcome. I'll look forward to using them with you."

Raja carefully examined the skillfully made weapon and was amazed at the craftsmanship of the bow. The set of arrows had black and white feather fletching. Jafar explained how these types of feathers helped the arrow to fly very true to its course. Raja touched the feathers delicately. She could hardly wait to try out her gift.

"Can we practice now?" asked Raja, who really wanted to learn the skill.

"Of course," said Jafar.

After their lunch, the two of them spent the afternoon shooting arrows. As evening neared they packed up their things and galloped their horses back to the palace where a magnificent meal was waiting for them.

The afternoon with Jafar had been exciting and Raja told him that she wanted more of the same outing. So the two of them rode their horses along the cliffs of the seashore, and spent every day shooting arrows for hours and hours. She couldn't seem to get enough of it. Raja's skills improved dramatically and she ended up becoming an equal match for Jafar.

Besides shooting arrows, Jafar scheduled numerous falconry outings. Raja enjoyed the events, gaining the trust of the falcons as they perched on her own arms. Jafar had never felt so happy as with Raja and grew more and more confident that she would now finally become his bride for real.

Chapter 16

A Complete Surprise

During the time in Dracon, Raja had her old chamber back, but she felt it was somewhat lonely without Shamra. However, the twin chambermaids were happy to see Raja and made her feel very welcome. The three of them got along very well, as if they were sisters.

Delighting in making Raja laugh, the twins bestowed upon her unusual and interesting gifts, such as pieces of jewelry made with tiny shells—very pretty indeed. The twins themselves wore numerous jewelry pieces of the same sort and hung all types of shelled jewelry around Raja's neck and arms to make the three of them look alike. Their generosity almost made Raja forget about the seriousness of her situation.

Jafar, of course, was trying his best to completely win Raja's trust and compensate for any feelings of uncertainty she had about staying in Dracon. Despite the wonderful time Raja was having, she of course knew the purpose of Jafar's affection, but she admitted he was doing a good job of winning her over.

At times the guards that lingered around her were very annoying. Today, she wanted to be completely by herself. Deciding to walk to one of the open pools of the palace, Raja asked the guards to leave, as the particular pool was only for women. The request was granted and after finding the pool, Raja lay on her back with her feet in the water.

Reaching under her sash, she pulled out her doll, as she usually did when she had to make a difficult decision. As usual she counted the twenty-four pearls and then took out the note that she always kept inside of the doll. Looking at the arrangement of letters, she smiled.

Ll'I eb ta eht dne fo eht lennut.

She contemplated why she was keeping this note and decided it was special to her because it was written in a secret code that she and Pavel had made up. She admitted Pavel did hold a special place in her heart. The note brought back memories of how he and others had risked their lives rescuing her. Perhaps they were searching for her right now. Yes, of course they were. She hadn't even thought of that. Her mother would be worried to no end about her, she was sure.

Raja realized that she hadn't thought through everything concerning staying in Dracon. True, she was safe for now, but that did not necessarily mean for the future. Certainly, Zurkia would fight to get her back, as she was royalty. And if Zurkia could not succeed in that, how could she ever be at peace with herself knowing that she had turned her back on her country and left her tzarina mother. Most likely, she would never be forgiven for that decision.

She was Zurkian blood and deep inside of herself she knew she could not stay in Dracon. Yes, the country was in turmoil and she would be in danger, but better to die doing what you know to be right than live the rest of your life in miserable regret. She would have to be strong and tell Jafar how she really felt. The time she spent here was exhilarating and Jafar desperately wanted her. She made him very happy, but she knew the feelings of the present situation would eventually fade. She wanted to make the right choice for a firm foundation for the future.

Raja thought about the right time to tell Jafar about her decision. She would ask to take a stroll in the Redvenus Garden. She went back to her chamber to get herself ready. After putting on her best Dracian costume, she asked that Jafar meet her in the gardens.

As Raja sat on one of the benches she saw Jafar approaching. He himself looked royally handsome.

"Why the urgent request, my Dracian princess?" Jafar bowed and kissed her hand.

"I must speak of my decision."

Jafar had a worried expression. "Is it not already made? We are in love. We will be married soon."

"Can we walk and talk at the same time?" asked Raja.

"Certainly."

The two walked beside each other, meandering along the curvy garden paths.

"Jafar, this is a difficult thing to tell you because I know how much you care for me, but I cannot stay here."

"But you love me," said Jafar in a firm voice. "This is reason to stay."

"I have never said that I did. I like you and it is true that we have a wonderful time together, but there are other matters that are pressing in on me. I cannot leave Zurkia."

Jafar stopped walking and turned Raja to face him with his hands on her shoulders. Forcefully, he said, "You must forget Zurkia and sit on the throne in Dracon with me. You must!"

"You do not understand my situation. I already have my own life in Zurkia. I have a family and many friends there. And I cannot turn my back on my tzarina mother."

"Doesn't love take precedence over those things?" asked Jafar. "It should be just you and me."

Raja spoke in a matter-of-fact tone. "I didn't say that I love you." She could see the hurt in his eyes and was tempted to change her mind, but then realized she had to stay strong and do what she knew to be right. "Please, let's continue our walk."

Jafar took his hands off of Raja's shoulders and the two continued their walk. Jafar desperately wanted to win this argument and tried to think of anything that would change her mind.

"But Raja, I have never forgotten our words we spoke during our duel in the courtyard."

Raja tried to answer as diplomatically as possible. "I only said words that I thought I was supposed to say, but everything changed after I went back to Zurkia."

"But now we are back together and we have enjoyed each other's company so much."

It was true, the time had been fun and relaxing for Raja, but she knew that those feelings wouldn't last. She would pay a consequence for her betrayal of Zurkia, even if her fears of the Dark Prince were valid.

After taking some time to respond to Jafar's proposal, Raja finally said, "There is something you need to understand. You cannot assume that I love you, especially under these circumstances."

"What circumstances and why not?"

"For one thing, I am very young."

"How old are you?"

"Sixteen."

That didn't seem all that young to Jafar. "That's not a good excuse."

Raja didn't particularly like that answer. "I have a destiny to fulfill and staying here doesn't seem to be part of it. My being here is not right."

Jafar thought about Raja's answer. "How is it not right? You have everything that you could ever want with me."

"Yes, you treat me well, and I'm the crown princess, but if I'm bought for a price, I'm still a slave."

"What does it matter how you came here, if I love you?"

"I can't believe you are saying that," said Raja, hurt by his statement. "Don't my feelings matter to you?"

"I'm sure we can work out your feeling in time," said Jafar.

"Not if I haven't been treated right. Doesn't it bother you that I have been traded for coin?"

"Not really. We will get what we both want in the end."

Raja knew Jafar was only speaking for himself right now. He just wasn't seeing her point of view. Turning to face Jafar, she said, "Well, it matters to me and I can't fall in love in this situation."

The conversation was beginning to frustrate Raja and she thought they should continue it another time. She turned and began walking away.

Jafar called after her. "I'm sorry." He walked after her. "I just feel so sure you will feel the same again."

Raja stopped and turned to face Jafar. "Please, you cannot order me to do that."

Jafar bit his lower lip. It was then that Jafar started to realize his folly. He admitted to himself that he could not force Raja to love him. "You are right. But I thought you would have seen it from my perspective, and be willing to give our feelings another chance."

Shaking her head to say no, Raja responded with less patience than before. "Perhaps you should see it from my perspective. You are not going to make things right by giving me whatever I want."

Jafar saw that he wasn't going to win Raja's heart by trying to convince her that it was right for them to be together. He began realizing he wasn't saying the things she wanted to hear.

"I'm sorry," said Jafar. "How can I make it up to you?"

Raja looked over to the sea. "I don't know that you can."

"There must be something," said Jafar.

Still staring at the sea, she said, "Actually, there is a way."

"Please," said Jafar. "Name it."

"Let me go back to Zurkia where I belong." Raja turned to look at Jafar, waiting for his reply. She saw sadness come over his face, but she stood her ground. "If you really care for me as you say, then that is what you will do."

Deep down, Jafar knew he couldn't insist that Raja leave her family to be with him. She may always hold it against him. He wondered if she would even forgive him now. He tried to say something to justify his actions. "Please understand I had you come to Dracon to find out your feelings for me. I had to do it."

"A part of me understands that, but another part of me is angry with you. I know it seemed like I wanted to be with you, but I was afraid of what might happen to me if I didn't obey your father."

A somber look came over Jafar's face. "Yes, I can understand that now."

Wanting to make Jafar feel better, she said, "Despite the circumstances I still like you."

Jafar's face lit up with a smile.

"Well like is next to love, and that will do for now."

Raja was satisfied with that answer. At least she had made some headway. She said in a very polite manner, "I need to get back to my country. You will let me go, won't you?" Raja had no idea what he would say to her request, as they both knew it would be dangerous for her to go back. She waited anxiously for his response.

"Under one condition."

Relieved, thinking it would be a simple request, Raja asked, "What is it?"

"I want to come with you."

"You want to what!"

"I want to leave my country."

"For good?"

"Yes, I want to be with you. There is no one else who is so skillful and intelligent, nor so beautiful."

This took Raja by complete surprise. She had not expected that he would defect from his country. However, she knew she could not tell Jafar to stay in Dracon.

"I understand how you could feel that way, but if you come to Zurkia we are not getting married," said Raja.

"Yes, yes, I can accept that."

Somehow Raja had doubts that he would, but nevertheless she wanted to get back to Zurkia. "Who will take over for you?"

"My cousin, Daxen Lionstronge."

"He's a royal?"

"Yes, he's next in line for the throne. We are very close and I trust him to take the responsibility of ruling the country seriously."

"Does he know about this?"

"Yes, I've already spoken to him about this possibility and he has agreed to it."

This was indeed a new set of circumstances for Raja. She had a hard time comprehending the idea, but after a while thought that it might be a very good plan, as he could prove to be valuable in solving their problems in Zurkia.

"Okay," said Raja. "When do we leave?"

Pleased that Raja agreed to his idea, Jafar smiled, showing his brilliant white teeth. "In two weeks from now, when the ship is ready."

Raja couldn't help but notice his handsome smile.

"Does that please you?" asked Jafar, hoping that he could eventually win her admiration for good.

"Yes, yes of course. I'm very thankful."

Raja was going to ask that she not be in Jafar's company for the next two weeks but then changed her mind, as she was very interested in continuing to improve her shooting skills.

As promised, when the time came, the ship was ready, but after having spent so much time with her new horse, Raja could not leave it behind, so Jafar agreed to take it on the ship back to Zurkia. In some way, the gift had made whatever pain she had endured coming to Dracon all worthwhile.

Bidding farewell to Jafar's cousin, who was now the new khan, and who would have to find another princess to fill the position of crown princess, Raja and Jafar went aboard the ship wearing their traditional Dracian outfits. Raja also brought with her the gifts she had received from Jafar and from the chambermaid twins along with clothing made in her favorite color, teal green, tailored with traditional Zurkian bell sleeves that drooped at least five hands in length.

The ship was set to sail and they were headed for Zurkia. Raja couldn't believe the quick turn-around she was making from Dracon. Everyone would be overjoyed to see her in Zurkia, as they were probably very worried about her, but she would have a new friend to introduce, who, she was sure, would prove invaluable in solving the turmoil in Zurkia.

"Can we make a bit of a detour?" asked Raja as she looked out onto the sea.

"Where to?"

"Kulaly Island."

"Kulaly Island? Isn't that the pirates' island?"

"Yes it is, but Captain Cham and her pirates live on that island. And as I told you, they have changed their ways and given up their piracy practices. The captain is now my friend."

"Since when did this pirate become your friend?" asked Jafar with a dissatisfied look.

"After the first time I was in Baku. She helped rescue me and for that she is in my good graces."

Jafar's judgmental attitude softened. "I can understand how she would now hold a place in your heart."

"I am thinking I could use the pirates to help solve the problems in Zurkia."

"All right. If that is your wish it is my command."

"And one more thing I haven't told you yet. Kuzma is Captain Cham's father."

"How surprising!"

"The captain is a very interesting person. I'm sure you will like her," said Raja.

Jafar decided the whole affair would be intriguing, especially to see a real pirates' island. In an enthusiastic voice he shouted, "Full sail ahead to Kulaly Island!"

Raja felt full of confidence as the wind brushed against her face in the sea breeze. Jafar couldn't help but notice how pretty she was. Raja saw him staring at her. She hoped he wouldn't continue to become taken with her, especially after they arrived in Kazan. Her thoughts wandered to her cousin Hannah, who was just as pretty, intelligent, and gallant as she was, if not more. She decided to tell him about her and began painting a very enticing picture, from describing her beauty to her mystifying personality. He half paid attention to Raja and then to be polite, said he would look forward to meeting her.

"I have a good idea for you," said Raja, still trying to spark Jafar's interest.

"What is it?"

"Perhaps in the future you could give the oval ruby jewel to my cousin."

"Perhaps," said Jafar.

"She is probably a better swordswoman than me. You would be very impressed."

Raja's comment didn't seem to affect Jafar.

"Like I said, I'll think about meeting her. But right now, I can't picture it," said Jafar.

Raja thought his answer sounded quite unenthusiastic, but she was sure he would change his mind after meeting Hannah in person.

Chapter 17

Shiver Me Timbers

Kulaly Island was now in clear view from the deck of Jafar's ship. Raja had enjoyed the sail from Dracon and the crew was gracious toward her. However, she noticed that there was one person who always kept a good distance from her. Today, she finally recognized him as the bailiff who used to serve at Victory Manor. He was a short older man who hid well inside a crowd. And now that she knew who he was, she felt as if he was always watching her. She was sure he was a spy and told Jafar about him. For that reason, Jafar decided to tell his crew to stay on the ship.

As the ship sailed closer to the island, Jafar raised the white flag to signal they were not a threat, but were coming as friends.

"Captain Cham will be so surprised to see me," said Raja.

"And me as well!" said Jafar.

"That can be counted on."

The crew anchored the ship and Jafar and Raja rowed a small boat towards the island. When they were close enough they waded in the water to the shore where Cham was standing.

"Shiver me timbers, if it isn't Raja!" said Cham, who had been watching them come to the island. "And look at you. Why ye be dressed like a Dracian away from Zurkia?"

"It's good to see you, Cham," said Raja.

Cham couldn't stop looking at Raja's hair and attire. "Me thought you be back in Zurkia. What happened?"

"I was kidnapped."

"What! You were forced t' go back t' Baku?"

"Yes, but I'm now headed to Zurkia again."

"Ye poor lassie, what a lot o' hoopla."

"It's all turned out for the good," said Raja, who turned to look at Jafar.

"And who's this bucko?" asked Cham, looking Jafar over from head to foot.

"This is Jafar. He's the Crown Prince of Dracon."

"Well, what be he doin' here?" said Cham as she put her hand on her cutlass.

Jafar did the same with his own knife.

Raja, standing between the two of them and extending her arms, said firmly, "It's okay Cham, he's one of us now."

"Speak, then," said Cham, who still had her had on her weapon.

Sounding like he had no regrets, Jafar said, "I'm leaving my country to live in Zurkia."

Cham squinted. "What hasty decision brought that on?"

Jafar shifted his feet. "Ah . . . well a lot has to do with Raja."

Cham looked suspiciously between the two of them. "Be that so, Raja?"

"We're friends," said Raja.

"What kind o' friends?" asked Cham, with a half-smile slowly appearing on her face.

"Just friends," said Raja. "And nothing else."

Cham relaxed her hand from her cutlass and then looked upwards. A crow circled above. "Raja, hold out yer arm."

Raja did so and Cham put a piece of dried meat in her palm. Swooping down, the crow landed on her hand, took the meat, and flew off. Cham gave Raja a few more pieces of meat. "Do that, 'n ye will 'ave yourself a new mate. His name be Cade. Found 'im fallen from a nest."

Smiling, Raja put the meat in the folds of her sash. She might have preferred to hold out her arm to Jafar's falcons but for the sake of Cham she would befriend her crow.

"Do ye want 'o hear me crow's secret?"

"I do," said Raja.

"He's trained to bring me a twig from people me know. But it has to be a two-prong twig."

"Like a wish bone?"

"Aye, he won't take it otherwise."

"Fascinating!" said Raja.

"Me show you his trick later."

"Yes, please do," said Raja. "I'd like to see it."

Cham then turned her attention to Jafar and asked in a taunting voice, "So, how is Raja bringing ye away from your country? Or need me ask by the looks o' ye eyes."

Looking at Jafar, Raja didn't think Jafar's sentiments toward her were that obvious. Seeing that Jafar looked a bit uncomfortable she thought she should answer for him. "Zurkia's in trouble. And Jafar has agreed to help me with my plans."

"I admit it's a sound excuse," said Cham as she eyed Jafar to see his reaction. Jafar bowed his head to show that his motives were sincere.

"I want to ask for your help as well," said Raja.

Concluding that Jafar was trustworthy, Cham agreed to consider the request. "Okay, why don't we talk about it over dinner?"

Jafar and Raja were pleased with the offer.

Cham motioned for them to follow her. "In the meantime, me will introduce Jafar, t' Yev and Ivan."

Raja was excited that she would see the boys again and wondered how they were doing. When she met them they looked taller, stronger, and a good deal more like pirates.

"Hi," said Raja.

"Hi," said the two boys.

"What are you doing here?" asked Yev.

"Just making my usual journeys," said Raja, who cast a sideways glance at Jafar. "But it's not my wish to elaborate right now." Raja extended her hand toward her new friend. "This is Jafar."

"Good to meet you," said both boys.

"Likewise," said Jafar.

"So how do you like living your life with Captain Cham?" asked Raja.

"It's great. I wouldn't give it up for anything," said Ivan.

"That's good to hear. You certainly fit the role," said Raja, looking at the boys' hoop earrings. "But I guess you have to look the part to fit the part."

"Oh, the jewelry," said Yev as he tugged on his chains around his neck. "All given to me by Captain Cham. It's nothing but the best."

"Looks good on you," said Raja.

"Uh um," agreed Jafar, wanting to be polite.

"Come this way," said Cham, as she walked towards their camp. She motioned Raja and Jafar to sit around the fire with Ivan and Yev and assured everyone the food would be good. "Me see the grub is comin'. You haven't tasted anything better."

Hungry, Raja and Jafar stuffed the roasted fish served in a tasty poached egg sauce into their mouths. It seemed a bit boorish to Jafar to eat with his fingers. He was used to using carved spoons, but nevertheless he did enjoy the change of culture.

"So you goin' to tell me why you came?" asked Cham.

"Terrible things have been going on. Peasants are being kidnapped from our castle estates," said Raja.

"Who's responsible for this?"

"We think it's the Tyhets but we also think the Dark Prince is behind it."

"So him again."

"He's also taken Hannah back to live with him."

"The poor lassie."

"Yes, I'm concerned for her."

"So how do you want me t' help?"

"I'd like you to take over one of the castles. It's called Levap Castle, which is on Pavel's estate."

"It be empty?"

"To begin with, it wasn't." Raja continued telling Cham of how the servants and knights disappeared and how Hannah went back to her father.

Cham looked seriously at Raja. "So the castle needs t' be occupied t' ensure the estate's protection from the enemy?"

"Yes," said Raja. "We need to get Hannah back and Levap Castle is a good place for us to rest. We haven't exactly made plans for this yet, but the idea of getting her back needs to be kept secret."

"Ye have me word."

Raja looked at Ivan and Yev.

"You have our word too," said the boys, who were very intrigued with the news.

"So does that mean we are going to live in a castle?" asked Yev, munching on some corn.

Cham looked around the group and then at Raja. "I'll accept yer request, under one condition, that we be sent maids and servants to help us. No one here is used t' livin' in a castle."

"I think I can make that happen for you," said Raja with a smile. "The castle also has the potential for making clay pots—a good way to earn coin for yourself and to pay Pavel for inhabiting the castle, as the estate belongs to him."

"Sounds interesting," said Cham. "I'll agree with that."

"Wow!" said Yev, "When do we leave?"

"I'd like to leave as soon as possible," said Raja. "The matters are urgent."

Cham agreed to the request.

Later in the evening, as everyone sat around the fire, Cham announced the plan to the rest of the pirates. The news was well received. Cheers went up and the pirates circled around the fire with music, singing, and dancing.

Raja watched Jafar's reactions. He seemed to be enjoying himself away from his responsibility of being a khan.

"How do you like your first experience with pirates?" asked Raja.

"Entertaining to say the least," said Jafar as he looked at the pirates all dressed in a slightly different costume. "No inhibitions here!"

Jafar turned his attention to the glow of the fire. He couldn't take his eyes from it. The flickering and crackling made its way right into his soul. He thought about the decision he'd just made to leave his country. He didn't have any regrets. He knew he had made the right choice for himself.

Cham's eyes drew upward as she noticed her crow circling above the group. It cawed loudly and repeatedly and wouldn't stop.

"Somethin' be happenin' at the shore," said Cham. "That caw usually means trouble. Quick, everyone t' the shore!"

The group dropped everything they were holding and ran down the path toward the shore.

Then, just as they got there, a huge explosion came from Jafar's ship.

"Shiver me timbers!" said Cham.

Chapter 18

Battle of Catapult

"Hailing stones!" shouted Jafar. "What is happening with my ship?"

The white flag on his vessel was down and a cannon was pointed to the shore. The first cannon ball fired from the ship had already hit one of the pirate huts and destroyed it.

"Get the catapult ready!" shouted Cham.

Branches were torn off the catapult camouflaged at the tree line of the shore. Ivan and Yev brought out grenades from one of the nearby huts. A team of pirates worked together as the arm of the catapult was pulled down and a coconut filled with powder and tar was put into the pouch. A pirate stood ready with a flaming torch beside the bomb hurler.

"Light the fuse," shouted Cham.

The fuse was lit.

"Release!"

A counterweight of stones pulled the beam down, flinging the grenade into the air at a tremendous speed.

As Raja watched the coconut bomb fly through the air, it hit the ship and exploded.

"Watch yer heads," yelled Cham over another explosion as a cannon ball shot towards the shore. It just barely missed Yev.

"That was close!" yelled Yev.

"Quit belly achin'! Reload the catapult!" shouted Cham. "We'll give them a taste of me hospitality."

Yev and the other pirates reloaded the catapult. This time the pirates flung several coconuts through the air all at once. Each one had a lit fuse, progressively burning toward the core of the weapon. The grenades turned into a blazing ball of fire and landed on the deck of the ship. Upon contact, they exploded, causing the ship to catch on fire.

The white flag was raised on the mask and the cannon balls ceased shooting from the ship. Screaming and yelling trailed across the water as the crew worked frantically to put out the fire. After a billow of smoldering smoke rose in the air from the drenched blaze, the crew pulled up the anchor and set sail. Jafar looked on with disbelief as his ship retreated.

Full of anger, Cham whipped out her dagger and held it to Jafar's throat. "What be goin' on with yer crew? We could 'ave been killed! You have something to do with this?"

Jafar swallowed hard as Cham's fiery eyes met his. Her rapid breathing hit his face like a hot flame. Jafar's dark eyes deepened and returned Cham's anger. "I have nothing to do with this! My crew's attack is preposterous!"

Raja quickly approached Cham and looked her in the face while pushing her away from Jafar. "Trust Jafar! He is not behind this!"

Jafar spat out his words in continued anger. "Why would I ask them to shoot cannons while I'm here on this island? That would be insane!"

Cham withdrew her dagger, collecting her emotions. His statement made sense. She instead said something sarcastic. "Obviously yer crew got tired o' waitin'!"

Raja joked, wanting to lighten the conversation. "Perhaps if they'd known we were making dinner for them they would have reconsidered."

"Seriously, me think they wanted t' raid us," said Cham, who again looked at Jafar as if it was his fault.

"I think my crew put two and two together on where I stood," said Jafar. "Traditionally, your pirates of this island have not been on the best of terms with Dracon. They really do not like you and your pirates."

Ivan joined the conversation. "So maybe your crew thought you were committing treason by joining the pirates."

"That could have been the case," said Jafar.

"Your crew probably thought it would be a good opportunity to raid us," said Yev, putting his arms across his chest as if to say he knew what was going on.

Cham agreed. "Me think that pretty much sums it up."

"And that was a good ship," said Jafar.

"Aye, it's bad yer ship be gone," said Cham.

"I was going to keep that ship and send my crew back to Dracon on a different ship that was headed that way, but I guess those plans are thwarted," said Jafar.

"My tzarina mother can give you a new ship," said Raja.

Jafar was feeling apprehensive about meeting Raja's mother but so far had kept those feelings to himself. "After what I've put her through? I don't think she'll want to give me anything."

"There's always forgiveness," said Raja. "My mother believes that any circumstance can somehow be used for the good."

"A hopeful way of looking at things. You and your family are very kind," said Jafar.

"Me can attest t' that," said Cham.

"Our duty," said Raja.

Cham looked up at the nearby hut. "Looks like we'll need t' fix that hut."

"Can it wait to be fixed?" asked Raja. "I think it's more important to leave for Zurkia."

"Aye, me can understand how ye feel, and I have no problem with that," said Cham. She turned around and looked at the damage made to the other huts. "Me wonder if the Dracians will be back t' raid this place while we're gone."

"That is possible," said Jafar.

"We don't want this island taken over," said Yev. "This is our island."

Ivan added to that declaration. "I think the crew should stay here to protect our land."

"Me agree with that," said Cham, who also did not want to give up what she felt was her property.

"We should take the smaller ship since there will only be six of us," said Ivan.

"That sounds good," said Cham, who then looked at Raja. "But on the other hand, what help would me have if m pirates stay here?"

"My mother will give you servants and guards so you can occupy Levap Castle without any hardship. I don't want anyone to rule the castle but you."

"All right then, that sounds like a fair plan," said Cham.

"Good," said Raja.

"I'm glad no one was hurt in the battle," said Jafar. "And I apologize for my crew's bad behavior. Those nasty scoundrels!"

Everyone laughed—bad behavior was a bit of an understatement. Cham thought there was more to it than just bad behavior. "It wasn't yer fault," she said. "Me sure there be a bad apple in th' barrel leadin' everyone astray. Me thinks someone on th' ship was connected with Raja's kidnappin."

Jafar thought about that and concluded that Raja was right about the bailiff. He was the bad apple. But at this point, it really didn't matter. The crew was gone and they weren't his responsibility right now. The bailiff would no doubt be found out after they solved the problems in Zurkia.

"We can be thankful for Cade, who warned us ahead of time," said Raja.

"Aye, every second counted in th' battle. Without me crow more damage could o' be done."

Raja looked out onto the sea. "Yes, and we can be thankful that they didn't take Cham's ships."

The others agreed.

"Aye, me ships are our lifeline. We wouldn't want t' lose them," said Cham.

"Nice ships," said Jafar.

"Thank you," said Cham. "The larger one be me father's ship, from when he was a merchant. Me took over th' ship when th' former pirate captain was mutinied for killing too many of his own crew fer makin' mistakes."

"Kuzma! Where is Kuzma?" said Raja feeling alarmed that she had not seen him.

"Me forgot t' tell you, he went up into the mountains t' do some thinking. He should have heard the explosions and will be here soon."

Feeling relieved, Raja smiled. "Perhaps he was inventing another story."

"Aye, he be very good at that."

"He'll be surprised to see Jafar here."

And just as Raja said that, Kuzma came walking onto the beach, barefoot and tanned. At that moment Raja thought he looked like the epitome of peace. She was sure there was a halo circling his head. Stopping, he stared at the group with a huge smile and shouted across the beach. "Is that who I think it is?"

Raja went running up to Kuzma and gave him a hug. She was so glad to see him. He had the same merry eyes and warm smile. His hair was just a bit grayer. Tears of joy welled in her eyes. He had been like another father to her.

"My princess! What are you doing here?" asked Kuzma. "I could not have expected anything more surprising!"

"It's a long story," said Raja, with a laugh.

"I'm sure 'tis true. And I can hardly wait to hear it."

"Come on," she said. Holding his hand, she half dragged him to the others. "I want you to meet Jafar, Crown Prince of Dracon."

"Did you say the Crown Prince of Dracon?" asked Kuzma.

"Yes, he's coming to Zurkia with me."

This was surprising news for Kuzma. He bowed his head for the prince but then got straight to the point.

"Abandoned your country, did you?" asked Kuzma.

"That I did."

Kuzma looked from Raja to Jafar.

Jafar gave an explanation. "Raja was captured a second time and taken to Dracon. I wanted to put an end to this kidnapping so I decided to leave my country and go to Zurkia."

"That's the way a boy in love thinks," said Kuzma.

Raja blushed. "It's not like that."

"Well, how is that going to stop the kidnapping?" asked Kuzma.

"We have plans, Kuzma. Don't worry," said Raja.

"As you say, my princess," said Kuzma. He looked around the beach.

"Is Jafar's abandonment of his country the reason for all of these cannon balls everywhere?" asked Kuzma.

"In a way," said Raja. "The crew turned their backs on Jafar and wanted to get rid of us."

"Not a surprising story," said Kuzma. "Hope they're not coming back."

"Don't worry," said Raja. "You will be coming back to Zurkia with me."

"What do you mean by that?"

"Cham, Yev, and Ivan are going back to Zurkia. And the pirates are staying here to protect the island."

"Well how did that come about?"

"How about if we have dinner and we will tell you all about it."

Agreeing to that, Kuzma walked with Raja to the camp where more food was being prepared as a reward for winning the small battle.

Staying behind to look at the catapult, Jafar said, "Cham, this catapult is magnificent. Where did you get it?"

"I made it."

"Marvelous, just marvelous," said Jafar.

"It comes apart. Me show you," said Cham.

"I'd like to learn."

Cham and Jafar spent the next hour taking apart the catapult and putting it back together as Cham thoroughly explained how it operated. Cham's suspicions and hostility toward Jafar had now turned to trust.

"Thank you for showing me how to operate this magnificent weapon," said Jafar.

"Yer welcome. It sure be useful," said Cham.

Jafar couldn't have agreed more. Thanks to the catapult they had won the small battle and were kept from tragedy. And because of that, Jafar named the attack the *Battle of Catapult.*

Chapter 19

Sunrise

The six passengers—Raja, Jafar, Cham, Ivan, Yev, and Kuzma—finally set sail for Zurkia on Cham's ship around mid-day a few days later.

"Cham, does your ship have a name?" asked Raja.

"Aye."

"What is it?"

"Hope."

"The meaning of my name!"

"It be carved on the bow o' the ship below the bowsprit."

Raja wanted to take a look at it but she could not bend over far enough to see the carving. She would have to wait until they were at Kazan. It was a sturdy ship and she felt good to be on it with the others—she thought it was rather fun.

The four who knew how to operate the ship—Cham, Ivan, Yev, and Kuzma— set about teaching Raja and Jafar how to sail.

They were both very eager to learn and it added to the fun of the whole situation. She couldn't wait to tell everyone about her new experience.

Raja was still thinking about Hannah. She didn't think Hannah's father would hurt his daughter, but, nonetheless, she was captive and needed to be rescued. Raja was certain her uncle would be afraid Hannah would leave again. So every now and again Raja worked at formulating a plan to rescue her cousin. But first she had to get the parchments from the trunk. Once she got in contact with Pavel again, they'd add the finishing details.

The traveling had gone smoothly so far, with just enough wind to move the ship along at a good speed. Everyone took turns at the ship's wheel and pretended to be the captain, which sent Cham into hysterical laughter.

The night didn't come too soon for Raja, as she felt exhausted from the ordeals she had been through lately. She found a comfortable spot in the cabin and fell asleep. But Raja awoke when she fell onto the floor from the bunk she was sleeping on.

"That's odd, I don't usually move around that much," she said to herself. She picked herself up to get back on the bunk, but suddenly the ship listed, causing her to lose her balance and fall to the floor again.

She heard shouting on the deck and loud groans coming from the ship. Opening the door, a horrific wind blew against her face and seawater sprayed the front of her clothes.

Again, the boat listed and Raja fell back to the floor. More water from the waves poured onto the ship's deck. The boys were working frantically to bail the water out of boat.

The already loosened sails whipped against the mast, threatening to completely rip themselves in two. Cham shouted orders at the three boys.

"Close the sails!"

Struggling to get to the ropes, the boys were knocked from their feet when another huge wave tossed their boat and more water poured into the ship. Cham and the boys slid away from the ropes and were thrown against the side of the ship.

At that moment the yard for the topmast sail splintered and ripped a long hole in the canvas of the sail. The canvas whipped against the other sails and was utterly useless.

Raja was sure they were going to die in this storm. The ship was now completely out of control.

"We need t' get off the ship!" yelled Cham.

"What?" called Jafar.

"We need t' get OFF the ship! We are headed fer rocky waters!"

"Raja!" called Jafar, who saw her standing at the door of the cabin. "Are you okay?"

"Yes!"

"We need to abandon the ship!" shouted Jafar.

Raja wanted to answer back but couldn't, as a huge spray of water hit her face.

"We need t' do it now or we feed the fish!" yelled Cham.

Raja thought they would die either way. Staying in a sinking ship or riding in a small boat in the middle of the storm was surely death in either case.

Ivan was at the rescue boat first.

"Raja first!" yelled Ivan as he held out his hand to help her. Yev helped Raja into the boat and followed her, then Kuzma, Jafar, and lastly Cham.

In between huge waves, Jafar and Cham used the block and tackle to lower the small boat onto the turbulent sea. The ropes were cut and in a matter of minutes the six of them were a good distance away from the ship and then in a few more moments, the ship crashed into a rock that was jutting from the water, nearly splitting the ship in two.

Raja hung onto the others as she looked on in disbelief. The ship was slowly sinking into the sea. They were still in a great deal of danger but at this point still alive. All were extremely frightened as each huge wave took them up and down like a yoyo.

It was rare that a storm in this part of the sea would be this ferocious and last more than two hours. Fortunately, the winds did die down and safety was again on their side—except for the fact that they were in the middle of the sea without oars.

"Who forgot t' put the oars in?" asked Cham.

"Not me," said Ivan.

"I didn't," said Yev. "I've never even been in this boat."

"Aye, me know that," said Cham, "but when we be gettin' ready t' leave whose duty was it t' check that the boat was equipped?"

Ivan looked at Yev. "It was his."

"No, it wasn't," said Yev.

"Well it be one o' ye two," said Cham. "But each o' you could have double checked the other. And, me suppose, I could have double checked ye both."

"A hard lesson to learn," said Kuzma.

"Hopefully not a deadly one," said Jafar. "We are going to be stuck here in the sun with no water or food."

"There's fish in the ocean," said Yev.

"And are you going to dive for them?" asked Ivan.

"No, but maybe we could think of something to catch them in."

"Okay, then we'll leave that to you," said Ivan.

"Well, we don't have anything else to do, do we?"

"How about twiddle our thumbs?" asked Ivan.

Raja looked perturbed. "Stop arguing, you two. That's not going to get us anywhere."

"I wish it would," said Yev.

Raja tried again. "Truly, we need to stay calm. Place your hands on top of mine."

The others fell silent. One by one they placed their hands together.

As the princess closed her eyes she felt a peace come over her and the others. Then just as she opened her eyes the first rays of sun come up over the horizon. The sun seemed extraordinarily beautiful on that morning, as if it were a message to not lose hope. The odds, however, of ever being rescued were zero to none. There wasn't another living soul around.

Raja kept her eyes on the beautiful sunrise and then saw something. "What's that on the horizon?"

Cham, who had very good eyesight, said, "Shiver me timbers, I think it be a ship!"

"You've got to be seeing things!" said Jafar.

"It be a ship all right."

"Gramercy!" shouted Ivan exuberantly slapping Yev on the back who returned the acts of complete jubilance.

"I am more joyous than a singing lark," said Kuzma.

"Now let's just hope it's not a pirate ship and that they even see us," said Cham.

Anxiously waiting, the six did not take their eyes off of the ship. And miraculously the ship headed straight for their little boat.

As the vessel came closer, they recognized it to be a Zurkian ship. The group waved their arms in desperation, not wanting the people on the ship to miss them.

They were spotted and someone from the deck yelled out, "Who are you?"

"Zurkians."

"Come aboard."

When the little boat was close enough to the ship a rope was tossed to them and the boat was pulled in. They climbed into another boat that had been lowered down to the water from the deck. In short order the group was pulled up the side of the ship.

Someone was there to help them aboard. A hand reached out to Raja.

"Raja?"

"Pavel! You came to rescue me!"

"Not really, just passing through."

Chapter 20

Table of Twelve

Even though Pavel was astonished to find the stranded six passengers out on sea, he had still managed one of his sarcastic comments. Raja gave him a perplexed look.

"Just joking. Of course I've come to rescue you," said Pavel. "I've been going out of my mind ever since you went missing."

Quickly relaxing and refocusing, she said urgently, "Pavel, please quickly escort Jafar and me to the aftercastle. Don't let anyone see us."

The three quickly went into the aftercastle of the Zurkian ship and closed the door. Pavel anxiously waited to find out why Raja and the others were in the middle of the sea in a tiny boat.

Raja began by introducing Jafar. "This is Prince Jafar, from Dracon. He is abandoning his country and joining forces with us."

Pavel nodded at Jafar and Jafar nodded back. Pavel wondered why he was abandoning his country. He looked at Jafar and then at Raja. He noticed she was wearing a ring with a jade stone. He didn't want them standing too close together and offered Raja a chair a little further away. Raja sat down.

"Our ship crashed in a terrible storm," said Raja. "And Jafar worked very hard to save us."

"Thank you, Jafar," said Pavel. "Everyone is lucky to be alive. I stayed in Port Caphanne last night so we happened to avoid the storm."

"Were you looking for me in Baku?"

"Yes, I was going to offer to buy you back. But the khan said you left with somebody named Jafar."

"Well yes I did, and here he is, but we can use Jafar in our attempt to get the parchments out of Antom's trunk."

"I see," said Pavel, casting a sideways glance at Jafar.

Pavel's awkward glance at Jafar did not go unnoticed by Raja. She quickly went on about her plans, hoping to avoid an escalation of unwanted emotions between the boys.

"Pavel, I think it's important that Jafar be involved in our mission and that his identity be concealed. I'm certain we can figure out how to dupe the person responsible for my kidnapping and find out what is going on."

As he thought about what Raja was saying, Pavel relaxed. "I agree that involving a person from Dracon would give us more options in devising a plan."

Sensing the ease in Pavel, Raja turned her attention to Jafar.

"Are you okay with concealing your identity?"

"Anything to help," said Jafar.

"It's agreed then?" asked Raja as she looked at Pavel.

"Okay, but for now I think we're safe on the ship."

"Why, who's with you?" asked Raja.

"Viktor, Shamra, Boris, Antom, and Arhip, who are all very trustworthy people."

"Excellent," said Raja.

"Shall we go out to meet the others?" asked Pavel.

"Absolutely," said Raja.

"And was that Kuzma I saw with you in the boat?" asked Pavel.

"Yes."

"Amazing that you are all here. I'll introduce Jafar to our other friends."

Pleased that Pavel was finally showing a mature attitude, Raja gave him a smile of approval.

The three then joined the others on the deck and saw that Ivan and Yev were already telling the story of the shipwreck.

"Pardon me for interrupting," said Pavel. "Everyone, this is Prince Jafar. He has come from Dracon, but he is now one of us. I hope that everyone will treat him as family."

Welcomed by everyone, Jafar already felt part of the close-knit group. Pavel encouraged Yev and Ivan to finish their story, which was being told in a very embellished manner.

Later that evening, the twelve sat at the long crew table ready to eat a delicious meal that had been prepared by Antom and Princess Shamra. Each person was served a trencher with a slab of fish on it, drizzled with parsley sauce. Just about everyone had their own dagger to eat their food with and only a few people had to share.

For desert, a large bowl of thick sweet plum sauce, with an array of sliced pouched pears, was set in the middle of the table. The bowl was passed around and everyone took turns using their dagger to spear the pears, being careful not to drip the sauce as they brought the savory cooked fruit to their watering mouths.

After the meal, Viktor stood up holding his cup. "Let us give a toast to the six people who survived near death."

Cheers went up for the toast.

Pavel also stood and raised his cup. "Let us give a toast to Jafar, our new member." Raja was impressed with Pavel's effort to welcome Jafar.

More cheers went up for the welcome. Then Jafar stood. "I'm elated to have come. Thank you all and I look forward to assisting you in your plans to overcome the oppression that plagues Zurkia."

Continuing to celebrate throughout the evening, the twelve eventually came to the point of discussing their ideas on how to get the parchments.

After listening to Raja's story of her capture by the Tyhet chieftain, and consoling her on how frightening it must have been, Viktor was the first to speak up about the trunk. "So you are certain the trunk wasn't in the hut?"

"Yes, I'm certain. I looked along all four walls," said Raja.

"Where do you think it is then?" asked Viktor.

Pavel offered his reasoning. "I think it's in Thrumb Castle. The Tyhets may now see it as something valuable, but hopefully they haven't discovered the secret side panels."

"Well if the trunk is in Thrumb Castle and the castle is occupied, how are we going to get it without a battle?" asked Viktor.

"I have a plan," said Raja, who had been thinking about it for days. "Who's interested to hear it?"

Everyone put up their hand and encouraged her to reveal her plan.

"Right now, the Tyhet chieftain thinks I'm back in Dracon and happily making a life with Khan Jafar."

She saw Jafar put his hands to his chin as she continued her proposal. "He has no idea that Prince Jafar is now on our side. As far as they are concerned, I am now married to the Khan of Dracon."

Murmurs of agreement came from everyone as Raja continued.

"So my idea is that the khan, with his new wife, which would be me, pay the Tyhet chieftain a visit to thank him for providing Khan Jafar with a beautiful wife."

"Brilliant," said Viktor. "And so once you are in the castle you can try to locate the trunk. Is that your idea?"

"Correct, and if I may add, I think our acting skills will have everyone convinced."

"And we do have the right attire," said Jafar.

"Yes, that we have," said Raja.

Raja thought she sensed a bit of tension in Pavel again as he and Jafar exchanged serious looks. She thought he probably didn't like the idea of her and Jafar pretending to be husband and wife.

Sensing the tension between the boys, Shamra quickly made a suggestion to keep the conversation flowing. "And since I used to be Raja's lady-in-waiting at Dragomir Palace I could fix Raja's hair in a customary style."

"Nice idea," said Raja. "No one would ever know that we were faking."

"I'm sure you would pass for a real couple," said Shamra, who then thought she probably shouldn't have said that when she saw Pavel's fiery eyes.

People turned their attention towards Jafar to see what he thought of Raja's proposal. "Are you in agreement with this idea, Jafar?" asked Viktor.

"Very much so. I don't think I would have any problem with the acting job." Raja thought he sounded a bit too enthusiastic.

"Good, we should set about making more plans," said Viktor.

"Whatever they are," said Raja, "Jafar and I must be kept absolutely secret. No word of us being in Zurkia must come out."

"We will hide you in Kazan Castle when we get there," said Viktor.

Raja suddenly thought about her mother. "What about my tzarina mother? Should she know or not?"

"I think she should," said Viktor. "I'm sure she will agree to continue to play the role of a tzarina mother who has a missing princess."

There were no rebuttals to the suggestion. Viktor continued. "When we land at the port, Raja and Jafar will stay on the ship while we all go to Kazan Castle to tell the tzarina what has happened and make appropriate arrangements."

Shamra, who wanted to help, suggested that she bring back some peasant clothes for Raja and Jafar to wear and emphasized that she would wash them first.

Raja appreciated Shamra's thoughtfulness.

And then Boris, who had been quiet the whole time, offered to stay on board the ship to see that no one entered it while the others were gone.

Arhip thought that was a good idea and added another comment. "The meeting with the tzarina and making arrangements could take a while. And there will be more time needed for the tzarina to be served her meals."

"Should Yev and I stay on the ship for added protection?" asked Ivan.

"No, me don't think so," said Cham. "It would look too suspicious. A few people guarding should be enough."

"Can we go into the castle?" asked Yev, who made a comically pleading expression.

Cham wondered when he was going to mature. "Aye, ye may go into the castle but mind yer manners. Ye need t' be very respectful of the tzarina. Follow me and don't wander off."

Yev politely agreed to make sure he got his way, and it was also decided that Cham, Ivan, and Yev would meet with the tzarina's council and start planning for the move to Levap Castle.

Antom, who had been quietly talking with Kuzma off and on, finally spoke at the end of the meeting. "I've decided that I should go back to Victory Manor to help with the affairs of the estate."

"And I will stay in Zurkia to help with the planning," said Kuzma.

The plan was further talked about and it was accepted that Viktor, Arhip, and Antom would go back to Victory Manor after the announcements were made to the tzarina. The meeting on the ship was later recorded as the *Table of Twelve.*

After the meeting Kuzma offered to lighten up the evening. "How about if I tell all of you one of my stories before we retire?"

The suggestion put a smile on everyone's face, even Pavel's, though he knew he had no choice but to accept the fake marriage scheme. The table of twelve huddled a little closer to each other to hear one of Kuzma's captivating tales.

Part 3

The Revelations

Chapter 21

The Letter

The one thing that wasn't considered during the last meeting of the *Table of Twelve* was the fact that there were no escorts or gifts in order for Raja's idea to work. After all, it would seem highly suspicious and against protocol if Jafar and Raja turn up at Thrumb Castle as a married couple unescorted and without a gift.

Since Jafar had told his cousin Daxen, who was now the new khan, everything that he could before he left, Daxen knew details of the missing trunk and the importance of the parchment papers. Daxen trusted Jafar and he totally understood why his cousin was leaving Dracon to go live in Zurkia with Raja. Although there was no commitment between Jafar and Raja, Jafar had told Daxen he secretly had hopes for a relationship beyond just friends. However, it was also true that Jafar was sincere in wanting to help Zurkia.

So, considering the trust between the two cousins, Jafar wrote a letter in his Dracian language requesting that his cousin send over trustworthy escorts and a substantial gift that could be presented to the chieftain. It was then decided that Pavel, Cham, Yev, and Ivan would go back to Baku to deliver the letter to Khan Daxen and to bring back the escorts and gifts.

The tzarina had also overturned the decision to leave Cham's pirates on Kulaly Island and asked that Pavel pick up the pirates on his way back. She wanted as many allies as possible and didn't want to give up more of her own military to Levap Castle considering her losses with the recent abduction of the whole castle.

The wait for Pavel and the others to make the trip to Dracon was hard for Raja, as she and Jafar were not allowed outside their chambers. The fake couple's presence in Kazan Castle was to be kept secret. However, the two of them secretly visited each other on several occasions, which was just like Raja to do so considering her somewhat mischievous nature.

As time went on, the day finally came when Pavel returned with three ships: the pirate ship, the tzarina's ship stocked with gifts and escorts, and a Dracian ship filled with more gifts and escorts. Raja and Jafar were finally let out of their rooms to join the new arrivals and a few trusted others at the hall for a banqueting meal. But they were ordered by the tzarina to begin playing their role as a married Dracian couple to nullify any suspicions about Raja that might leak out to the enemy.

Jafar and Raja were both amazed at how many people from Dracon were at the feast. Raja recognized various people in the group, two being the twins that Raja had liked as chambermaids, and one other person, who was a complete surprise for Jafar.

"What are you doing here?" Jafar asked his cousin, who had his feet crossed up on the table, his hands behind his head, and, as usual, his pet cockatoo on his shoulder.

"I decided to do what you did," said Daxen as though nothing was wrong. He picked up a piece of small fruit from a platter and gave it to his bird.

"You what? Do you mean you left Dracon?"

"That's right," he said, giving the cockatoo another piece of fruit.

"For good?"

"Well not exactly for good."

"Isn't this a little irresponsible since you agreed to be the Khan of Dracon?"

Daxen drank from his goblet and then picked one up and offered it to Jafar.

"It's not irresponsible if you want to find a girl," said Daxen as he leaned forward and poured some wine into Jafar's goblet.

Daxen smirked confidently. Jafar thought a girl could certainly fall for his teasing smile, especially with such straight white teeth against his olive complexion.

"Ah . . . well I guess I can't argue with that," said Jafar a little slowly, knowing he himself left Dracon for Raja. "Welcome to Zurkia, then." The two cousins clanked their goblets together and sipped their drinks.

"Thanks, and I brought a lot of escorts with me as well. I'm sure after we help the tzarina she won't mind giving me a castle to live in while I'm here," said Daxen.

"You are presumptuous, aren't you?"

"Not at all, I've brought the tzarina lots of expensive gifts."

"Very generous of you, but aren't the Dracians going to be angry with you for leaving the country?" asked Jafar as he took a seat beside Daxen.

"No, I've worked that out. I had a choice of two cousins that I could ask to take over as khan while I'm gone. They're the sons of our Aunt Mereethea."

Jafar thought about their cousins. "Do you mean the one who doesn't know how to hold a sword and the one who doesn't know how to ride a horse?"

"Exactly."

"The Koffer twin brothers?" asked Jafar.

"Yes, the ones that are famous for their Cavalry Horse Farm."

"Or perhaps they are famous for their hilarious antics?" said Jafar.

"Yes, I suppose both."

"So which one of the Koffers did you choose?"

"The one who doesn't know how to ride a horse."

"Smart," said Jafar, "at least in a battle he can be a foot warrior and defend himself. And if need be he can ride in a chariot."

"True," said Daxen as he rubbed his chin, "although he may be the only one in a chariot on the battlefield."

"By the way," said Jafar, "I guess I can't trust you after all like I thought I could when I left Dracon. You said you would take on the responsibility to rule the country."

"Don't worry, I've got everything under control. There's a reason for my actions. You need me here." Daxen took some of the delicacies that were being passed around. "I see the way you're always watching Raja."

Jafar smiled. "You are a dedicated cousin, aren't you?"

Daxen gave Jafar a mischievous look, but then quickly cleared his throat and took a sip of his drink after catching Raja looking at them. "Ah yes, but what I really mean is I can help you come up with a clever plan to get the parchments from the trunk that Raja wants."

Raja turned away and Daxen continued speaking. "But I think you would be interested in hearing exactly how it can be done."

"Go on," said Jafar.

"It involves the identical chambermaid twins that I brought. Two people looking alike can be very useful in deceiving someone."

"It seems like a clever idea, but you'll need to fill me in."

"Certainly, it involves Raja and you," said Daxen, watching for Jafar's reaction out of the corner of his eye.

Jafar's face brightened. "I'm starting to get interested."

"You'll like the plan. And I think Raja will have no choice but to agree with it. Why don't we talk about it tonight?"

Jafar agreed and wondered how close Raja's own ideas would be to Daxen's plans.

Later that evening, after all new introductions were made, Raja, Pavel, Jafar, Daxen, Shamra, and the twins, whose names were Isa and Quinn, met in private to discuss more of Daxen's plans in detail. Raja was a bit dubious of the plans but in the end admitted that it was necessary to succeed in the mission.

"I also think Kuzma is a valuable person to take with us," said Raja.

"I'm thinking the same," said Pavel. "He would make an excellent distraction with his mesmerizing stories."

Raja looked at Daxen. "Do any of your escorts know how to dance?"

"Yes, I've already thought of that and brought the best ones with me."

"Perfect, another good distraction."

"Now, I think it would be a good idea if a letter stating the intention of our visit was delivered first," said Daxen. "And I could be the one to deliver the letter."

"Fabulous idea," said Pavel, who was trying not to convey any negative emotions about Raja and Jafar being together.

Daxen continued. "And I will also present a gift to the chieftain so he won't be able to refuse our visit."

"I can tell that you have thought about this ahead of time," said Pavel.

"I have and I think now would be a good time to construct the letter."

"Whose handwriting should we use?" asked Raja.

"I think it should be mine," said Jafar, "since I am the one to make the request."

Everyone agreed and contributed their ideas to the letter. In the end it turned out to be three long sentences. Daxen read the final version of the letter to everyone present.

To the Great Chieftain Tallboten, whose generosity is known far and wide

I, Prince Jafar, would like to personally thank you with gifts and dancing girls for the most beautiful princess of all time, which you have brought to me as a wife. I have come to Zurkia to thank you in person, as not being able to do so would never have shown enough gratitude. If it so pleases you, I would like to be your guest in three days from today to show you how happy my wife and I are together.

From your ever so grateful friend of the south, Khan Jafar of Dracon

Jafar then spent a long time rewriting the letter in a most skillful manner. During that time, Raja and Daxen took the opportunity to further explain details of the plan to the twins, Isa and Quinn. They also studied the maps of the castle so they would know every detail of its passages when the time came to carry out their mission.

When Jafar had rewritten the letter, Daxen suggested that he practice reading it. He began walking around acting as if he were a very important person. Then, sitting his cockatoo on his forearm and using a very eloquent form of speech, he began reciting the letter to his bird in a humorous fashion.

As he walked around with his funny antics, everyone noticed that he gave Shamra more attention than anyone else and was very successful at making her laugh. Feeling very proud that he could make Shamra laugh, his hilarious actions only heightened and he had everyone rolling in stitches. Daxen could certainly brighten up everyone's mood when he wanted to.

Chapter 22

In the Solar Room

Two days later, Daxen rode on his horse, presenting himself as a noble Dracian in the center of four escorts. Carrying crossbows by their sides and arrows at their backs, each man also held a small shield of wound wicker covered with leather as they rode past the village on their way to the Thrumb Castle.

Scurrying out of the way, the peasants stared at the group of horsemen with a mix of fear and curiosity. The riders wore protective armor composed of small iron and leather scales. Their helmets were cone shaped and were made of numerous steel plates. Long strands of horsehair protruded from the tops of the helmets. Long chain mail neck guards fell from the sides and rear of the helmets.

It was enough to make any man think twice about getting on the wrong side of these Dracians, which was the exact image that Daxen wanted to convey. Carrying the blue and white Dracian flag, Daxen rode to the entrance of the castle and handed the letter to a Tyhet warrior, who then went inside to deliver the message. Given the situation, the wait seemed horribly long but proved to be worthwhile, as the same warrior came out and allowed Daxen to enter the castle.

Upon removing his helmet, Daxen was ushered along by the Tyhet warrior.

"The chieftain will see you in the solar room," said the warrior.

That sounded very promising, as only good friends were invited to the solar room. It seemed the letter had been honored.

Daxen was led through the smaller hall and down a corridor, through another room and up a set of stairs to the second level of the castle. From there they went down two separate corridors and into the solar room. The Tyhet went down the opposite corridor and Daxen was left standing there. But soon the Tyhet returned with the chieftain, who then entered into the solar room with Daxen following.

The chieftain was a tall man with a rather tough-looking face. Not someone you would want to meet in the dark. He held out the letter for Daxen to see. "About this letter, I think it would be more official if you read it to me."

Daxen was wondering why he should read the letter and then guessed it was because the chieftain didn't know how to read. He held out his hand to receive the letter. "Certainly. I will do the honor of reading the letter."

The chieftain gave the letter to Daxen and he read it just as he had practiced it.

"This is quite unexpected," said the chieftain, trying to sound important.

"Not so unexpected," said Daxen, maintaining an air of sophistication. "The Dracians are known for their gifts of thankfulness in return for favors."

"So, you are returning the favor?"

"Yes, if it pleases you I have a gift for you right now."

Daxen presented the chieftain with a large goblet filled with gold coins.

The chieftain's eyes grew wide. "This is unexpected. I accept your gift."

The chieftain motioned for Daxen to sit while taking a seat himself. He offered him some cold leftover tea from a pot.

Daxen accepted, not wanting to offend him.

"I hear you are well protected," said the chieftain.

"Yes, I came with four escorts, since from what I hear protection is needed in these parts."

The chieftain looked Daxen over and wondered whether he was referring to the disappearing peasants. He grew a bit suspicious. "Where is your party staying?"

"Ah, that is a good question."

The chieftain met Daxen's gaze with an air of aloofness, waiting to see if his answer was worth believing.

"In my ship, which is the largest sailing ship in the Land of Rousse," said Daxen.

The answer seemed to satisfy the chieftain and he went on to ask more questions. "Three days is short notice for a banquet, don't you think?"

"Perhaps, but it is us who will arrange the banquet. And the dancers are eager to perform and I wouldn't want to disappoint them."

The chieftain's eyes flew open. His large lips formed a child-like smile, letting out a series of little hiccups. Then suddenly, trying to act more sophisticated, he shook his head violently, flapping his lips from side to side while making a gurgling noise. With a straight face he spoke a matter-of-factly. "No, of course not. I would never dream of doing such a horrid thing. I have more sense than that."

Daxen could see he was making good progress. "Yes, yes, I know you wouldn't. And might I add, we would not want the food we have brought to spoil."

"You brought food?"

"Yes, all the southern exotic foods one can think of."

"Spices?"

"A lot of them."

"Drink?"

"Plenty."

"Very good," said the chieftain. "I am low on food here."

"What happened to your food?"

"It's all gone to the north, as well as a lot of other things."

"To the north?"

"Yes, at the will of my ally."

"Is this ally the Dark Prince?" asked Daxen.

"You know about him?"

"I have heard about him in Dracon." Daxen tried to be nonchalant. "Will he be coming here?"

"Not for a good while."

Daxen felt relieved. "What's his business?"

"He's a slave trader."

"There must be coin in that," said Daxen.

"Lots, particularly when he deals with the Grand Padesha."

"So, the Dark Prince goes to Odyhun?"

"Yes, he does."

Daxen thought the conversation was going well, as he had no problem getting answers to his questions, but at the same time he didn't want to be too direct. "Well, it must be nice for him to have all of that coin. Does he share it with you?"

"Not really, he uses the coin for his projects, and that's why I have very few servants right now." The chieftain looked a bit unhappy.

Daxen noticed the chieftain's attitude and said, "I can understand why not having servants would pose a hardship on you."

"It does, but on the other hand, the Dark Prince promised to compensate for it later."

"Are you in the business too?"

The chieftain got up to look out the window. "I am. There's good coin in it, but it's all gone to the Dark Prince. He keeps saying its coming but I haven't seen it yet."

Daxen almost forgot about one of the reasons he'd come to Thrumb Castle. Still sitting, he quickly took the opportunity to look around the room for the trunk. It shouldn't be too hard to find with one of its legs broken.

"You say you have very few servants," said Daxen, as he continued his search for the trunk.

"Yes, and I'm angry about it."

Daxen looked along the south wall. "Perhaps my servants can make up for it when they arrive in two more days."

Contemplating something, the chieftain continued to look out the window. "I'm glad you brought that up."

"How so?" Daxen was sure he spotted the trunk next to a chaise lounge that was along the north wall, but it didn't have a broken leg. He got up himself and wandered closer to the trunk.

The chieftain finally revealed his thoughts. "I want to offer that your servants and the Dracian couple stay here over night after the festivity."

Daxen was sure it was the trunk. It had three bear heads. He took a chance and bent down to examine it more carefully. He then saw that one of the legs had been repaired. Daxen straightened up and continued talking to the chieftain. "Ah yes, that sounds like a perfect solution." However, Daxen had not been completely engaged in the conversation and suddenly realized what he had just agreed to.

"Good, that will solve both of our problems," said the chieftain.

"Yes, of course. The better for both of us," said Daxen, wondering how Jafar and Raja would feel about the new turn of events. He truly hoped they wouldn't be put out by the overnight invitation.

"You can return to the khan and tell him about my decision and that I will be looking forward to seeing him."

"Indeed, I will."

Daxen sat back down in the chaise. "There's one more thing."

"What's that?"

"I'd like to tell you about one of my gifts."

Sitting down again, the chieftain waited for Daxen to continue.

"Among my servants I have twin maids."

The chieftain looked interested.

"It is our belief in Dracon that it is extremely lucky to be served by twins and even more lucky if they have rare eye color. And if you are so fortunate to be in those circumstances good things will come to you."

The chieftain's eyes looked like two round wheels. "How fortunate for me to come upon this." This indeed put the chieftain in a good mood and he began to chuckle. "Tell me, what good things?"

"All of your wealth will more than double."

Starting to laugh at his good fortune, the chieftain pointed at Jafar and said, "You know that I will be richer than the Dark Prince." His own comment put him into a fit of laughter and he was barely able to speak. "A good belief system, indeed." The chieftain doubled over with squealing chortles, holding his stomach to ease the pain from laughing so hard.

Daxen laughed along with the chieftain. "You should have no problem replacing the servants taken by the Dark Prince. He will have to beg you for more with your new status."

The laughing continued for some time, but stopped when Daxen's face became serious. He spoke in a low voice. "But in order for all of this to transpire you must do one thing."

"And what's that?" asked the chieftain, whose own face looked like a cold stone.

"Everyone must join you in your keeping room so as not to defile any other space of the castle while the ritual is taking place."

The chieftain sat back and chuckled in a relieved manner. "A small request."

"I appreciate your cooperation," said Daxen, who now spoke in an uplifting manner. "The ritual takes place at midnight."

"I shall be ready by then. I look forward to the evening," said the chieftain.

"You will be well entertained," said Daxen.

Daxen and the chieftain stood at the same time and bid their farewells, and then Daxen was ushered back to the castle entrance by the Tyhet warrior. The four Dracian escorts were waiting for Daxen's return and the five of them traveled back to Kazan Castle.

Chapter 23

The Ruby Ring

Raja and Jafar were walking in the Soladecorus Gardens of Kazan Castle and talking about their act as a married couple. Jafar was explaining the Dracian customs to Raja.

"I don't think I want you kissing my foot," said Raja.

"It's not so much the kissing as the laying of your toe on the sword," said Jafar. "The art of just touching my sword with your toe signifies that whoever dares to touch my wife will die by the sword. Then after that I seal the warning with a kiss. This is always done in meeting new people who hold a title, such as the chieftain."

Raja looked displeased. "The chieftain probably doesn't even know the Dracian tradition so I suggest not doing it."

"Be sure, he does know it. My father would have seen to that. His own wife was extremely beautiful and when dealing with the slave trade he didn't trust anyone. That's why he invented the ritual. If we don't do it, the chieftain may doubt the authenticity of our marriage and then we will be in huge trouble."

Raja did not for one second like the idea of Jafar kissing her bare foot, but she could see Jafar's point of view. "Okay I'll go along with it, but please remember it is only to be a very short light kiss."

"Yes, of course. You can trust me." Jafar smiled, happy that Raja had consented, and took her hand in his. "Shall we practice it now."

Raja pulled her hand away and gave Jafar a hands-on-the-hip look. "Of all the nerve! I've a mind to ask Pavel to be my husband instead."

Jafar quickly went down on one knee. "Okay, okay, just joking," said Jafar. "My apologies, please."

At that moment Raja saw a group of horsemen ride over the arched bridge. "Daxen's back!"

"Hopefully he hit the nail on the head," said Jafar.

The two of them ran to the castle to the end of the garden pergolas. A number of servants were already there to meet Daxen and his four escorts. The servants quickly took the horses into their own care.

Daxen dusted himself off as if his mission duping a chieftain was an everyday occurrence. "Is there any food? I'm starved."

Ignoring Daxen's request, Jafar impatiently asked, "What's the verdict?"

"Do I look unhappy?" asked Daxen.

"That you don't."

Daxen stepped his feet forward one at a time letting a servant brush off his dusty boots while taking his time to answer the question. He looked as calm and collected as ever. "He grabbed onto it like a leach."

"Unbelievable," said Jafar.

"Not really, I don't think he is that smart. The Dark Prince has him wrapped around his finger."

"You talked about the Dark Prince?"

"Uh uh," said Daxen as he took a wet cloth to swipe the dust and sweat from his face.

Not wanting to continue the conversation in public, Raja suggested that they continue talking around the dinner table. The others agreed and the three of them went into the hall where food was immediately served to them.

Jafar jeered at his cousin over the fact that he had succeeded in convincing the chieftain to partake of the prosperity ritual. "You think you're quite good, don't you?" he said, leaning back on his chair.

"I know I'm good."

"A little arrogant, wouldn't you say?"

"Goes along with getting things done."

"I suppose, but look who's going to be the center of attention next," said Jafar with a proud smile.

"It seems like you're looking forward to that," said Daxen, giving his cousin a wink.

Raja raised her arm, threatening to give Jafar a swat. "A little too much, I would say. Remember to keep your promise."

"I will. I will," said Jafar, who held his arm up, pretending to defend himself from Raja's squat. "Don't worry, you can trust me."

Seeing the sincere look in Jafar's face, she was then eager to find out what else Daxen knew. "So, what about the Dark Prince?"

Daxen first took another mouthful of food before he answered. "He's a . . ." He took his time to chew his food a little more thoroughly. ". . . slave trader."

Raja sat back in her chair. "Well, that's not too surprising."

Daxen continued after swallowing his food. "And he's got some project going on up north."

"What about the chieftain? How is he connected?" asked Jafar.

Daxen talked with his mouth full. "Like I said, it looks like the prince has him doing his bidding. He is in on the slave trading too."

"Brutal," said Raja. "I hope we're not going to meet the Dark Prince at the castle."

Daxen helped himself to seconds. "Apparently he's busy up north."

"Busy and up to a lot of no good," said Jafar.

Raja noticed that Jafar did not have the mentality of his father. She wondered what had caused him to be so different and admitted to herself that she liked that side of him.

"And you're not going to believe this," said Daxen.

"What is it?" asked Raja.

"I saw the trunk with the bears."

"Amazing," said Raja.

"Where were you in the castle?" asked Jafar.

"In the solar room." Daxen stopped talking for a moment to eat some of his food. "It's on the second floor."

Jafar thought about that information. "That could pose a problem."

Daxen shook his head and swallowed. "Not really. We have the maps of the castle."

"True," said Jafar. "But the twins seem to have difficulty reading the maps."

"I'll go over the maps very thoroughly with them again," said Raja.

"And please, more than once," said Jafar.

"Don't worry," said Raja.

But despite Raja's promise, Jafar still had a worried look. Raja stood up and put her hand on his shoulder and assured him she was a good teacher. She then told Jafar and Daxen that she would be spending some time saying farewell to her mother before they left on their mission.

Raja left the hall and told one of the servants to ask the tzarina that the two of them have a farewell visit. The request was granted, and when Raja arrived at her mother's solar room, Pavel was in the room sitting and talking with her mother. Raja and Pavel greeted each other with a curtsy and a bow. Pavel then left the room so the princess and the tzarina could have some time alone.

"Please, sit down," said the tzarina. She called for Bettalia, who was in the chamber area.

Bettalia quickly came over and curtsied in front of Raja and then the tzarina. "My highness," she said.

The tzarina spoke with kindness. "Please retrieve my small jewelry box."

"Yes, right away."

Raja looked at her mother in surprise. "You have given me so much already. What more could you want to give me?"

Bettalia returned with the box and set it in front of the tzarina. Opening the lid, she said, "Princess Raja, your mother has been talking about this for a long time."

The tzarina reached into the box and then looked at her daughter.

Raja held her breath.

"Yes, I have," said the tzarina. "And I feel now is the right time to give this to you."

"What is it?" asked Raja, slowly releasing her breath, very much in suspense.

The tzarina took a piece of jewelry from the box and handed it to Raja. "It's a ring that your father gave me before we were married and I want you to have it. Think of it as a gift from your father."

"It's beautiful," she said. "But I couldn't take it."

"Yes, I insist. I have other keepsakes. I want you to have something to remember your father by, so I am giving this to you."

Raja turned the ring over, admiring the ruby. It was an exceptionally deep red color. She tried the ring on. It fit perfectly. She felt very touched that her mother would give her something to remember her father by, but she was saddened that she didn't have real memories of him.

"I shall cherish it always, thank you, Mother."

"You're welcome."

Bidding her mother farewell, Raja gave her mother a kiss on the cheek.

"Keep safe," said the tzarina.

"I shall."

"And no more running away by yourself," said Bettalia with a serious look.

"I shall try to heed the advice," said Raja.

Raja curtsied and left the room.

That same day Raja and her friends left Kazan Castle on a group of horses and headed for Port Alexandra. They rode past the monastery and on down through the streets. People darted out of their way with their carts and donkeys. Suddenly, a woman ran out in front of her and Raja had to quickly stop her horse.

"Get out of the way," shouted Daxen.

Not listening, the woman held out something in her hands. "For you my princess. It is a gift."

Raja saw that she was a Berzation. The woman looked quit poor. Raja always wanted to take time for the poor so she reached down and received the gift. Even though the Berzation said it was a gift, Raja gave her a coin. Grateful, the woman bowed and went back to her stall.

Examining the gift, she saw that it was block soap.

Raja looked at Kuzma, who rode beside her. She remembered Kuzma saying that block soap came from the native people of Zurkia from the west. Raja held the soap out for Kuzma to examine. "Does this comes from the Montia region?" she asked.

"Yes, it does. I recognize it well from when I was a trader."

It had a beautiful lilac fragrance and she was glad she'd taken the time to receive the gift.

The group continued their ride and finally boarded the Zurkian ship, where the escorts had already prepared for their mission. They set sail down the Kazanka River for the Sap Tributary, which was about three quarters of the way up north along the country's shores. Everyone had a nervous sort of excitement for what lay ahead. During the sail, Daxen, Jafar, Raja, Shamra, and the twins met in the captain's quarters and studied the details of the maps, especially the map of the second floor. They talked late into the night, discussing how they would try and retrieve the parchments. One very important decision made was that Daxen would carry the maps.

Every so often, Raja snuck a peak at her ring. She wondered what her father had been like and really wished she could have known him. From what her mother had said, he had been a very noble and kind person, and also very strong and brave. Her thoughts quieted her spirit and a peaceful mellowness came over her as with everyone else. One by one, the noble voyagers found a spot to sleep in the ship for the night.

No one was uncomfortable in terms of space, as the ship was most certainly the largest of its kind. Most people could sleep in the hold or in the aftercastle and forecastle. A few had to sleep out in the open on the deck. Raja, Shamra, and the twins were given the captain's quarters to sleep in and in the girls' minds it was turning out to be one of the best times they had ever had.

Chapter 24

Glazed Eyes

"You're joking," said Jafar, who stood on the deck of Daxen's ship at Sap Tributary.

"No, I'm not," said Daxen. "I'm sorry I didn't mention this earlier, but I forgot to tell you."

"I guess I'll forgive you, seeing as how I probably don't have a choice. You must have really made a good impression for the chieftain to invite us and the crew for the night."

"I'm afraid so. But I think what he was really interested in was spending more time with the dancers."

Jafar raised his eyebrows.

"Don't worry," said Daxen. "I'll have it under control."

The ship had been docked at Sap Tributary for some time and people were getting ready to make the trek to Thrumb Castle. Raja was with Shamra, who had taken three hours creating the perfect hairstyle for Raja.

Jafar continued the conversation with Daxen.

"So what do we do? Should we leave Thrumb Castle in the middle of the night, or wait it out until morning?"

"We should wait it out until morning, otherwise it won't seem like the real thing."

At that moment, Raja walked out onto the deck with her hair all done in an unusual style and wearing her Dracian costume. Bell trinkets adorned her hair and beads intertwined the hooped braids. Her dress glittered with stones of red, white, and black and trailed behind her, which had to be held up by Shamra and the twins.

"Don't you look like a Dracian princess, or rather, I should say, a Dracian khanum," said Jafar.

"I'm taking it you like my hair," said Raja, who touched her hairstyle to make sure it was all in place.

"Well, I'm not so sure," said Jafar.

"What does that mean?" asked Shamra.

"Oh, I do like Raja's hair but we're not in Dracon and I'm beginning to like Zurkian ways better."

"Do you mean it sticks out too much?" asked Raja.

"Perhaps just a little," said Jafar.

Raja smiled back. "Well, your ponytail on the top of your head sticks out so I guess we are even."

Everyone laughed at the comment.

"Nonetheless, a dashing couple indeed," said Daxen. "Your dark turquoise robe looks exquisite."

Jafar tightened the gray sash around his waist. "Thank you. Are we ready to go?"

"I'm ready," said Raja.

"What about Shamra?" asked Daxen.

"She's staying here with some of the escorts," said Raja.

"Is that fine with you, Shamra?" asked Daxen, concerned that she not feel afraid.

"Yes, it's fine," said Shamra.

Daxen strode over to one of the escorts and had a word with him. He then turned to Shamra. "You will have everything that you need."

"Thank you," said Shamra, feeling a little flushed that Daxen would pay her so much attention.

Daxen bowed his head at Shamra while she curtsied.

Then Daxen, Raja, and Jafar led the group away from the ship along the Wooded Path that followed the Sap Tributary.

Every servant carried a different bowl with a different type of food for what would end up being a huge feast. Raja walked in the middle of Daxen and Jafar and enjoyed all of the attention.

Jafar turned his head to Raja. "You look very beautiful tonight," he said.

Daxen cleared his throat. "I shall add that you look more lovely than a sunset."

Raja smiled and fluttered her eyelashes to be funny. "Thank you. You both look handsome as well."

"Do we have the maps?" asked Jafar.

"Yes, I have one," said Daxen, "And Quinn has the other map."

Raja looked at Daxen. "So you chose Quinn to get the parchments?"

"Yes," said Daxen, hoping he had made the right decision.

"Sounds good," said Raja.

The walk to the castle didn't take them much longer than an hour. They walked around to the front of Thrumb Castle, where Tyhet warriors let them in after they crossed the drawbridge. In single file the group passed through the two barbicans and into the gatehouse. Once everyone was inside the castle, the drawbridge was taken up and warriors were posted to the main entrance and the stables.

The large group from the ship continued into the courtyard. From there, the servants who had brought the food were led into the kitchens, and the entertainers, the escorts, and noble Daxen were led into the keeping room. Jafar and Raja were led into the great hall to greet the chieftain, who was by the hearth.

An enormously long table extended the length of the room. At the far side of the room was a dome shaped area with a stone fireplace in it. Chaise lounges were placed in front of the fire. A large man was sprawled out on one of the lounges.

The couple walked to the seating arrangement and stood before the chieftain. The air felt warm and the fire crackled. Shadows from the light of the fire fell on each person's face. From where Raja was standing she could now see the chieftain. He appeared monstrous to her. She recognized him from when he had kidnapped her, which made chills go up and down her spine—especially as he had held a knife to her face. He wore a black metal cap over his head and Raja was sure he wore it to make himself look important. Strands of straggly hair fell from underneath the brass cap onto his bulky shoulders.

The chieftain's eyes fell upon Raja in a lofty manner. Raja maintained her composure and reciprocated the gaze with a matter-of–fact look. It's true he had won the sword fight during their first encounter, but tonight she was sure she would be the one to win by getting what she'd come for.

The chieftain checked to see that his cap was on straight. He looked at Jafar with a furrowed brow, as if he didn't quit believe they were married.

Jafar motioned for Raja to sit down. He pulled off her already loosened boot, making sure that her dress covered her foot, all except for her big toe. Then taking out his sword from his sheath, he knelt down and laid it on the ground. Raja cast a steely look at the chieftain, tilted her head up, and put the tip of her toe on the gleaming metal of the sword. Jafar bent over and kissed the end of Raja's toe.

Feeling like the ordeal wasn't that bad, Raja waited for Jafar to put her boot back on, but instead he kissed her foot a second time and then a third. Knowing that wasn't part of the agreement she instinctively pulled her foot away and hoped the chieftain hadn't noticed.

Jafar quickly took Raja's hand and kissed it. He whispered, "I'm just trying to look real. Play your role."

Raja managed a small smile as she tilted her head upwards again with a look of arrogance. She looked at the chieftain out of the corner of her eye to watch his reaction. He was still looking at her foot, which suddenly made her feel angry. Raja had a sudden urge to say something nasty.

Jafar noticed Raja's change of mode and quickly put her boot back on. He got up and stood in between Raja and the chieftain. Holding his sword in front of him with the tip pointing upwards, he spoke with authority, looking straight at the chieftain's face.

On my wife, linger no eye or hand
Or die by the sword I will command

The chieftain mumbled under his breath.

My eyes and hands shall not loath
Your wife I honor to keep my oath

The chieftain was obviously schooled in Dracon's culture and knew what to say, which surprised Raja a good deal. Nonetheless, Raja wondered if the ritual did any good, as the first thing the chieftain did was look at her with a mean expression. His haughty look amplified his odious disposition. She tried to maintain an air of confidence, showing that she was not bothered by his scornful mannerism.

Then, in an instant, the chieftain's expression turned mellow as if he suddenly realized what he was supposed to say.

"Ahh . . . your wife, yes, no harm will come to her. I am pleased you are both here."

"Likewise," said Jafar, trying to act as mature as he could with a slight coolness in his demeanor. He put his sword back into his sheath.

"Pleased to meet you," said Raja, following Jafar's cue.

"I hear you are happy," said the chieftain, looking at Raja from head to toe.

"Very," she said, managing a slight smile.

"Ah good, it was the right decision for you then." The chieftain looked up at Jafar. "Sit down and let's talk."

Before sitting down, Jafar handed the chieftain a bag of gold coins. "Please accept my gift as my way of thanking you for giving me a beautiful wife."

The chieftain looked in the bag with wide eyes. He lifted the bag up and down to test its weight. "I see business with you is already good."

"It's no other way," said Jafar, with raised eyebrows.

"And you know what kind of business I'm talking about, right?"

"Of course, of course," said Jafar. "Very lucrative indeed."

Hating every moment of the conversation, Raja tried to keep from going over to the chieftain and saying just what she thought of him. Of course, that would ruin everything and so she just kept on thinking of the good she was doing while she was here at the castle.

"I'm looking forward to our new friendship," said the chieftain.

"I'll keep in touch," said Jafar.

The chieftain twirled his hair in his fingers. "I will personally come to Dracon myself and pay you a visit so we can talk."

Smiling to himself, and doubting his proposal, he agreed wholeheartedly with the chieftain's every word. "I will look forward to your visit."

"I'm not sure when I could come. I'll have to check on things up north first."

"No rush," said Jafar.

"Good, I don't like to be rushed," said the chieftain. "But on the other hand, some things might need to be rushed. I'm certainly getting low on all of my supplies."

"Well, I think I can do something about that tonight," said Jafar, who thought he had better get things moving along. "Shall we go into your keeping room? I'm sure my entertainers are anxiously waiting for you."

"The sooner the better. I'm looking forward to it."

The chieftain got up from his chaise, as did the couple. He stood at least one head above Jafar. But Raja thought of him as a big oaf, which made him less intimidating.

The chieftain led Jafar and Raja toward the keeping room. Jafar reached over and held Raja's hand. She didn't try to pull it away and he shot her a little smile. As they entered the room, the musicians readied themselves to play their instruments and the dancers stood and arranged themselves in various groups. The chieftain, looking very pleased, took his seat of honor.

"May the evening of festivity begin for the chieftain," shouted Jafar, raising his hand to signal the entertainers to begin their dancing.

The room was filled with lively music. There were three rebecs with round pear-shaped forms, and two psalteries, which were a cross between a harp and a lyre, then one lute, which stood about six feet tall. And to make the music livelier there were numerous drums and cymbals.

Dancing girls swayed and swerved around the chieftain, placing flowers in his long hair. Every time a flower was placed in his hair he giggled with delight. His eyes floated from one girl to the next with an amusing expression on his face. All in all, he seemed like a very immature man.

Cheese pies, custards, doughnuts, and ale were served to everyone throughout the evening, including the Tyhet warriors. However, more ale was especially served to the chieftain. Not missing any of the food or drink, the chieftain's eyes became more and more glazed as the evening wore on. At one point, he stood, wanting to dance along with the girls, but he lost his balance and fell to the floor. His metal cap rolled across the stone surface. A few dancers gasped. Daxen quickly helped the chieftain to his chair. He retrieved the cap and put it back on. There was a small grunt from the chieftain as he tried to make sure the cap was on straight.

The dancing continued and the chieftain feasted his eyes upon the beauty of the dancers and their graceful moves, however, in not too much more time, he lost his balance as he tried to grab one of the girls. She moved away just in time as he plummeted to the floor. His metal cap shot across the floor this time causing a surge of laughter among the escorts, servants, and warriors. Feeling jovial, the escorts started playing with the cap by kicking it around the room. Desperately hoping the incident wouldn't offend the chieftain, Daxen helped him back on his chair and demanded the cap back from the escorts. He quickly set it back on the chieftain's head.

Thankfully, the drunken chieftain had not realized that his hat had rolled away. He had been fully occupied getting up from the floor and was focusing on trying to stay on his chair. Daxen seriously hoped it was getting close to the end of the festival, as helping the chieftain back onto his chair was not an easy task.

Fortunately, the time was nearing midnight. Feeling relieved that things would now move along, Daxen waited for the timepiece to indicate the precise moment. Then Daxen lifted his arm as a signal for everyone to stop what he or she was doing.

Daxen called out in a firm voice. "It is time for our final gift!"

Swaying on his chair, the chieftain looked at Daxen with blurry eyes.

Daxen made his announcement. "Every single person must be in attendance in this room."

The chieftain, barely being able to raise his arm, called out. "Warriors!" He motioned Daxen with his hand to give the orders to the warriors.

"Bring every one into the keeping room. No one must be allowed out of this room until the rituals are complete!" shouted Daxen.

The warriors in the castle were brought into the keeping room and all eyes were now on Daxen. He clapped his hands. The twin girls, who hadn't shown themselves yet, came and stood in front of the chieftain.

"Lovely specimens," said the chieftain, in a slurred voice with a hiccup.

The twins stood poised and ready to carry out the rituals. They looked absolutely identical except that Quinn was wearing a blue robe and Isa was wearing a red robe.

"Let the ritual begin," said Daxen.

Chapter 25

Chloe

The twin girls went back into the kitchen inside Thrumb Castle.

"Here is my robe," said Quinn.

"Okay, thanks," said Isa as she took the blue robe and laid it aside.

Quinn took out the map to make sure she would be going in the right direction.

"As soon as you get out that door, you turn left," said Isa, looking at the map.

"Then I walk down the corridor and go through this room?" asked Quinn, pointing to the map.

"Yes, and then you should be at the bottom of the stairs."

Quinn nodded and studied the map.

"When you get to the top of the stairs, turn right down the first corridor and left down the second one. This should lead you into the solar room."

Quinn nodded again even though she wasn't entirely sure of all the directions.

"Remember what Daxen said. There is a chaise lounge against the north wall, which is in that direction," said Isa, pointing to where she thought north was.

"Okay," said Quinn, hoping that somehow she would find the right place, as the directions were rather confusing to her.

Isa continued. "The trunk is right next to the chaise lounge. It has three carvings of bear heads on it. Do you remember how to unlock the pins?"

"Turn to the right," said Quinn, imitating the rotation.

"Yes, but that is left."

Quinn rotated her hand the other way.

"Good," said Isa.

Quinn rolled up the map.

"Good luck."

"Thanks," said Quinn. She turned and walked through the kitchen. At the exit, she turned left and was gone.

* * *

Isa took a bowl filled with tarts and reentered the keeping room.

As soon as she entered the room, soft music began playing and Isa sang in a beautiful voice. Holding her tarts high in the air, she circled the room.

After she circled the room twice, Isa came and offered a tart to the chieftain, who obediently took it and ate it. Daxen then offered strong ale to the chieftain, who was only too glad to drink it.

At that point, Kuzma stood up and walked in front of the chieftain and began telling a tale in a most hypnotic way. All eyes were on Kuzma as he told his story.

Three Princesses and Three Bears

There once were three beautiful girls who were princesses and who loved to do good deeds. Each princess had a basket of magical precious stones. One day they met a poor farmer and his wife. They were both crying because their things that they needed to farm with were ruined and now they had no way of providing for themselves.

The girls asked the couple how their belongings had become ruined. They said that three large bears had torn them apart, and they themselves had barely escaped their treacherous acts by climbing up onto their roof.

The princesses comforted the farmer and his wife and then each girl gave them a precious stone. Immediately, the stones turned into a horse, a plow, and some seeds. The couple was overjoyed and wanted to get to work right away. They promised the princesses that they would be rewarded for their kindness, but the girls said that they were not looking for a reward and that the farmer and his wife could keep all of their harvests.

But then, by surprise, the three bears came back to the farmer's house. They growled and snarled to frighten the girls, and then grew to a gigantic size. The bears opened their mouths so wide that they swallowed the plow, the horse, and the seeds. Leaping at the girls, the bears wanted to swallow them as well. But the girls were very nimble and ran away from them.

The bears chased the princesses and were catching up with them, but when the bears got close, each princess threw out one of their stones and as soon as they hit the ground they turned into small boulders. The bears stumbled on the rocks and hit their heads, which caused them to cough up the horse, the plow, and the seeds. After that, the bears slowly became smaller until all that was left was their pelts. The princesses returned the robbed items to the farmer and from then on, all of the farmer's harvests were very bountiful.

Every escort clapped and cheered for Kuzma as he finished the tale. Raja thought the tale was very odd and watched for the chieftain's reaction. At first, he didn't clap and looked a little puzzled, but then, after a few moments, he joined in with the clapping as if nothing could be better.

* * *

Quinn had made a wrong turn and frantically retraced her steps. She got out the map and tried to make sense out of Isa's directions, but the directions and the map just didn't pair up. She rolled the map back up and decided she would try to find it without the map. Going on intuition, Quinn came to what she thought was the solar room. The walls were filled with tapestry that came from her country. One tapestry was an image of three older girls with flames for hair. They were watching three bears approaching them. When Quinn saw the bears, she was sure she had the right room.

Quinn looked along the north wall but did not see a trunk. She looked along another wall but no trunk. Then along the third wall she saw it. Yes, the trunk was beside a chaise lounge. She thought it was probably the south wall and Isa had it wrong. She noticed that there was a large crumpled blanket on the chaise, probably due to the lack of servants. She had an urge to fold the blanket in a neat square but she resisted.

Hurrying to the trunk she tripped over a bowl that was on the floor. It made a loud thud. She told herself to be quieter or she would have everyone up here in a flash.

Gently kneeling beside the trunk, Quinn opened it. It was full of trinkets. She would have to empty it in order to unlock the pins so she took out the items as quickly and as gently as she could. One of the things she picked up was a red glass bottle. It felt slippery from some of the liquid having run out of the bottle. She read the label in a whisper. "Red Oboedensglee." That was a strange sounding name. She uncorked the bottle to smell it. It smelled like sugar cane and had a red color. Then, as she tried to put the cork back on, the bottle slipped from her hand and fell onto the floor with a thud. The red liquid spilled out of the bottle.

Quinn heard a sound coming from the chaise lounge. Her heart felt as though it had stopped beating. Someone in the bed sat up.

It was a young girl. Relief suddenly swept over Quinn. She immediately rushed over to the girl and covered the girl's mouth with her hand.

"Shhh. I'm here to help you," said Quinn in a barely audible voice. "I won't hurt you. You can trust me. Tell me who you are."

Quinn slowly let her hand off the girl's mouth.

"I'm frightened," said the girl.

"Okay, I'm here to get you out of here. Try to be very quiet or you might be heard."

The girl nodded.

"First, I have to get something out of this trunk. Can you wait for that?"

The girl nodded.

Quinn took the rest of the things out of the trunk and found the locking pin. She turned it to the right. It loosened. She turned it round and round until it came out. She carefully lifted up the side panel. There it was, a paper. She quickly did the same to the other side of the trunk and got a second paper. Putting the parchments inside her sash, she reassembled the trunk.

"Wait here and I will be right back," said Quinn.

The girl agreed. "Please hurry. I want to get out of here."

"I will go as quickly as I can."

Reentering the kitchen, just as Isa walked in, Quinn felt relieved. Speaking, out of breath and with great concern, she said, "I've discovered . . . I've discovered a little . . . a little girl in the solar room."

"You what?" asked Isa.

"There's a girl in the solar room upstairs."

"Of all the horrid things," said Isa. "She was probably abducted."

"What are we going to do?" asked Quinn.

Isa set down the plate of tarts. "Wait here, I will get the maps from Daxen."

She was just about to leave when Quinn rushed over to her. "You forgot to change your robe. Remember, you're are supposed to be me when you go back out."

"Thank you," she said, feeling slightly embarrassed at her mistake.

Putting on the blue robe, she now carried the tray of halvah. Kuzma was still telling his tales when Isa reentered the keeping room. There was a big burst of laughter from the audience. Isa went over to several of the Tyhet warriors and offered them a piece of halvah. Then, as naturally as possible, as if it was part of the ritual, she went over to Daxen and offered him the delicacy as well. Isa then whispered to him that she needed the maps. He got up and started gracefully twirling in circles with Isa, while holding the bowl.

As Daxen moved more towards the back of the crowd, he inconspicuously handed her the maps. Isa quickly concealed them inside her robe. Twirling back to the chieftain, Isa offered him a piece of halvah. He took it and stuffed it into his mouth while still mesmerized by Kuzma. Daxen then offered him more ale and the chieftain drank it without any thought.

Isa left the room and went back into the kitchen.

"I've got the maps."

Isa quickly unrolled them and found the one she was looking for. "This is a map of the underground secret passages. You need to get the girl out of here."

Quinn looked at the map in confusion.

"It's not that hard," said Isa as she traced the route with her fingers. But from the look on Quinn's face, Isa could tell Quinn thought the map was difficult to read.

"Do you want me to go get the girl?" asked Isa.

"Yes," said Quinn.

"Okay."

After looking at the map one more time for details, Isa gave them to Quinn to take care of. She was about to leave when Quinn spoke up. "You're still wearing the blue robe."

"Thanks for reminding me," said Isa and took off the robe.

Quinn put on the red robe and went out with a bowl of sugared fritters. She wondered if Daxen would notice she wasn't Isa. In a way she thought it was funny, but then again, the situation was serious.

* * *

Isa found her way up to the solar room and the young girl was still sitting on the chaise lounge.

Rushing over to the girl, she wrapped her own shawl around her. "Come with me. We need to get out of here."

But before leaving, Isa quickly made the blanket seem like the girl was still sleeping underneath it.

Carrying a torch and holding onto the girl's hand, Isa hurried down the stairs. Going down the hall, she came to an engraved bear's head on the side of the wall. Remembering where she saw that on the map, she then went a short distance and turned into the storage room. Isa looked for the secret passage. Her eyes rested on what she believed to be the correct entrance. Isa walked across the room and lifted the wooden lid of a stone well.

It was in fact a real well, but it was also the way to a passage that led under the moat. Isa could see there were places to put one's feet to go down into the water hole. There were also iron rungs to hold on to. Isa told the girl to step carefully.

Still holding onto the torch, Isa lowered herself into the hole with the girl following her. Before they got to the water, they found the entrance that led into the secret passage. The girls went into the opening and climbed down the incline. After some time, the opening leveled and they were able to stand up, but unfortunately, their torch went out and it was pitch dark. Isa and the girl walked along the passageway, feeling the sides of the wall, making sure each footstep they took was on solid ground. It was scary and exhausting, to say the least, but really there wasn't any choice but to keep moving forward.

To Isa's relief, after a good half hour, she saw a bit of light at the end of the tunnel. They exited through a hole in the side of a small mound that was hidden behind a large boulder, and came out beside the Sap Tributary. Isa and the young girl found the Wooded Path and fled to the ship, guided by the light of the bright full moon.

Chapter 26

My Turn

At two o'clock in the morning the chieftain finally fell off of his chair in the keeping room and refused to get back up. He kept on telling Daxen to leave him alone so he could sleep.

"Get me a cushion," said the chieftain in a slurred loud voice, trying to raise his arm. Daxen could see the chieftain wasn't going to be awake for much longer. And, within a couple of moments a loud snore erupted through his large nostrils.

Quinn went over to Daxen and whispered something in his ear. Daxen gave a look of surprise and then hurried over to Jafar and Raja. He whispered the same thing into their ears. Glancing at Quinn, Jafar and Raja nodded in agreement. Quinn then continued to whisper the same message to the escorts. The escorts hurried around the room letting everyone know the message.

Trying to look busy and act as if everything was fine, the escorts finally went into the kitchen to clean up. Daxen and Jafar stood over the chieftain, arguing who was going to take the legs and who was going to take the arms. Finally, Jafar volunteered to take the lead. The two boys began by sliding him across the floor making their way to the stairs. Once they got there, each boy took one arm and dragged him up the stairs.

"Try not to hit his head," said Daxen.

"Too late," said Jafar. Luckily the chieftain only grunted when his head banged against a step. It was a huge struggle to pull him and the boys had to stop several times to rest.

"He's heavier than five sacks of potatoes," said Jafar.

"And just as smart," said Daxen.

"Don't insult the potatoes," said Jafar.

The boys laughed.

"Which way do we go?" asked Jafar.

"I think it's down this corridor."

By the time the boys were in the chamber they were breathing heavily and perspiring. Then, with one last burst of energy, they pulled him up onto his bed.

"Should we cover him?" asked Jafar.

"Why should we?" asked Daxen.

"He might sleep longer that way."

"All right."

The boys threw a blanket over him and put a flower beside his nose.

"Sleep well, my little one," said Daxen.

"Stop, you're going to make me die of laughter," said Jafar.

"Come on, let's get out of here," said Daxen.

They quickly walked out of the chamber, rushing down the stairs and into the storage room. Without any problem they found the secret passageway leading into the well.

"You stay here and I'll see to it that all the escorts get here," said Daxen.

"Okay, check on the warriors. If they are not sleeping offer them more strong ale."

Daxen agreed.

The first four people to arrive at the well were Raja, Quinn, and two of Raja's escorts.

"I'll go first," said Raja. "Once I'm out of the passage, I'll stay back and point people in the right direction."

"Okay," said Jafar. He looked at Raja. "By the way, you did a great job of acting."

"Thanks," said Raja. "It was rather fun, but I'm still upset with you kissing my foot more than once.

"My apologies," said Jafar, thinking he'd like to do it again. "It was just a duty."

Raja let it go, concentrating on the task ahead.

After the first group ascended the well, four more escorts arrived and the new group started making their way down the water hole. In numbers of four or five, all the escorts and servants made their way through the secret passageway. Once everyone was outside the castle, they ran all the way to the ship. When the group was aboard, Daxen gave the command to set sail and everyone was off to Kazan.

Their mission had been successful! They had left a little earlier than expected but for a very good reason. Of course, by morning they would be discovered, but it was all worth it for the little girl.

Quinn felt proud of her accomplished mission and handed over the papers to Daxen, who handed them to Jafar. Shamra, Isa, and the young girl were found in the aftercastle. The young girl had fallen asleep with her head on Shamra's lap. Raja and Quinn joined them.

"Do you know anything about her?" asked Raja.

"No, she didn't want to talk about anything," said Shamra. "How did it all go?"

"As planned. The chieftain didn't have a clue as to what was going on," said Raja.

Raja looked at Quinn and Isa. "You girls were amazing."

"Thanks," they said.

"The best part was dancing with Daxen," said Isa.

Raja looked over to see how Quinn would respond.

"When did you dance with him?" asked Quinn with a pouty face.

"When he gave the maps to me," said Isa.

"I think Daxen already likes me," said Quinn.

"He likes me," said Isa.

"That's not true."

"Stop arguing. You'll wake up the girl," said Shamra.

Giggling, the twins quickly apologized and forgave each other.

"Where do you think the girl has come from?" asked Shamra.

"She could be from any village. It may be difficult to find out."

Shamra combed the girl's hair with her fingers. "I'm sure a victim of the slave trade."

"No doubt," said Raja feeling angry. "We'll get to the bottom of this."

Just then the girl woke up. She sat up beside Shamra.

Raja smiled at the young girl. "I'm Raja. And these are my friends. We are here to help you."

"Where am I going?"

"We don't know that for sure," said Raja. "Where did you come from?"

"I don't know."

"Do you have a mother or father?"

The girl shook her head.

"Did you like it where you came from?" asked Shamra.

"No, I didn't."

"You don't have to go back there. We'll take care of you," said Raja with a soft voice.

"Would you like that?" asked Shamra.

"Yes," said the girl as she moved closer to Shamra.

"What's your name?" asked Isa.

"Chloe."

"That's a nice name," said Isa.

"How old are you?" asked Raja.

"I don't know," said Chloe.

Raja thought perhaps the girl was around eight, a little younger than Fedor when she'd found him.

Noticing that Chloe's hair was all tangled, Shamra offered to comb it. "May I fix your hair?"

The girl nodded.

Shamra began gently working through the long hair. "You have very thick, long hair for a young girl."

"I should say," said Raja.

"Could I have a turn at combing her hair?" asked Isa.

"Okay," said Shamra reluctantly.

"Then it's my turn," said Quinn.

"I want a turn too," said Raja running her fingers through Chloe's hair. "I've never seen such silky soft hair before."

The others agreed with Raja's compliment. Chloe's wavy hair shimmered in the candlelight as the girls fussed with it. She was actually an extraordinarily pretty girl with hair the color of gold.

"I think we should style your hair in braids for the tzarina," said Shamra. "Would you like that Chloe?"

"The tzarina?"

"Yes, you will be meeting the tzarina."

A worried look came over Chloe's face.

"Don't worry. She is a very nice person. In fact, she's my mother," said Raja.

Chloe's eyes grew wide. "Are you a princess?"

"Yes, and so is Shamra."

"Will I be a princess too?" asked Chloe.

Raja smiled. "Maybe."

"I think we should try and get some sleep," said Shamra.

The others quickly agreed, as they all felt exhausted. They fell asleep huddled together on the floor of the aftercastle.

Chapter 27

Revelations

When the ship arrived in Kazan, Daxen decided he would return to his country in the morning along with his escorts. After the chieftain awoke, he would know he had been duped. Daxen didn't want to be held up by any danger, as he needed to check in with the Koffer cousins in Dracon. He would return later to Kazan with twice as many escorts as before, which would surely be the start of a more positive relationship between Dracon and Zurkia.

The tzarina and Pavel, who had some very good talks together while walking in the Soladecorus Gardens, were relieved that everyone had come back safely. They were all welcomed into the castle. Making a huge fuss about Chloe, the tzarina wanted to find out about her, but Chloe offered no information. The tzarina thought the girl's life so far had surely been abusive. She knew it would take time for Chloe to adjust to something different. The tzarina said she would try to find out about Chloe's past.

Everyone noticed how Chloe and Shamra seemed to take a liking to each other. Raja thought Shamra would be a good mother. Shamra was a bit young to be her mother, but seeing as how Chloe had no one, the situation seemed to be leaning in that direction.

The tzarina, who was beginning to tire, suggested that they all go to their sleeping chambers and continue their discussions in the morning.

Raja and Shamra shared a room with a warm fire burning inside the rounded fireplace. All three of the girls fit on the bed. Chloe instantly fell asleep. Raja and Shamra whispered to each other.

"Do you ever think of Hannah?" asked Shamra.

"Yes, I do."

"Is it hard?"

"Yes, but I trust God is with her. I believe she will come back with our help."

"I believe that too."

The girls smiled at each other.

"There's something I need to tell you," said Shamra. "I'm going to Dracon with Daxen in the morning and I'd like to take Chloe with me."

"Why do you want to go to Dracon?"

"I thought sailing with Daxen would be fun."

Raja sensed a bit of eagerness in Shamra and smiled. "You have my permission."

"Thank you, your highness."

"I hope you have a good time," said Raja.

"Thank you."

"Good night."

"Good night."

The morning came very soon. Good-byes were made to Shamra, Daxen, and Chloe, and all of the other Dracians. The tzarina looked forward to seeing them when they returned with more escorts.

A little later, sitting around the breakfast table, the sketch of the peasant that had been found in the trunk, now being called the *Trunk of Antom,* was being passed to each person. After looking at the sketch, Pavel and Jafar turned their attention to the other parchment from the trunk.

Kuzma, Raja, and the tzarina stood together and looked at the sketch of the peasant by themselves.

"There is something about this sketch," said the tzarina. "Every time I look at it, I think I see someone."

"Who do you see?" asked Kuzma.

The tzarina didn't want to say. Her face became strained and tears started to swell in her eyes.

"Tell us mother."

With trembling lips, the tzarina said in a quiet voice, "Your father."

"My father is dead."

Trying not to cry, the tzarina said, "Yes, I have told you that, but this image looks like him."

She put her hand to her eyes to catch her tears. "I still wonder whether he is alive. Deep down in my soul I sometimes feel he is."

The revelation that her husband might still be alive sent a surge of emotion through her body. She started to sob. "Oh God, please let it be true."

Raja put her arms around her mother. She turned her head to look at the sketch. She thought he was a handsome man but at the same time his face looked drawn, like someone with a wounded soul.

At that moment, Kuzma directed his attention to Jafar and Pavel. "What does the parchment say?"

"We don't know, it's all written in a code," said Pavel with his head bent over the paper.

"See what you can make of it," said Kuzma. "The tzarina and I will talk on the balcony."

Still holding the sketch, the tzarina went out onto the balcony to talk with Kuzma.

Pavel started a conversation with Jafar and Raja. "This is no ordinary peasant. Only an educated person could do this." He looked at everyone around the table with serious eyes. "We will have to put our heads together to try and figure this out—step by step."

Heads nodded as Pavel went on. "First, take a good look at this code." Pavel passed the parchment around.

V NZ . . . JNF NOQHPGRQ OL GLURGF NAQ GNXRA GB BQLUHA. ZL UNYS-FVFGRE-VA-YNJ FBYQ URE GJVAF. GLURGF GENQRQ GUR GJVAF GB BQLUHA, JUB GENQRQ GURZ GB QENPBA . . . OYHR NAQ TERRA . . . UNTNGUN UNF . . .

"Part of the message at the end is missing, but we can try to figure out the other parts," said Pavel. "Now if you look at the first word, it is a single letter. Does anyone have an idea of what that word might be?"

Raja's hand went up.

"I think it is the word 'I' because he would want to say who he is."

"I agree, so let's find all of the other 'V's' and put an 'I' on top of them."

Pavel, Raja, and Jafar wrote the correct letters on top of the code letters.

"I see something," said Raja. "I think 'VA' stands for the word 'IN.'"

"I think that's safe," said Jafar.

They wrote the letter "N" on top of any letter "A".

"And the next word is 'LAW,'" said Raja.

They all wrote "L" on top of "Y", "A" on top of "N", and "J" on top of "W".

"And "FVGRE" is 'sister,'" said Pavel.

"Right," said Raja.

Pavel looked at another word with only two letters missing. "This word must spell 'TYHETS.'"

"I think you're right," said Jafar. "There are two words like that."

Everyone agreed and marked the letters in the right spots.

From there it was easy to translate the whole message. And it was Jafar who finally deciphered the code pattern. Pavel finally read the message.

I am . . . was abducted by Tyhets and taken to Odyhun. My half-sister-in-law sold her twins. Tyhets traded the twins to Odyhun, who traded them to Dracon. . . . blue and green . . . Hagatha has . . .

"His name is faded," said Raja.

"And a few other words in the message," said Pavel.

"It looks like we have a middleman here," said Jafar. "The Tyhets are doing the dirty work for the Odyhuns."

"And what about the name Hagatha?" asked Raja.

No one could answer that question, however Jafar contributed information about Dracon. "Dracon deals a lot with the Odyhuns. There's no doubt that the people being sold to Odyhun are then sold to Dracon for a higher price."

Raja agreed, remembering the obvious affluence of the Dragomir Palace.

Pavel read the message again. "But this person could not have stayed in Odyhun if this is the same person in the sketch."

"What do you suppose that means?" asked Raja.

"Well, for some reason the Tyhets want him in Zurkia. And we know that the Dark Prince seems to have the Tyhets on a puppet string. It could have something to do with the Dark Prince."

"But how would this person who wrote the message know anything about the twins mentioned in the message?" asked Raja.

"Obviously he had some connection with the Odyhuns," said Jafar. "The Dark Prince probably goes back and forth between the Tyhet region and Odyhun to do his dealing. And it could have been that the person who wrote the message overheard what was going on."

Pavel agreed. "What do you make of the twins? We know they went to Dracon but the question is why did his half-sister-in-law sell them?" he asked.

"I can't imagine it," said Raja.

"Perhaps because they were twins," said Jafar. "Twins in Dracon are thought to bring good fortune. It's a convenient way to get coin."

"We do know a set of twins," said Raja. "And each of the twins has one blue eye and one green eye. And most likely that is what the colors refer to in the message." Raja had never said anything about Quinn and Isa's unusual eyes because she thought it would be offensive to the girls and unfair, but now of course it would help in their identity.

"I agree," said Jafar. "And definitely their eye color would add to their value."

"That sounds logical," said Raja. "And if that is the case that would be two more identities uncovered."

"Which makes total sense because of their rare eye features," said Pavel. "We know no one else who fits that description."

Kuzma and the tzarina returned from the balcony. "What did you find out?" asked Kuzma.

Pavel summarized the coded message, making sure to mention the woman's name. The tzarina could offer no explanation of Hagatha, but she connected to the other parts of the message and became very concerned over what she heard. Putting her hands on the table and leaning in, she spoke forcefully. "You have to find this man! This half-sister-in-law could be my half-sister!"

Everyone was silent as it took a while to absorb that statement.

"Are you saying that this man could be your husband?" asked Pavel.

"Yes."

"The tzar?"

"Yes, that's right, the tzar."

Chapter 28

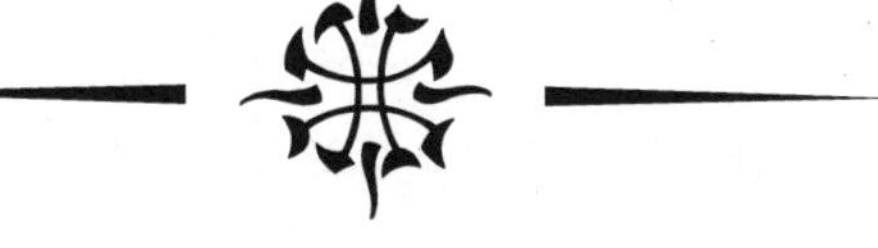

Deductions

"Raja's father?" asked Pavel, as he looked at the tzarina.

"Yes," said the tzarina. She looked at everyone seated around the breakfast table having a discussion over the parchments found in the *Trunk of Antom*. "We need to find him. I always thought he was dead, but if he was abducted it could have been made to look as if he died in an accident."

"True," said Pavel.

The tzarina looked at the sketch she was holding. "The sketch looks like him, especially the eyes."

Seeing the strong emotion in both the tzarina and Raja, Pavel took initiative. "I think we should begin planning right now."

"I give you my full support," said the tzarina.

"What happening at Levap Castle?" asked Pavel.

"Cham, Ivan, Yev, and the rest of the pirates are at the castle," said the tzarina.

"Good, I'm glad the castle is secure. We will be needing it."

The five continued to pursue the question of how they were going to find who they believed now to be the tzar.

"According to the message, it is probable that he could be in any of three locations, Odyhun, Thrumb Village, or further up north," said Pavel.

Jafar was the first to make another comment. "It is more probable that he is either at Thrumb Village or up north as the trips they would make to Odyhun would not be that often." He looked around to see if there were any objections. There were none. "Further, it appears that these projects the Dark Prince has up north are very important to him and he most likely spends a good deal of his time there."

Heads nodded around the circle.

"All right then," said Pavel. "We look up north first."

As no one said anything to the contrary, Pavel continued. "Any suggestions as to how we locate his quarters?"

"I remember that we followed the Tyhet's tracks heading to Thrumb Castle but they disappeared about half way, so we know it is further up north from there," said Raja.

They all agreed and there was a short silence with everyone trying to think of what to say next. Kuzma was the first to speak.

"I think his projects would most likely be around a water source. I know there is fresh water in the northern part of Zurkia, not too far from the mouth of the Volga River. The tributary is called Larchwood Tributary. It flows from the east into the Valley of Durlabh and runs into the Strait of the Golden Sun. So you might want to follow the Volga River continuing up from Levap Castle."

Pavel continued to expand on that idea. "If you are right, the Tyhets we saw riding on horseback could have come from Bolger Village and were cutting across land to the Larchwood Tributary."

Kuzma continued. "That is a good deduction, according to what has been happening. Peasants have disappeared from all three of the castle estates in the Plotria region of Zurkia and the Tyhets would have traveled along the Oak Trail to get there."

"So, it looks like our best route to find the Dark Prince is to travel along the Volga River," said Pavel.

"Yes, I believe so," said Kuzma. "But you will need to follow the Ardua Trail which is about halfway down the Iris Trail. The trail leads down to the Volga shore and from there you should have an easy ride."

Everyone was satisfied with the instructions.

"Sounds good," said Pavel and Jafar.

Raja looked at her mother. "It'll work out, Mother. Don't worry."

A look of hope appeared on the tzarina's face.

"I remember the words you spoke to me," said Raja. "Hope restores broken dreams."

"Yes, thank you for reminding me. I shall cling to hope."

The meeting concluded and was named the *Meeting of Patefactio*.

Chapter 29

The Little Boy

It was decided that Pavel, Jafar, and Raja would cut across land, riding along the Lapsus Trail, and go directly to Levap Castle. The small group would have to make sure not to cross paths with the Tyhets if the warriors happened to be on one of their destructive missions. Kuzma stayed behind to give the tzarina emotional support during this trying time.

After beginning their ride heading northeast, the three friends found the terrain in these parts to be much more mountainous and rugged. Situated along the ridges of steep cliffs, the trail was narrow and rocky in many parts. During their journey, they had come to a rockslide created by a huge downpour of rain and it took them two days to find their way around the boulders with their horses.

The going was slower than they were used to and their water supply was getting low. Fortunately, they came to the Varyclude

Waterfall, where they refilled their water skins. And at the same time, they took the opportunity to stand under the falling water, clothes and all. It felt good to get the dust off their faces and out of their hair. Afterward, wearing cold and clingy clothes was a bit uncomfortable for them, but the discomfort was worth being clean.

"Viktor once told me about Noware Cave. It's in this area and there's a path that leads from the waterfall to the cave," said Pavel. "We could find it, make a fire and dry off. And then stay for the night."

Jafar and Raja thought that was a good plan. They set off in the direction of a rough-cut path they had found. They hadn't gone far when Raja noticed smoke in the air.

"Do you smell that?" she asked.

"Yes," said Pavel.

Pavel got off his horse and threw some bits of fine dry grass up in the air.

"The wind's coming from that direction. It's most likely that the smoke is coming from the same direction."

"Should we investigate?" asked Jafar.

"I think we should," said Pavel. "The fire is probably not far from here."

"Maybe it's coming from the cave," said Raja.

"Let's get off our horses and walk," said Pavel.

The three kept going for another short while. The smell of the smoke became stronger and eventually they heard voices in the distance.

They were finally close enough that they could hear what was being said. They stayed behind some thick bushes.

"Is that a child I hear crying?" asked Raja.

"Shhh," said Pavel.

* * *

A voice boomed out above the others.

"Keep that child quiet!" shouted a man. "What's the matter with you?"

"The child is frightened," said a woman's voice. "Not that you care!"

"Don't you know how to look after children at your age!"

"I never had any."

"That doesn't matter. Just do your job or I'll leave you here."

Raja was shocked. "That voice sounds like Alma!"

"Shhh," said Pavel, trying to listen to more of the conversation.

"You've taken this child away from his home. What can you expect?" said the woman.

"I expect you to keep that boy quiet!" shouted the man.

"Why don't you just leave the hollering one here," said another man.

"That's a good idea. The crying is aggravating," said the first man.

"You wouldn't!" yelled the woman.

"Shut your mouth or I'll leave you too!"

The woman clung onto the child and they both screamed.

"Let go of the boy!" yelled the man. "We are leaving and we are leaving now."

"Stop," screamed the woman. "You cannot leave the child to die."

"Tie them both up," yelled the second man.

"No, we need the woman," said the first man. "Get her on the horse and I'll take care of the boy."

"Come on, let's get out of here," said Pavel.

They quietly retraced their steps and when they were far enough away, they got on their horses and quickly went down the rest of the path.

"We've got to hide ourselves until they're gone," said Pavel.

They took their horses deeper in the bushes and waited.

"I can't imagine what Alma and the child are going through," said Raja, who was nearly in tears over what was happening.

"Well, we were here just at the right time," said Pavel in an assuring voice.

Realizing that Pavel was right, Raja got more control of herself. They hid where they could still have a view of the abductors as they came down from Noware Cave. In a short time, the group could be seen.

"Tyhets," said Pavel.

Raja could see Alma on a horse with a child as she rode in between the warriors. Her face was in deep distress as she silently sobbed. Raja recognized the red cloak she had given Alma in the Manor Village.

"Brutal," said Jafar. "I'd like to go down there and get my hands on those Tyhets' necks."

"Calm down," said Pavel. "You'll get your chance. Well maybe not quite like that, but we will put a stop to this."

They waited until the Tyhets left and then went back up towards Noware Cave. After arriving there, they quickly dismounted their horses.

They found a little child tied inside the cave, lying lifeless on the ground.

"I hope he's not dead," said Raja.

"If he is . . ." said Jafar, whose blood was boiling.

Running to the child, Raja scooped him up in her arms. Raja put her head to the child's face. "He's still breathing."

Pavel opened his water canteen and had it ready for the little boy. "The child is no doubt extremely exhausted."

The little boy's eyes opened for a second and closed again. Raja held the child close to her body and rocked him back and forth. The three cared for the child throughout the night giving the boy water at every opportunity.

By morning the boy awoke and he seemed to have made some recovery. He stared at Raja with wide eyes.

"You're safe now," said Raja "And we'll get you back home."

"Ask him what his name is," said Pavel.

"What's your name?" asked Raja.

The little boy didn't say anything. Instead he stretched out his hand for some food that was lying on top of Pavel's pouch.

"That's okay, we can find out what his name is later," said Pavel as he gave the little boy some nuts and dried fruit. Raja felt relieved that the boy was well enough to eat.

Shortly afterwards, the group continued their journey along the Lapsus Trail.

CHAPTER 30

THE SECRET ROOM

Each person took turns riding with the boy as Pavel, Jafar, and Raja finally completed the journey to Levap Castle after six nights. Cham had already known from the cawing of her pet crow that people were coming to the castle. From on top of the tower, Cham verified that the group was safe when Cade came back with a two-pronged twig. It was Raja who had thought ahead of time and had the twig ready.

Once inside the castle, Raja eventually found out that the boy's name was Ridge. He was amazingly well behaved and became the center of attention. Everyone thought he was the brightest little child they had ever come across. He was cute and had curly hair the color of a tawny tiger.

Ivan and Yev agreed that they would make a trek to Victory Manor with the child to put him into Maya's care. Before the two boys left with Ridge, Raja told Ivan to tell Viktor how Ridge was rescued at Noware Cave and to allow him to stay in the manor. And Raja requested that Viktor know about their aspirations to recover the other child that they had seen with Alma.

Cham then ordered the pirates and their wives to prepare a feast. The news from Raja that the tzar could be alive was good reason to celebrate and the meal was just what was needed before the upcoming dangerous mission. Speeches of every good will and cordiality were expressed throughout the meal as goblets rose in the air.

It appeared to Raja that the pirates had adapted to their surrounding very well and had become self-sufficient. She thought they were much happier here than on the island. And they definitely seemed to be acquiring a few more manners.

"You look like you are enjoying it here," said Raja to Cham.

"I'd be tempted t' stay here."

"I'd like that."

"But I better be careful. If I stay here too long I could become a landlubber."

"I doubt it, you have too much sea in your veins."

Pavel and Jafar came over to join the conversation.

"So, when do we leave for the north?" asked Pavel.

"What about tomorrow morning?" asked Raja. "I think the situation is urgent."

"I agree," said Jafar.

"What be yer plans?" asked Cham.

"First, we are going to find out exactly where the Dark Prince is and assess the situation from there."

Cham waited for Pavel to explain more of the plan. She brushed some breadcrumbs together for Cade to peck at.

"Then, if we feel we need help to either find or rescue the tzar, we'll come back."

Raja added her thoughts. "I think we may be doing more than one thing at a time, according to what we've witnessed with the stolen children."

"I agree that the children are also an urgent concern," said Jafar.

"Right," said Pavel. "Like I said, we will have to determine what to do once we get there."

"Okay," said Cham. "We be here if ye need us. We been practicin' our skills with all the swords we found in the castle."

"You found swords?" asked Pavel.

"Aye, lots o' them and some other weapons."

"Where did you find them?"

"There's a secret room in this castle that I guess no one knew about since its last occupants." Cham smiled to show she was proud of herself. "I am good at findin' secret rooms."

"I have no doubt about that," said Pavel. "Let's have a look at it."

"Okay, follow me."

The group followed Cham to the end of a hallway. The sides of the hallway were decorated with large wooden panels. Cham showed the group how she put her finger into a small hidden space behind one of the panels. She pushed on a latch and the panel was free to slide behind the other panels. Sliding it over revealed the secret room.

"How did you discover the secret panel?" asked Pavel.

"I noticed that the panel was worn on this area, so I investigated it. I saw the space between the panel and wall and suspected that it was a door. And when I banged on it I could hear it wasn't a solid wall."

"Smart thinking," said Pavel as he entered the secret room. He held up the torch so they could see.

Raja was completely surprised. "What are these doing here?"

"I was wonderin' that myself," said Cham.

Pavel and Jafar were just as surprised to see the three thrones.

"Well, let's bring them out again," said Raja.

"Okay," said the others, and together they carried the three thrones out of the room and back to where they belonged.

Standing back, Raja looked at the royal chairs and said, "The Dark Prince will not keep us off of these thrones."

The others agreed whole-heartedly.

"I wonder who hid them in the secret room in the first place," said Raja.

"That is a good question," said Pavel.

Raja went over in her mind who could have hidden the thrones and why.

The four went back down to the secret room to look at the weapons.

While they were in the room, Jafar, who had a great deal of knowledge about the design of secret rooms and passages, discovered some bricks in the wall that came out. Behind the bricks were diagrams of the secret passages of the castle. The three couldn't believe the great discovery they had made.

However, any writing on the diagrams was in a foreign language. Pavel knew the Zurkians did not create these passages and asked Cham and her pirates to make changes to confuse any previous enemy who had intentions of invading. The request was obeyed and plans for the changes would begin in the near future.

Part 4

The Horse and Rider

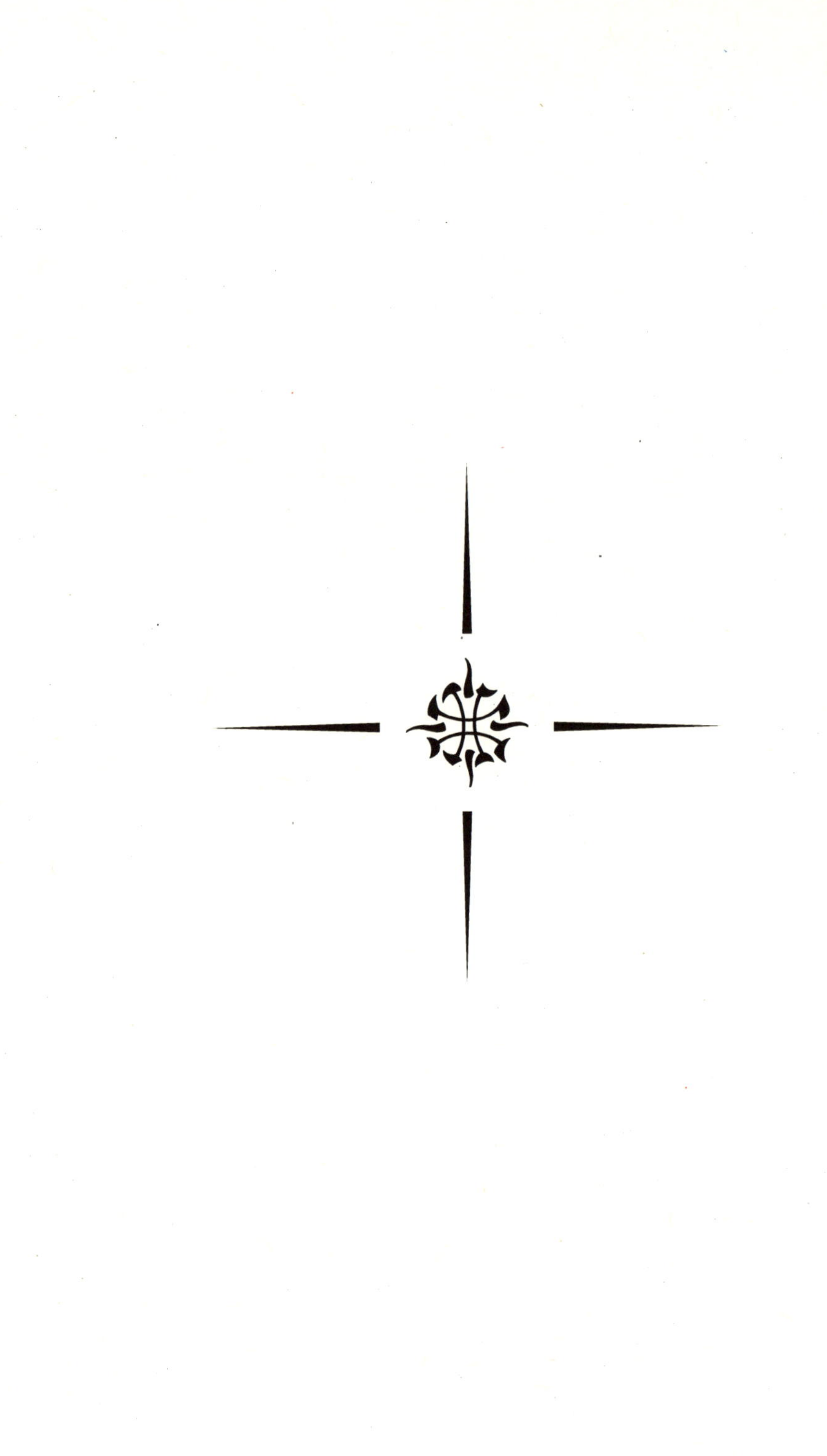

Chapter 31

The History Lesson

The three friends, Raja, Pavel, and Jafar, left Levap Castle riding north on the Ardua Trail. The incline was very steep and Raja feared several times her horse would lose footing, but despite this she was able to look around and take in the view of the ancient Pallaton Bridge that crossed over the Volga River at the bottom of the bluffs. It had a large round stone arch for the ships to pass through. Cham had said she was making use of the bridge to trade with the Berzation tribe across the river. Then, before Raja knew it, having been lost in her thoughts, everyone had managed to ride down safely to the shores of the Volga River.

Heading toward the northern region along the shores, the three friends found it to be very different from riding in the southern parts. Craggy rocks shaped the high and steep mountain range that went along the sides of the river. The peaks, all very narrow and sharp, cast intermittent shadows, blocking the sunlight sooner than the group was used to. The air was cooler and crisper in these parts.

The further north they rode the narrower the river became, with small islands of rugged rock interrupting its flow. The shores were wide just as Kuzma had said, and there was no problem riding the horses along the river. The three went at an easy pace, along the now-named Shora Trail.

As the evening progressed, it became too cold for Raja to continue, as her hands were turning numb. Fortunately, Jafar spotted a cave along the wall of a mountain and they decided to settle in for the night. They were extremely thankful to find a cave and decided to call it Gratias Cave. They built themselves a fire and warmed their bodies.

After letting the warmth of the fire rejuvenate him, Pavel thought this would be a good time to let Raja and Jafar know about the things Kuzma had told him while they had been at Kazan Castle. Poking the wood in the fire with a gnarly crocked branch, he began.

"Kuzma told me he at one time lived in the northern part of Zurkia in the Valley of Durlabh." Pavel bit into a piece of barley bread. "He gave me a history lesson."

"I like history," said Raja.

"Kuzma traveled with a group of peasants to look for gold in northern Wsyrut, which is the country north of here. They were told not to come back unless they found gold. Kuzma said he lived there for about one year."

"Did they find gold?"

"He did, and they threw it down the Abyss of Ogin on a small island that is close to the mouth of the Volga River."

"Abyss of Ogin?" asked Raja.

"It's a dead volcano. They threw the gold down there as an appeasement to the Ogin spirit."

Raja and Jafar ate some dried meat as they listened for Pavel to offer more explanation.

"Kuzma says there is something very mysterious about the abyss and he heard some peasants say that the Abyss of Ogin was cursed and that people who go to the far side of the island never come back."

Thinking that it might not be true, Raja asked, "Did the peasants ever look for those people?"

"No, they were too afraid. But Kuzma thinks it is to do with Duo Cave at the bottom of the abyss." Pavel took a bite of fruit. "He told me something else that was very interesting."

Raja and Jafar went on listening with some skepticism.

"The island has an old castle on it. It's called Norx Castle. And hear this, the peasants in Norx Village were making large amounts of bricks during that time."

"Strange," said Jafar.

"Did he know anything more about the castle?" asked Raja, who took a few bites of goat cheese.

"He said the island was overtaken from Wsyrut about one hundred years ago.

Wsyrut built the Nexum Bridge across the strait and that's how the country took over the castle."

Pavel spent some time eating some of his dried seaweed, a gift from Jafar, and then continued. "But fifty years ago, Zurkia took back the island and called it Yurx Island. Some of the castle on the island was damaged during that battle."

Raja thought back to Pavel's estate. "Did they ruin the castle at Levap Estate as well?"

"Correct," said Pavel and turned to Jafar to explain further. "The standing parts of the old castle on Levap Estate are the remains of a Zurkian castle that was ruined during the battle with the Wsyruts. It was called Isumca Castle."

"Jafar, that was our lookout tower," said Raja, remembering she had explained the not so pleasant dungeon incident to Jafar.

"I see," said Jafar. "So, was Levap Castle built by Wsyrut?"

"Yes," said Pavel. "And that's why I've asked Cham to change the secret passages of the castle."

Jafar nodded. "Good plan."

Pavel munched on another piece of fruit before he continued. "And have you ever wondered how the Tyhets have come to occupy Thrumb Castle?"

"Tell us," said Raja.

"The Wsyruts had damaged Thrumb Castle in a battle as well, but then rebuilt it. But when Zurkia got all three estates back, the two castles remained empty. And so the Tyhets moved into Thrumb Castle."

"What about Norx Castle on Yurx Island?" asked Raja.

"It was never restored."

Suddenly, Pavel recalled something else he wanted to say. "I have some history about the thrones."

Raja waited for Pavel's information with curiosity.

"Before the siege of the three castles by the Wsyruts, each of these castles had a throne. Right after the ruin of Norx Castle and Thrumb Castle, the thrones had miraculously been untouched and were taken to Isumca Castle. The third throne at Isumca Castle was also untouched during the battle. The three thrones eventually were moved into Levap Castle."

Pavel took some more bites of his fruit and chewed before speaking.

"It was the hope of Zurkia that these castles would be recaptured and each of these thrones would one day be put back in their rightful places."

"Strange that the thrones were untouched during the battles," said Jafar. "It seemed like they were being protected for a reason."

"And it seems like they are still being protected because we found the thrones in the secret room," said Raja.

"I agree," said Jafar.

Pavel took out the sketch of the peasant from his pouch. "Do you have this image memorized?"

Jafar and Raja looked at the sketch again.

"May I look at it closer?" asked Raja.

"Certainly." Pavel handed Raja the sketch.

Raja looked at it in deep contemplation. To think that it could be her father was overwhelming. If it was her father, she knew that he had gone through a horrible experience.

"I hope that it is my father and that he is still alive," said Raja, staring at the sketch with a sorrowful face. "I can only imagine that his hope has been destroyed after all these years."

"I'm sure it has been extremely difficult for him. But you need to remember that a person can go through an awful lot and still survive and have hope," said Jafar, who also sat and starred at the image.

Raja turned to Jafar and then instead imagined her father having a strong will and mind. "True," she said. "Very true."

Chapter 32

Entering the Valley of Durlabh

Catching whiffs of algae, the three friends knew they had reached their destination. Traveling seven days had brought them close to the mouth of the Volga, which poured into the Skyep Sea. The mountain range was now getting narrower and steeper. Conveniently, they found a path that went in between the mountains to the east and decided to go in that direction. It didn't take them that long to see the end of the narrow valley. All three of them were hesitant to ride out into the open and so decided to leave their horses hidden and climb to the top of the mountain so they could see their whereabouts without being noticed.

The climb wasn't that difficult, as there were a lot of footholds along the rugged rocks, and the mountain had natural ledges for them to rest and catch their breath. Reaching the top of the mountain, they hiked to the other side and came to the edge of a cliff. From there they had a full view of the valley and Yurx Island.

The first thing that caught their breath was the huge castle that was positioned very close to the edge of the island. Coming from a large base was a tall tower with three turrets on top of one another, creating a very high lookout. Behind the tower were numerous other towers and turrets with tall and spiky points.

"I can see where this castle has an extraordinary lookout scheme," said Pavel.

"Did you know this existed?" asked Raja.

"No, you cannot see it when you are at the mouth of the Volga and ships cannot sail in the narrow passage between the island and the mainland. However, I see that the bay opposite the castle has a small ship in it. The water must be higher there."

From where they stood, the island looked habitable, except for the high vertical rock bluffs that surrounded the island.

"It looks like the only way to the island is by crossing the bridge over the chasm," said Jafar.

"Yes, and I can see why the island is unpopulated, as the bridge obviously belongs to the castle," said Pavel.

Two tall stone arches that rested at the bottom of the deep gorge supported the bridge. Guards stood on either end while a trail of people crossed the bridge.

"Those people are tugging something over the bridge," said Raja.

"It looks like they are building something," said Pavel. "The valley is filled with working peasants."

"I think we know where the Levap occupants have gone to," said Raja. "And the other peasants who have gone missing from their villages."

"That seems like a probable conclusion," said Pavel. "They have been turned into slaves for the Dark Prince."

"What do you conclude about the military that is riding around the area?" asked Jafar.

Pavel was aquatinted with the military markings owned by the countries that made up the Land of Rousse. "They're wearing hemispherical helmets and black cloaks, so it appears the Dark Prince has brought forces in from Wsyrut. They call themselves the warnorres."

"Which could also mean some of these peasants are from there, because there are so many of them," said Raja.

"I agree. The people probably use Larchwood Tributary to travel back and forth to their country," said Pavel as he pointed in the direction of the waterway, which curved along the valley and flowed north to the Skyep Sea.

Jafar added further detail. "And I can see a number of rowboats at that small inlet along the tributary."

"There's also a trail along the river," said Raja.

The three of them continued to look over the valley. Next to the trail, in the eastern part, were a large number of huts. But no activity was seen surrounding the huts. West to that was an area of land dedicated to the activity of the peasants. They worked in various groups, and there were more peasants than any of them could have imagined.

Then, along the shores of the Skyep Sea, was a row of three small white castles, which were the stables, as horses were being led in and out of the structures for feeding purposes in the fields. The grass fields were beyond the huts to the south, where a large group of white horses were grazing. But it was obvious that the horses would need additional hay for survival.

The most prevalent thing growing on the land was the tamarack tree, as there was an abundance of them along the tributary and at the base of some of the hills. A work party was falling some of the trees. The land near the huts, where more peasants were working, looked barren, with no crops or gardens. The people appeared to be carving long thick beams.

Raja, feeling like she wanted to know exactly what the peasants were doing, asked, "Can you figure out what is happening in this huge accumulation of people?"

"Let's watch them for a while," said Pavel.

The three studied the maze of peasants, trying to figure out what they were doing. Most of them were working in the center of the valley, where heaps of rock, sand, and clay were dispersed around large mortar-like structures. Workers holding long thick rods operated large rocking barrels. They slowly and strenuously mixed the contents of the barrels. Other groups were shaping long rectangular blocks of material, which were being cut into smaller pieces after it hardened.

"I think they're making bricks," said Jafar.

"Look, there's a group over there leaving towards the castle," said Pavel, pointing to his left.

A group of peasants with rope tied around their bodies towed a large pallet with heavy stones and bricks. One of the peasants stumbled, which caught the attention of a nearby warnorre. The warnorre shouted at the man to get up. When the man didn't get up the warnorre raised his whip and whipped him. The peasant was then taken from the group and left lying on the ground.

The three friends were horrified as they witnessed the brutal scene.

"That is outrageous!" said Raja. "There needs to be a stop to this!"

The rest of the peasants continued to tug the palette toward a bridge that extended over the deep chasm connecting the island to the mainland.

After the group of peasants crossed the bridge, more peasants came from the opposite side and collected the stones and bricks and put them onto smaller pallets. The peasants then carried them to the castle.

"I think they are building onto the castle," said Pavel.

"It looks like they've been doing that for a long time," said Jafar.

Just then Raja saw that the peasant who was whipped was being helped. "Look, a woman is helping the fallen man." They watched as the woman took the man into one of the huts.

"Thank goodness the man was helped," said Raja.

Feeling distraught by the cruelty of the whipping, the three friends knew this slavery had to stop. They wanted to discuss their plans immediately.

"How many peasants do you estimate there to be?" asked Jafar.

Pavel scanned the area. "Maybe one thousand."

"A good guess."

"How are we going to find the man in the sketch with so many people?" asked Raja.

"Somehow we're going to have to go down there," said Pavel.

Jafar and Pavel looked at Raja.

"Why are you looking at me?"

"Because we think you are the best one. A woman is always less suspicious than a man."

Agreeing that was true, Raja still wasn't going to be persuaded this time.

"I think you should come with me."

Pavel gave it some thought.

"You may be needed," said Raja. "We don't know for sure how things will transpire."

"I think Raja is right," said Jafar. "I'll go back to Gratias Cave and attend to the horses."

Jafar patted Pavel on the back. "Remember, you are doing this for who could be Raja's father."

Pavel became serious. "You're right, and I'm honored to do it."

Then, turning his attention to the Valley of Durlabh, Pavel said, "Let's stay up here and watch the routines of the people. I think that will help us figure out how to go about this plan."

"Okay, but can we make a fire?" asked Raja, rubbing her hands together.

"No, not if we don't want to be found out, but there should only be about two more hours of daylight before we go into Norx Village," Pavel said in a reassuring voice.

The light was beginning to fade and the activity slowed. A loud bell sounded from the castle. The workers walked away from their places of toil. Small lines of peasants joined larger lines.

"It looks like they're going back into their huts," said Raja.

Then suddenly, a rider on a white horse came from one of the small white castles.

"Who do you think that is?" asked Pavel.

"It's definitely a woman. Look at the long train trailing behind her," said Raja.

As the rider came closer alongside the peasants, Raja had a much better view of the woman. She was sure the woman's hair was red.

"I think that's Hannah," said Raja.

They watched to see what she would do.

"It appears she is giving things to the peasants," said Raja. "Each time she passes something out, the peasants bow to the ground and back away."

"I think you're right," said Pavel.

A thought came to Raja. "I wish I knew where Alma was."

"That would be extremely helpful. Let's look for her," said Pavel. "Do you remember what she was wearing when we saw her at Noware Cave?"

Raja recalled seeing her ride on the horse with the Tyhets. "Yes, of course, she was wearing the red cloak I had given her a short while ago."

Looking for anyone wearing a red cloak, Raja thought she spotted someone.

"Look the rider is stopping by a person with a red cloak and is passing something to her. I think it's the same woman who helped the peasant."

Pavel saw the woman. "That must be her. Let's keep an eye out to see which hut she goes into."

As their eyes were constantly fixed on the red cloak, they saw that the person went into one of the huts situated on the edge of the village.

Raja counted the huts. "It's the ninth hut from the end."

"Okay, are you ready to go?" asked Pavel.

"Yes, do you have the sketch?"

Pavel felt inside his cloak. "Yes, I have it."

Raja took the sketch and put it inside her cloak.

"What about your sword?" asked Jafar.

"I'm taking it."

"Isn't that risky?"

"It's the chance I'm taking."

"Keep it well hidden."

Raja nodded and her and Pavel went back down the mountain the way they had come and walked along the path to the east between the two mountains. They came out amongst the trees to a place just outside the Valley of Durlabh. They waited where they couldn't be seen until it was dark.

Chapter 33

Alma

Raja and Pavel set out across the Valley of Durlabh toward the hut of the woman with the red cloak with a mission to search for the man in the sketch. At Raja's suggestion, they had dressed in peasant clothes before they left on the journey. She held a sickle that had been hers at the age of thirteen, which she had used to cut down wheat for her peasant father. The feeling of her fingers wrapped around the handle brought back memories of how laborious her life had been. She imagined herself back in her village. Her and Pavel had both taken off their boots and hid them under their cloaks, and then dirtied their feet and faces. Raja wasn't used to going barefoot anymore and the rocks hurt her feet. The pain brought back more memories of her past life. She made a new vow right then and there that she would never forget the plight of the peasants.

Then, unexpectedly, a horse galloped up from behind them and blocked their way. It was one of the Wsyrut warnorres. He had bright red hair and a white face that was partly covered with metal from his helmet. His hemispherical helmet had two bands of medal going across the center at the front and sides. Even sitting on a horse, the warnorre seemed to be very tall and rather broad shouldered. Raja put her head down and tightened the cloak around her face.

"Who are you and why are you here?"

Pavel wasn't prepared for this, but quickly thought of something to say. "This is my sister. She is sick. I'm taking her to her mother's hut."

The Wsyrut warnorre looked at their feet. "No soles?"

"They got wet and are drying," said Pavel.

The warnorre laughed but seemed satisfied with the answers and rode away.

"That was close," said Raja.

"Very."

"Are you counting the huts?"

"I've lost track."

Pavel and Raja backtracked to recount the huts. They finally came to the ninth hut.

"This is it," said Pavel.

"Let's go in one at a time so we don't overly frighten who we hope is Alma," said Raja.

Pavel agreed.

Walking quietly into the hut, a sense of relief came over Raja as she saw that it was Alma sleeping on the floor. Surprised but elated, she saw the abducted child sleeping beside her. The child was a girl and Raja guessed her to be about six. She quietly walked over to Alma's side and knelt down.

Bending close to her face, she said, "Alma, Alma."

Alma woke up with a start. Raja put her hand over Alma's mouth and said, "It's Raja."

Immediately, Alma sat up. Intense joy filled her face. "I knew you'd come." Tears swelled in Alma's eyes. Raja hugged her for a long time and then looked into her face.

"I'm so glad that I found you. Pavel's here, too."

Raja got up and went to the entrance. She motioned for Pavel to come in.

"My lord," said Alma.

Pavel bowed his head.

"Please come and sit around the embers," said Alma.

"Thank you," said Pavel.

"We need to talk," said Raja as she warmed her hands by the coals.

"What is it?" asked Alma.

"We think my father is in this village."

"Oh my!" said Alma. "How did you find that out?"

Raja retrieved the sketch from her cloak. She showed Alma the sketch. "We think this is my father."

"Where did you get that from?"

"Antom sketched it." Raja continued to tell Alma the story of how they got the sketch.

"Amazing!" said Alma.

"It is. I'll tell you the rest of the story sometime after we get out of here."

"How did your father know to go to Antom?"

"He must have seen me in Thrumb Village when I was a little girl. That's what I think," said Raja.

Alma looked at the sketch. "I don't recognize him."

"I didn't expect that you would with so many peasants in this village," said Raja.

"Sorry," said Alma.

"That's okay, we'll find him."

"How?"

"We'll have to become peasants," said Raja and looked at Pavel. "Can you do that?"

"Ah . . . yes, of course."

"I know that will be extremely hard for you to do but just keep thinking of my father and this child," said Raja as she pointed to the young girl.

"The only concern I have about being a peasant is that I hope I don't get whipped," said Pavel.

"Yes, that could be a problem," said Raja. "Just work hard."

Raja looked at Alma. "We're going to take the girl with us when we leave this village."

"I'm so glad. I can't bear the thought of her being sold. She is supposed to be taken away somewhere north of here."

"Do you know where to?" asked Pavel.

"I don't know exactly, but I think Wsyrut," said Alma.

Pavel was surprised to know that Wsyrut was involved with the abductions as well and was thankful he could prevent those evil plans from happening to this girl. "We've come at the right time then," he said.

Alma nodded at that good news, but then crumbled as an incredible sadness came over her and she couldn't speak. She bent her head and put her hand to her forehead. Her face grew distorted with grief and after a few moments she started to sob.

Raja put her arm around Alma's shoulders. "Tell me what's suddenly made you feel this way."

In between her sobs, Alma managed to say a few words. "There was . . . a . . . a child."

"Please, don't cry," said Raja. "I know about that child."

"The boy?" asked Alma, who looked up into Raja's face.

"Yes, while we were traveling to come here we discovered the group of Tyhets in Noware Cave and heard everything that went on. After they left we rescued the boy."

"A miracle," said Alma. She looked into Raja's face and started to cry again, her face tearful and joyful at the same time.

"Thank God," said Alma. "I couldn't sleep at nights after that, always waking up and thinking about the boy."

"Don't worry. He's safe now."

Alma nodded with her head down, wiping her tears away.

"Do you know where the boy came from?" asked Raja.

"No, I don't."

"I'm sure Viktor and Maya will try and find out. He will be in good hands."

Raja looked into Alma's eyes. "We can take you back to the Manor Village."

Alma looked up at Raja. "No, I can't go with you."

"Why not?"

"I need to stay here to help the peasants."

"Are you sure?" asked Raja.

"Yes, they need me. The treatment here is very cruel."

"This is a great sacrifice," said Raja. "May you be rewarded for your kindness."

"Thank you," said Alma. "It is what I must do."

"I am truly humbled by your bravery and sacrifice." Raja waited a bit before she asked her next question. "Who is the woman rider on the horse?"

"Hannah."

"I thought so."

"She's kind but I don't know whose side she's on. You should be careful with her," said Alma.

Raja thought about that but decided she knew Hannah well enough to not worry about Alma's fear. Hannah would never side with her evil father, unless she herself became that way, but Raja just couldn't imagine it.

"I see you brought your sword with you," said Alma.

"I did."

"Keep it well hidden. If that's found out it will be used to end your own life."

Raja heeded the warning and kept her sword covered. The small group stayed up a little longer talking about how they were going to get Raja's father rescued. They came up with all sorts of ideas, but in the end they didn't really have a clear plan. It seemed like it was going to be one day at a time, searching for the lost face in the sketch.

Chapter 34

Horse and Rider

Alma made breakfast in her little hut, but the only thing she could serve was pea pottage with a few herbs. Even after eating, Raja and Pavel were incredibly hungry but they couldn't do anything about it and had no choice but to step out onto the village path and follow Alma.

Other peasants were emerging from their huts and joining in various single lines, taking them to their place of work in the Valley of Durlabh. They looked worn and depressed, as if all hope was gone. They were nothing but walking lifeless humans.

It was hard for Raja to deal with, but she needed to look into the face of every peasant. For now, their plan was to try and spot the face that they had seen drawn in the sketch while still acting as peasants.

Pavel ended up joining a team of men who were mixing mortar. Since he didn't know what was going on, he thought the best thing for him to do was to become the mixer.

He took over the job of a peasant who looked much too underweight. Pavel didn't know how the man could continue with the hard task of stirring the heavy material with such scrawny arms. The man seemed relieved to be given a different job.

"I haven't seen you here before," said one of the men who poured clay into the mixer.

"I just came," said Pavel.

"From where?"

"The south. What about you?"

"Wsyrut."

"What is it like in Wsyrut?"

"Not much better than here."

"That's pretty bad."

"They promised us better things here, but it never happened."

"Like what?"

"Food, good shelter, and more independence."

"Where does your food come from?"

"Wsyrut."

Noticing an approaching warnorre, Pavel quit talking. The warnorre rode in front of the group and stopped. He starred at Pavel. Not wanting any conversation, Pavel looked down and worked as hard as he could. The warnorre moved on.

His back started to ache and he wondered how all these people could do what they were doing. Perhaps not all of them survived. Pavel was sure people would just plain wear out and die from exhaustion or illness.

Pavel felt he could not move another muscle and just at that precise moment a bell rang. He didn't think he had ever heard a more welcoming sound.

The people left their tools and joined in a line. Pavel spotted Raja up ahead with Alma. He wondered how she had done. She seemed to be moving very slowly, probably from aching all over. Perhaps her feet were raw.

Then the great white horse with its magnificent rider emerged from the northern white castles. Pavel could see that she was beautiful with her long wavy red hair and fair skin. Her attire was majestic, revealing a purple and black cloak with white fur. Flurries of white mane and tail whipped in the wind as the elegant beast approached.

Raja looked back and caught Pavel's attention. She inconspicuously moved down the line closer to him. Pavel waited. She had managed to get right in front of Pavel. The rider came closer, stopping in front of Raja.

Looking into the face of the rider, Raja wanted to burst out crying. It was indeed Hannah. Raja longed to wrap her arms around her and tell her how much she had missed her and how often she had thought of her.

However, her cousin stared at her and showed no expression at all. Her face was like ice. Moments of confusion swept over Raja. Perhaps Hannah had turned to her father's side. Perhaps she and Pavel would now be found out and become captives just like her father and all the other peasants. She tried to dismiss those thoughts.

No, Hannah was only playing the part. Raja hoped that she was right. She would take the chance. And if she were wrong it wouldn't matter in the end anyway. They would be discovered either way.

Raja stepped closer to the horse and held her hand up. Hannah looked around her from side to side. Raja steadied her hand. Then, after what seemed forever, Hannah finally bent down from her saddle and gave Raja a handout. At the same time, Raja placed the folded sketch into Hannah's hand. Relief swept over Raja as Hannah took the parchment that was folded up into small sections. Raja bowed and backed away. Hannah looked at Pavel. She made eye contact with him, but that was all. She then rode by.

The peasants filtered into their huts one by one, including Raja, Pavel, and Alma. The little girl was lying on a bed of moss. Raja assumed she had stayed in the hut all day. She felt sorry for the girl and wondered what she did in all that time. Alma likely had orders to keep the child in the hut. The young girl looked sad and despondent, but she had a sweet face with curly auburn hair.

"What's your name?" asked Raja.

"Lynadia."

"That's a pretty name."

The girl continued to lie on the bed of moss.

"How old are you?"

Lynadia shrugged.

"Do you have parents?" asked Raja.

The girl shook her head to say no.

"I don't know where she came from," said Alma, who had begun to make a fire. "She and the boy were already with the Tyhets when they abducted me."

Sitting down beside the girl, Raja inspected her own feet. They were very sore and had a few cuts. Pavel's feet seemed to have fared better. Then she picked up the handout. It was a dried piece of meat—granted, these people needed all the food they could get. It was kind of Hannah to do this, but Raja also believed there were other reasons why Hannah was involved with this activity. She always had ulterior motives.

Raja gave some of the meat to Lynadia, who took it very willingly.

"I gave Hannah the sketch."

"I saw you do that," said Alma.

Raja thought she had been more discrete than that. The peasants no doubt would report anything suspicious.

"Do you think that was the right decision?" asked Pavel.

"I thought about it all day and felt that's what I should do."

Pavel understood this part about Raja—going on instinct. "But how do we know what Hannah is going to do?"

"Trust," said Raja.

"Trust?"

"Yes, Hannah is very intelligent, I trust her to think of something."

"With no communication between the two of you?"

Raja nodded.

Alma, who had started making a meal, said, "Can you trust her?" She threw some food scrapes to her hen. "I saw her stare at you, cold as ice."

"I realize that, but that is Hannah. She is perfect at concealing her true self."

By the look on Alma's face, Raja knew she wasn't convinced. Raja pictured Hannah again on her white horse. It was true there wasn't a flinch of expression in her face to indicate that she was on their side. She certainly looked beautiful and the white castles she rode from were magnificent.

"Are the small white castles the stables?" asked Raja.

"Yes, they're called the White Stables," said Alma. "The prince puts a lot of pride in his horses and it's his objective to build up his herd. Hannah spends a lot of time at the stables and manages what goes on there. I tell you, she's on her father's side."

Alma gave Raja one of those looks, as if she was right and Raja was wrong. But Raja decided that, for now, she was still going to believe that Hannah was on their side. Ignoring the look, Raja turned her attention to the young girl. She would try and do some good while she was here and play with the child. She asked Lynadia to help her make an outline of the numerals one to five with tamarack needles. Then, as if playing a game, Raja asked Lynadia to match groups of tree needles with the right numeral. She was pleased with the way the girl caught on so quickly.

Alma continued to make the dinner from what very little they had for the four of them. Pavel willingly offered his help. Despite the meager variety of food and the small amount, the food tasted good, especially with the egg the hen provided. Raja was thankful.

Chapter 35

Bars of the Dungeon

Both Raja and Pavel were a bit stiff the next morning when they got up off the ground of Alma's hut. They were not used to such heavy labor. They ate breakfast as before and joined the lines of peasants at the sound of the bell. Raja cringed with every step she took on her cut bare feet. She would have to put her boots back on if she was going to continue working as a peasant.

Thoughts crossed her mind of possibly never getting out of this situation. What if she never escaped from Durlabh Valley? Perhaps she was wrong about Hannah and she really was on her father's side. She tried to force those thoughts away and kept on thinking they were here for a purpose and it would work out. She didn't know what Pavel was thinking but he didn't look all that happy. She wondered if he was having trouble with the same negative thoughts she sometimes had.

"It could be days here," said Pavel.

"Possibly," said Raja.

"I'll be thin and weak like the rest of them."

Raja was right. Pavel was not in good spirits. She tried to be positive. "The others are surviving and you'll survive."

"You don't know how many die here."

Raja knew that was true and they were taking an incredible risk to be here.

"Remember to trust," said Raja.

At the moment, Pavel was finding it difficult to do that.

"I'll see you at the end of the day," said Raja.

"All right."

The Princess of Kazan went off in the same direction as yesterday to work at shoveling sand with Alma, a very dusty and strenuous job. She continued to keep a look out for the peasant in the sketch. At one point she thought she saw Zolf and she hoped that if she was correct he hadn't notice her or Pavel. Or perhaps she had already met Zolf. She didn't exactly know.

Pavel joined the same group that he was in yesterday. With fortitude that he didn't know he possessed, he managed to work throughout the day. However, he had never been so thirsty and hungry in his life. He and Raja kept on looking for the peasant in the sketch but never saw him. It was hard to keep hoping that they would see him, especially knowing that he may be secluded from the other peasants.

During the day, Raja and Pavel noticed Hannah riding in and out of the peasants, most likely keeping an eye on everything that went on, but Hannah never came close enough for them to see her face. And in the evening when Hannah came out she always passed them by and didn't even look at them. Raja later said it was all part of Hannah's plan, although she admitted she did not have a clue what it was.

Doubts entered Pavel's mind of never escaping. His fears of the days lingering on and on were turning out to be true. The days turned into a week and then two weeks. He wondered how Jafar was doing in Gratias Cave. Thankfully, they had packed a lot of food supplies for the three of them so Jafar's food should have lasted until at least now. Pavel hoped this would somehow end soon. He and Raja had lost a lot of weight and he knew they looked deathly tired and he certainly felt it.

Pavel had moved on from being a mixer to towing one of the pallets of bricks. He wasn't sure how many pallets he had towed that day, with each one getting more difficult. It was on this last trip that he was expected to pull a huge load of bricks across the deep chasm of water. He couldn't seem to muster any more strength to do his share of the pulling. The pallet was harder to pull over the bridge and it was just being tugged on to the bridge when it happened.

"Pull!" shouted a warnorre. "Pull!"

Pavel heard the word but he could not respond to it. He felt he had no more strength to pull, try as hard as he might.

A sudden searing pain spread over his back. It weakened him even more.

"Pull!"

He turned to see the whip come down again. He felt faint. He was caught in a situation where there was no way out. Death, injury, ruin were all words that crashed into his mind. He fell to the ground, partly off the edge of the bridge. One little jar would push him off the edge. The warnorre lifted his whip again and was ready to strike. Surely, the next whip would cause him to plummet to his death.

Then, in that same moment, Pavel heard another shout. But, it was a female voice. "Halt! Don't lay another stroke on him!"

It was Hannah on her horse. Upon seeing what was going on, she had galloped over to the bridge.

"What's going on here?" asked Hannah.

"He's not doing his share of the work," said the warnorre.

"Pull him onto the bridge and take the ropes off him."

The warnorre did as Hannah asked.

"Throw him into the dungeon!"

Pavel couldn't believe what was going on. Wasn't Hannah on their side? Perhaps she really was on her father's side. Pavel couldn't even struggle and had no choice but to be dragged along by two warnorres. He was thrown into the dungeon of the middle White Stables.

Raja, who wasn't that far away, had seen what was going on.

"Alma, look! They're taking Pavel away!"

"I told you. Hannah can't be trusted anymore. Who knows what will happen to him now!"

Raja didn't want to believe that. There must be a reason for this.

"People who go in there never come out," said Alma.

Raja knew that and started doubting her situation again. They really would be here forever and would never get out. They would both die here. But then, a quiet thought entered her mind. "Trust."

At that moment, Hannah came galloping up behind her. She shouted to a warnorre who was close by.

"Take that girl and throw her into the dungeon!"

Raja whipped out her sword and challenged the warnorre who had suddenly approached her. The unexpected threat with her sword stunned the warnorre but he was still quick to defend himself. The two were immersed in a frantic battle. Hannah jumped from her horse and put her sword to the warnorre's back and shouted, "Halt! Drop your sword!"

The warnorre dropped his sword and Hannah resumed the sword fight with Raja. Confused and caught off guard by Hannah's actions, she was not at her best. Raja's strength had deteriorated from all the days of working in the valley and Hannah was much stronger than she was. In a few seconds Hannah had won the match and confiscated Raja's sword. Hannah ordered the warnorre to take her to the dungeon.

Handling her roughly, two warnorres grabbed her arms and forced her toward one of the White Stables. Half running and half walking, she stumbled along as the warnorres walked forward at a swift pace.

The bars of the dungeon cell opened and she was thrown in so hard that she fell. Pavel was in the same cell. He helped her sit up.

"Pavel, I'm so sorry."

"I'll live." And he really hoped he would.

"This must be all part of Hannah's plan," said Raja, who didn't want to be wrong about trusting her cousin and at the same time wanted to convince herself she was right.

"Are you sure?" asked Pavel.

Raja admitted that she could be wrong. She wasn't sure whether she believed it was part of Hannah's plan or not—perhaps it was only a plan to get rid of them. "I don't know what to think," she said.

Pavel winced as he spoke. His back was throbbing with pain, but he still wanted to have some sort of hope. "If we escaped the last dungeon, I'm sure we can escape this one."

"Okay, let's at least wait until it's dark to see what we can do," said Raja, who was now fully doubting that Hannah was in their favor.

Pavel agreed, as he couldn't move much anyway.

In the late afternoon, about an hour later, they heard footsteps coming down the corridor.

Raja's heart almost stopped. She feared what might happen next.

A Wsyrut warnorre forced a peasant up against the bars of the dungeon. Opening the barred door, he ordered the peasant to go inside the cell with Pavel and Raja.

The warnorre sneered at the peasant. "It doesn't matter that these two are here with you because they won't be alive for much longer anyway. Enjoy the company while it lasts."

The warnorre left the dungeon, his feet thudding loudly, and then there was silence.

Not alive for much longer? Raja wondered how Hannah could have turned this evil. She suddenly felt very anxious.

The peasant, however, didn't seem to be bothered by the threat or maybe he didn't have any energy left for emotions. Looking at him, he only appeared somewhat worn and not as thin as the other peasants. Raja wondered who he was. She leaned toward him and with compassion put a hand on his shoulder. She said, "It's going to be okay. We will all get out of here."

The statement must have done something for the peasant because he looked up and starred at her for some time.

Raja again said something. "When we get out we'll bring you with us."

The peasant still didn't speak.

Raja was a little taken back with the man's face, as she thought he looked like the man in the sketch, but then decided that would be too coincidental and dismissed the thought.

"What's your name?" asked Raja.

The peasant didn't answer but instead asked, "Who are you?"

Raja, not quite knowing what to say and wondering whether it really mattered at this point, answered the peasant. "I'm here because I'm looking for my father."

"Who's your father?"

"He is the tzar of Zurkia."

The expression on the peasant's face suddenly became distraught with emotion.

"I'm he," said the peasant.

Raja couldn't believe what she was hearing.

"Father?"

"Chamaris."

It really was her father. No one else would know that name.

"You sound like your mother and you look like her."

Raja put her hand to her mouth in disbelief.

"I see you are wearing your mother's ring."

"Yes, it's true," said Raja, in a barely audible voice.

The tzar reached over to touch it. "I have been thinking of you all of these years wondering what would become of you."

"I became the Princess of Kazan."

"So, you are back with mother?"

"Yes."

The tzar put his hand over his daughter's hand with the ring and started to cry. "What a beautiful gift for me to see you here. I don't understand how this could have possibly happened."

Raja leaned over to hug her father and she could not keep the tears from pouring out of her own eyes. She was sure the ring brought back a flood of memories for her father. Raja would give it back to her mother now that her husband was alive.

"I always thought you were dead, but here you are alive," said Raja.

"I am at a loss for words," said the tzar. "This is a miracle for me."

"And a dream come true for me," said Raja. "I finally have found my birth father."

"And I have my daughter. We will have so much to talk about."

Pavel sat in disbelief with the reality that he was sitting next to the lost peasant in the sketch and that he was no less Raja's father. But even though he appreciated the moment, he thought he would bring everyone back to the dire circumstances. "I hate to tell you this, but you will have nothing to talk about if we all stay in this cell. We will all most likely be dead by tomorrow."

The tzar leaned back. "And who is this?"

"Pavel Ramazon. He is the lord of Victory Manor, from which I came."

"Are you here by choice or force?" asked the tzar.

"By choice," said Pavel. "But I didn't think we would end up in the dungeon."

"We thought you were still alive and we came here to look for you," said Raja. "But now Hannah has thrown us into this dungeon."

"I see that," said the tzar. "Is she on our side or her father's side?"

Raja knew Hannah was good at concealing her true self, but Raja had lost faith in Hannah. "I thought she was on our side, but now I don't know."

At that moment two pairs of footsteps were heard coming from down the corridor. Both a heavy and light clunking of boots against the stone made its way into the ears of the victims. The three sat tense as they waited to see who approached.

In the next few moments, Hannah and her father stood in front of the cell bars. Despite the Dark Prince wearing a black hood that partially covered his face, Raja knew it was Hannah's father because of his slender face and deep-set eyes. Hannah herself looked very different. Her attire encompassed heavy adornments to accentuate her beauty. She had a ring on every finger, evenly spaced sparkling diamonds around the base of her raised hairstyle, and golden necklaces hanging around her neck.

"Good work, Hannah," said the Dark Prince.

"It was nothing, Father. Once I discovered they were here, I took action right away."

"I will end their interference. But it will have to wait until the morning."

"Understandably," said Hannah.

Raja looked back and forth between Hannah and her father, wondering how Hannah could have switched sides.

The Dark Prince looked at Raja with cold eyes. "I didn't think I would see you again so soon, but your timing is impeccable, for tonight I celebrate with wine. Say your farewells now, for they will be your last."

It was torture for Raja to think how her cousin had betrayed her. She didn't think it would ever happen, but her father had obviously influenced her to join his side.

"Hannah!" said Raja desperately. "Don't let your father do this. Don't you remember the words you spoke to me? We are friends forever!"

Hannah spoke with a stone face. "Yes, I remember. But this is now and not then. It will be as my father says." She banged down the scepter she was holding.

"Enough spoken!" said the Dark Prince. The two of them turned and walked out of the dungeon, leaving the three captives in a state of fear.

Raja could feel her legs trembling. Slumped on the floor, she put her face in her hands and began to cry. "This can't be! How could she do that?"

"Easily," said Pavel. "He's her father."

"But, but I thought she would never . . ."

"Switch sides?" asked Pavel. "I guess you were wrong."

"How are we ever going to get out of this mess? We could be dead by tomorrow morning."

"I know that and I have no idea of what to do," said Pavel.

Raja and Pavel looked at the tzar.

"Father?" asked Raja expecting that he have a solution.

He gave no answer, except to bow his head and close his eyes, probably for the one-thousandth time.

Chapter 36

Fading Footsteps

Footsteps woke Raja from her very light sleep.

Within moments, there stood Hannah at the dungeon cell. She was dressed in a flamboyant dress that tapered at the waist and spread out at the hips.

Raja leaped up and hung onto the bars, her face etched with desperation.

"Hannah, whose side are you on? Why have you thrown us in this dungeon?"

Hannah's white face was emotionless.

Raja screamed at Hannah, wanting to get through to her. "I thought we were friends forever!"

Hannah's face was a mask. She starred at Raja without a flinch of expression. Everyone was quiet. Her eyes suddenly became shiny and a tear silently rolled down her cheek. It broke her emotionless, placid look as more tears drained from her eyes.

"I'm sorry," said Hannah. "I didn't want you to go through all of this pain."

Raja tried not to look at all of Hannah's adornments. She wanted to see the real person beneath her jewelry and makeup. "Whose side are you on!" she yelled.

Hannah's eyes of steel turned soft. "How could you think I would betray you?"

Raja broke down in tears gripping the bars until her knuckles turned white. Her lips trembled as she screamed out her words. "I thought we were doomed to die!"

"Forgive me. There was no other way," said Hannah. Her eyes glimmered with sorrow.

"It was hard to trust you!" said Raja. "Pavel nearly died!"

"I can understand how you feel, but now you need to trust me more than ever to rescue yourselves and your father."

Raja wished she could pull the cell bars apart. "In a dungeon! I can't!"

Pavel got up and stood beside Raja. He put an arm around her shoulders. She covered her distressed face with her hands.

Hannah began speaking to Pavel, who was much calmer than Raja. "My father thinks I'm on his side again."

"You had me fooled," said Pavel.

"Throwing you in the dungeon was the only way I could get all three of you together," said Hannah, who looked compassionately at Raja and then at her father, who was still sitting against the wall.

Despite the tzar being tired, a look of new understanding came over on his face.

Raja turned and looked at her father. His intelligent eyes spoke to her. Her soul quieted and she nervously reached out and touched Hannah. "I'm sorry for yelling. Thank you for helping us."

"I will always be there for you," said Hannah with great sincerity.

Tears swelled in Raja's eyes again.

"It's going to work out," said Hannah. She handed Raja some food. "Here, take this. All of you will need the energy."

"Thank you," said Raja, who took the food through the bars, which made her feel all the more dependent on Hannah.

Pavel looked at Hannah and spoke with curiosity. "Did the sketch help?"

"Yes, otherwise I may not have known precisely why you and Raja were here. I had no idea that you knew your father was here until I saw the sketch."

At this point Raja's father got up and walked to the bars. "You had a sketch of me?"

"Yes, Raja gave it to me," said Hannah.

The tzar looked at Raja. "So, you found it in Antom's trunk?"

"Yes," she answered. "And we found your secret message, which is what helped us figure out that you were probably in Norx Village."

The tzar put his fingers to his eyes. "In all of these years, I always stayed hopeful that the sketch would do its work."

Raja knelt beside her father. "Providence - especially knowing that the trunk always stayed in the village."

Looking at Hannah, Raja asked, "When you got the sketch did you know he was my father?"

"I did, but I never knew about the tzar's captivity prior to coming to Norx Castle. My father wanted to keep him alive, but he wouldn't tell me why."

"Why didn't you help him to escape before this?" asked Raja.

Hannah's expression softened. "I couldn't have. Your father would never have made it. He was too weak. Ever since I've been here, I saw to it that he got extra food and more rest. Now is the right time for him to escape."

"Thank you for your kindness," said the tzar. He got up and walked across the floor. Putting his arm through the bars, he touched Hannah's hand.

Hannah bowed her head and put her own hand over his.

"You had me fooled, but not completely. You were too kind to me," said the tzar.

"You are perceptive," said Hannah.

The tzar took back his hand and let his years of captivity drain from his spirit. His shoulders shook as he wept uncontrollably. Raja went to her father and wrapped her arms around him. She spoke softly to him. "It's over now."

Gaining back his control, the tzar spoke quietly but loud enough that everyone could hear. "What was only known in part will be fully revealed."

Raja could feel her spirit of fear being replaced with faith and strength. She looked into Hannah's face with new determination. "Please, get us out of here quickly. There is more work to accomplish."

"You must listen carefully," said Hannah, "and make no mistakes." She looked down the corridor to make sure no one was coming and then pulled out something from her waistband. "This is the key for the cell padlock. Hide it on yourself."

Raja took the key and put it inside her cloak.

"My father and his warnorres will be having a feast tonight. Then later he will be walking along the Vulcan Path to the abyss. He makes appeasements to the spirit almost every night on account of the orb."

"The orb?" asked Raja.

"Yes, he thinks an orb is in the abyss."

"That sounds strange."

"I know. He goes down the side of the mountain on the Bell Path to check the sea level in Duo Cave."

"Why does he do that?"

"I don't have time to explain it to you. I must go." Hannah held out eight fingers, which meant the end of the twenty-fourth hour. "Escape at midnight."

"How will we know it is midnight?" asked Pavel.

"A wolf cry," said Hannah.

Pavel remembered when he had taught the wolf cry to Hannah.

"There will be horses waiting for you in the first of the White Stables, closest to the castle. The horses are black. As soon as you get out of the dungeon, cross over the moat and turn to the right. The horses will be in a stall next to the entrance. They are strong and ready to ride."

Pavel nodded at Hannah's instructions as she continued with a serious face. "Can you take the girl?"

"Yes," said Raja. "The girl can ride with Pavel."

"Good," said Hannah. "Ride straight to Alma's hut. After you take the girl from the hut, ride across the valley towards the bay. It's called the Hid Bay. You will see the Nar Path that will take you to the shores of the Volga River." Hannah wanted to make sure the tzar was strong enough to make the escape. "My tzar, do you feel confident riding or do you want to double?"

"I can ride," said the tzar with a look of determination.

"All right," said Hannah. "There is a full moon tonight so you will be able to see well enough to ride."

"An appropriate night," said the tzar. "A true gift."

Raja couldn't help but ask the next question, although she had a sinking feeling about the answer. "Are you coming with us?"

Hannah shook her head. "No, I need to stay here. Stopping my father from all he is doing will depend on me." Hannah starred into Raja's face catching her full attention. "I saw you on the mountain when you first came."

Raja looked surprised. "You did?"

"My room in the highest point of the castle and it was I that distracted everyone's attention, to keep them from noticing you. I knew you would see me on my white horse."

Pavel and Raja were humbled. "Thank you," they both said. They could see how they were spoon fed right into Hannah's plans.

Raja's cousin continued. "Nothing will change if I leave, but no one else must ever know of my intentions."

Raja knew that Hannah was right, even though she missed her desperately. Her work was dangerous and she was a heroine to continue. Raja spoke some words of encouragement. "You are brave, Hannah, and together with the help of others, we will put an end to this."

Hannah's face became serious again and she nodded. She said a few more words and then left with the train of her garment flowing behind her. Her clunking footsteps soon faded into silence.

Raja wished Hannah had let them go right now. It was agony to wait. Riding out with her father to escape this horrible valley was still only a dream wanting to come true. There were warnorres around the valley and things would have to go just right before they actually made it out of this place. But her one consolation was that now she trusted Hannah again. It gave her a new confidence. Raja thought her cousin was very cunning and intelligent indeed.

Chapter 37

Grace

Raja was thankful for the bit of food that Hannah had brought for everyone. She passed out some of the dried meat to her father and Pavel. Raja was so hungry that she couldn't eat her meat fast enough. She started a conversation between mouthfuls of food.

"Did you ever think . . ." Raja took a few more bites of the meat and continued, ". . . that you would be sitting with me in a dungeon?"

The tzar tilted his head back and smiled.

"Certainly not," said her father. "Not what I expected at all."

Raja tore a piece of dried meat with her teeth. "I agree . . ." She tore off another piece. "It's not the most pleasant way for a reunion."

The three of them managed a little chuckle over the ordeal with Raja nearly choking on her food. She put her hand to her mouth and chewed more thoroughly.

"You are very brave to have done this," said the tzar.

"Thank you, it is the least I can do. You are my father." Raja stuck the last bit of meat in her mouth and chewed until she swallowed it. Finally, she spoke again, wanting to justify something in her mind. "Did you know that little girl was me in Antom's hut?"

"Yes."

"But why didn't you do anything about it?" asked Raja.

"Please understand. If you would have been discovered the Tyhets would have killed Antom."

"No doubt," said Pavel.

Raja nodded, understanding Antom's plight.

"I was hoping the parchments in the trunk would be discovered and lead to my rescue. Then I surely would have come for you."

"Yes, I'm sure of it, Father."

"But now you, my daughter, have rescued me."

"If all goes well," said Pavel, who still feeling the pain in his back.

Raja sympathized with Pavel, but wanted to speak again to her father. "I understand your desire of wanting to work things out in the safest manner."

"Thank you for saying that and not taking on any resentment," said the tzar.

Nodding in response, Raja gave her father a loving, reassuring look.

"Where did you move to after you were in Thrumb Village?" asked the tzar.

"Victory Manor, owned by Viktor Ramazon."

"I see," said the tzar. "How did Pavel find out you were a princess?"

"He rescued me from having to marry at a very early age."

The tzar addressed Pavel. "Did you know Raja was of royal blood?"

"No, but I thought there was something special about her."

"You did, did you?" said Raja with a smile.

"Well, not that special."

"I don't believe you," said Raja.

"Okay, well maybe a little special," said Pavel.

"Even in rags?" asked Raja.

"Even in rags," said Pavel with a sincere look. "It's the inside of a person that counts."

Raja tilted her head with a little smile, pleased with Pavel's answer. Thinking the conversation was amusing, the tzar laughed. Raja turned her attention to her father again. She was amazed he could laugh. "How did you survive all these years? It must have been extremely difficult."

"Very. I've seen a lot of cruelty."

"But for what?" asked Raja, whose feelings turned to anger.

"Control, fear, greed . . . all sorts of reasons. The Dark Prince believes acquiring wealth by having a large castle will give him power to rule Zurkia."

"What does the Dark Prince want with you?"

"I don't know exactly. It has something to do with his childhood."

"That goes back a long way."

The tzar thought for a moment. "Yes, but I know someone who might be able to shed some light on this mystery."

"Who?"

"Your Aunt Vermisha Flutturwing."

"I didn't know I had an Aunt Vermisha."

"She lives in Valetta Castle in the Trumia region of Zurkia. Her castle is right along the Volga River. After her own aunt passed away she took over that castle."

Raja recalled the secret message that her father had written. "Who is Hagatha?"

"She lives in Marsh Castle, but she used to rule with members of her family in Bolger Castle. I believe she has strong connections with the Dark Prince."

"I see," said Raja. "I'd like to visit Vermisha in Valetta Castle. Perhaps she knows about Hagatha."

"If we get out of here," said Pavel, who felt anxious about the escape.

"We will," said Raja.

"How did you survive this place?" asked Pavel, looking at the tzar with a puzzled expression.

"I prayed."

The lord looked at the tzar wanting more out of his answer. After all, he was captive for twelve years in what seemed unbearable circumstances.

"It strengthened my mind."

"Truly, you must have a strong mind."

The tzar leaned towards Pavel. "The mind is very powerful. It can either destroy you or save you."

Pavel was in awe at how the tzar survived considering he'd been in captivity for close to twelve years. He could barely imagine it.

"I learned how to control my negative thoughts and fears," said the tzar.

Pavel thought back to that very day in the Valley of Durlabh and how he had done the opposite and gave in to fear. He was sure Raja must have been guilty of that as well.

The tzar continued. "It's not that I didn't ever have fear, but it's whether or not I let it control me. I knew fear would kill me so I constantly replaced my negative thoughts with the hope of one day escaping."

"It must have been a tough battle," said Raja.

"It was, but in this last while I was given grace in the form of Hannah. Even though she did not let on any of her motives, I felt grateful towards her for the extra food she gave for me."

Raja was thankful. She remembered how devastated she felt when Hannah was forced to go back to her father, but now she could see how it was used for good.

The tzar continued. "I thought Hannah was on her father's side, but on the other hand she was so kind to me. It was hard to believe."

"Your intuition was right," said Raja. "Now she is helping you escape."

"And she was wise to not have allowed it to happen before this," said the tzar.

"True," said Raja. "I can understand how she needed to first build trust with her father."

"Yes, and besides that I wasn't physically strong enough before she started to care for me." The tzar waited a few moments before he spoke again. "Her patience has made this work."

"Not quite yet," said Pavel. "We still need to escape."

Just then they heard the cry of a wolf.

"I think it's time to get out of here," said Pavel as he looked at the tzar.

The tzar agreed. "Who's got the key?" he asked.

Raja shrugged her shoulders.

"I don't have it," said Pavel.

They looked at the tzar.

"Don't look at me. No one gave it to me."

"Don't you have it?" asked Raja.

"No, I don't," said Pavel. "I think you do."

"As a matter of fact, I do," said Raja, with a little smile.

"Do you think you are funny?" asked Pavel.

"Quite."

"I was beginning to sweat," said Pavel.

"Just keeping you on your toes."

"Okay, I appreciate that but we need to get serious," said Pavel.

"Okay," said Raja and got out the key.

Chapter 38

What Hannah Had Said

Raja put the key in the iron padlock that hung from the bars of the Norx Castle dungeon. She turned it but the pad did not unlock. In exasperation she tried again, but to no avail. Then, she accidentally dropped it outside of the cell.

"Now look what you've done," said Pavel.

"Sorry," said Raja. "I think I can get it."

Fortunately, her arms were small enough to fit through the bars, but the key was just out of reach.

"Now what?" asked the tzar.

"I know just what to do," said Raja.

Retrieving her doll from under her cloak, she held on to it as she put her arm through the bars. She was then able to swish the key towards her.

"Brilliant," said the tzar.

She carefully got the key and brought her arm back through the bars.

"The gift I gave you is certainly proving to be useful for getting out of dungeons," said Pavel.

The comment put a smile on Raja's face.

"Now put it in the lock and wiggle it a few times," said Pavel.

Raja followed that advice and the lock opened.

Relieved, Raja said, "Thank goodness."

The tzar breathed a sigh of relief.

"Come on. Let's get out of here," said Pavel.

The three captives walked down the narrow corridor and up steps that zigzagged back and forth. Having no door at the entrance, Pavel looked around to the sides of the building. He didn't see anyone. He motioned for Raja and the tzar to follow him and led the way to the first of the White Stables. Without difficulty the three of them entered the stable. The black horses were waiting for them as Hannah had indicated.

The three mounted the beautiful horses. The second the tzar was on his horse he was in full control. To him it seemed like only yesterday that he had ridden. The three riders left at a gallop, heading towards Alma's hut.

Safely making it to their destination, Pavel jumped off his horse and ran into the hut. Alma was not in the hut, but he found the girl sleeping on the moss. He wondered where Alma was, but right now had no time to think about it. Pavel immediately woke up the girl, who seemed to be expecting him, because without hesitation, she got up and handed Pavel a sword. Surprised, Pavel saw that it was Raja's double-edged sword. He took the sword and put it next to his own.

Pavel quickly led the girl outside the hut and then gave Raja her weapon. Raja caught Pavel's attention with her sword against his shoulder. She wanted him to believe as she did and spoke with conviction. "A lost gift found is a prophesy for strength." He affirmed her belief with his reassuring eyes.

Pavel then hoisted the girl on the horse, telling her to hang on to the horse's mane. Pavel put his foot in the stirrup and swung his leg over the back of his horse. Holding the girl with one hand and the reigns with the other, he shouted to Raja to lead the group.

The three horses took off galloping across the Valley of Durlabh toward Hid Bay. Then, coming from the White Stables, Pavel saw two warnorres galloping on horses toward them. Closing in on them fast, Pavel had a feeling of dread. He wished they could go faster, but he was unable to while hanging on to the young girl. Perhaps they weren't going to escape after all.

The warnorres were closing in on them quickly. Pavel was sure they were going to be captured. Beads of sweat formed on his forehead. At that instant, he felt their escape had failed.

Then, out of the trees and almost directly in front of Pavel, a rider on a white horse appeared with a torch. It was Hannah. She cut in front of the warnorres and held up the torch.

The pursuing warnorres stopped with a cloud of dust surrounding them. Hannah shouted something to the warnorres, which put an end to the chase. What Hannah said was unknown to Pavel, Raja, and the tzar at that moment, but whatever it had been, it was enough to turn the warnorres away.

The three adults with the young girl continued galloping to the Nar Path headed toward the Volga. Raja was so glad to be getting away from the nightmarish village. She felt triumphant that she was leaving with what she'd come for—her father and the little girl. But she also felt pangs of guilt leaving the slaves behind. But perhaps it wasn't their time to be free from the tyranny. It was still in the future. She could live with that last thought for now.

Riding along the Shora Trail, the riders finally slowed their horses to a trot and then a walk. Pavel found Jafar waiting in Gratias Cave. The first thing Jafar asked Pavel was why he had taken so long. Pavel said it was a long story and told Jafar not to complain because he had gotten the easy job. Quick introductions were made with the tzar, and the group continued their escape with the four adults and the child, each riding their own horse.

The hours passed into days and Raja wondered what Hannah had said to prevent any of the warnorres from following them. And what was more, she wondered what Hannah would say to her father with the fact that the tzar was missing. Raja hoped to hear the story from Hannah soon. Raja knew she would think of something that would convince her father that his daughter had nothing to do with the escape. She would find a way. Raja thought her cousin was definitely extraordinary. She hoped it wouldn't be long before she could see Hannah again.

Chapter 39

New Plans

The group was just reaching the beginning of the Ardua Trail. With only a few rocks sliding down the steep incline, they safely made it to the top and it wouldn't be long before they would be riding on the Iris Trail, which would lead them right to Levap Castle estate. Raja began telling her father about the castle.

"Just to warn you father, there are pirates in the castle," said Raja.

"What! Pirates!"

"It's not what you might think. They have become our friends."

"I can't believe you have pirates staying in the castle."

"They're good pirates," said Raja.

"She's right," said Pavel. "Cham is the captain and she helped to rescue Raja. She fought in the *Battle of Orsus* to win back the Zurkian throne."

"I see," said the tzar. "That changes things. I'll look forward to meeting her then."

"And I'm sure you'll enjoy the experience," said Raja as she went on to explain about Cham's pet crow. The tzar found Cham's attraction to the crow peculiar but interesting.

They were finally approaching the Levap Castle estate. And as Raja had explained, Cade circled the air above them, indicating that Cham knew a party was close by. Raja held out her two-prong twig for the crow and it took the twig, flying off to the castle.

As the group reached Pavel's estate they were taken up in the basket and all of the appropriate introductions were made. The pirates decided to have their traditional way of celebration and made a huge bonfire. There was lots of food, grog, dancing, clapping, and singing. Raja was right, the tzar was well entertained long into the night. He hadn't had so much fun in a long, long time.

The Princess of Kazan also had a wonderful time taking care of Lynadia. She thought up more counting games to teach the little girl, who eagerly played all of them. Raja even let her hold her double-edged sword. True, Raja had lost the match with Hannah, but for a good reason. It was all a part of the plan in rescuing her father. Raja would make sure to have another match with Hannah just to satisfy herself that she was still Hannah's equal. She smiled to herself at Hannah's intelligent ways.

"I have something for you," said Lynadia. "The rider on the white horse told me to give it to you."

"What is it?"

Lynadia took out a piece of paper that had been folded inside the sash that went around Lynadia's dress. She handed it to Raja.

The princess slowly unfolded the paper. It was the sketch of her father. Tears filled Raja's eyes at the thoughtfulness of Hannah. The paper was crumpled and filled with creases, but it somehow added to its charm. It was certainly an unforgettable gift that she would always cherish.

"Thank you," said Raja. "I'm so glad that you remembered to give it to me."

"You're welcome. Thank you for rescuing me."

"My princess duty. I know you will love your new home."

Lynadia smiled with sparkly eyes.

Raja decided that when the time came to go to Kazan, they would first stop in at Viktor Estate. Raja would insist that Lynadia stay in the manor to be cared for. She had a feeling Maya would be delighted with the idea.

During the evening, Cham came over to make conversation with the tzar.

The tzar had no trouble finding something to say. "I think we should put a door on Levap Castle."

"Why? Don't you like goin' up in a basket?" asked Cham.

"It's not my taste. I'm afraid of heights," said the tzar, trying to be funny.

"I understand," said Cham with a chuckle. "I don't like going up in the ship's crow's nest either."

"Do you expect me to believe that?"

"No, but I don't believe you either," said Cham.

"Okay, it was not the truth, but I still want a door."

"I understand. Anything for the tzar."

"Good, I think we should make new plans for the castle as well."

"What would that be?" asked Cham with interest.

"I'd like you and your crew to build a better defense system for this castle. I'll help you with the architecture. It's my forte."

Cham was elated with the offer. "At yer command, Tzar."

Continuing the conversation, the tzar commented on some information that Raja had given him. "Apparently Daxen is coming back to Zurkia with a ship load of escorts. I'm thinking they could help with the construction."

"The more the merrier," said Cham.

Cham thought this would be a good time to mention the secret passages. "Pavel asked me t' change the secret passages so we've been workin' at that."

"Good. I'd like to see the new plans later."

"Aye, me be delighted. Care for some more food?"

"No, I couldn't eat another mouthful," said the tzar, who would have to get used to eating normal portions of food again. "But thank you for your generous hospitality."

"You are welcome."

"It sure feels good to be free," said the tzar.

"I know what yer sayin," said Cham. "I used t' be a slave in me own way."

"So I heard."

"But I guess I can say yer daughter rescued me as well."

The tzar agreed. They were both rescued but in different ways. It was something the tzar thought they had in common. And they were both very thankful to Raja.

The two continued to chat as the evening wore on and eventually everyone retired just before sunrise.

Chapter 40

Roboris Alas

Word had been sent to the tzarina that her husband had been rescued and that he was recovering quickly. She, of course, was overjoyed and the next day hastened to organize a huge celebration for his eventual return. After receiving the letter, she immediately wrote back saying how thankful and grateful she was and that it would be difficult for her to wait until the occasion of seeing her husband.

The tzarina continued to say that Daxen and his escorts had arrived from Dracon. However, Daxen and Shamra decided not to stay in Kazan and had returned to Dracon with Chloe. Before Daxen's departure, the tzarina had taken the time to present him with the Order of Acumen for showing exceptional ingenuity for helping to devise a plan that played a part in rescuing the tzar. He was presented with a shield bearing a symbol of a lion, representing strength and leadership.

In due time, the party from Levap Castle arrived at Kazan Castle and the reunion of the tzarina and tzar was made in hugs and tears of joy. The tzar told his wife that she looked as beautiful as ever and she returned the compliment saying that he looked as handsome as ever. Her compliment wasn't quite true, but it didn't matter to her. Underneath his worn face he still had that good-looking charm and he was her gallant prince.

Raja, Pavel, and Jafar were also recognized at the celebration for their bravery in rescuing the tzar. Pavel received the order of the Shield of Royalty given to young men who are not yet knights but showed bravery in protecting and rescuing a royal. The shield given to him had a symbol of an archangel, signifying the tzarina's desire for Pavel's emotional healing of the turmoil he felt during the last two years. Raja received the Royal Order of Crown, which was awarded to royals for protecting the tzarina or tzar. A golden crown was given to her with seventeen red ruby jewels for blessings upon her life. And Jafar received a shield with a symbol of an eagle, representing renewed life in Zurkia. At the same time he was given the Order of Valor for bravery in helping to discover where the tzar had been held captive.

New shields were also presented to both Viktor and Raja. Viktor was awarded with symbols of horses and swords on a red and white background. The tzarina commented on his swiftness of action and intelligent decisions. Raja was given a new shield trimmed in gold with three symbols, which were a crown representing victory, a cross representing hope and grace, and two arrows representing protection.

After the formalities of the presentation of orders and awards, people were given the opportunity to relax and eat small sweets that were being passed around. Raja looked over the many guests at the celebration and spotted the twins who were sitting amongst the escorts that had arrived from Dracon. Beforehand, Raja had spoken to her father regarding his secret message about the twins and it was confirmed that they indeed were the girls of his half-sister-in-law.

Raja summoned Bettalia. "Do you see the twins sitting over there?" she asked.

"Yes," said Bettalia.

"Tell them to come to me."

"Certainly, my princess."

The twins, being a bit surprised, came over to Raja. "We are at your service, Princess Raja," they said as they curtsied with bowed heads.

"I need to find out something about you twins," said Raja matter-of-factly.

The twins were inquisitive, but perplexed. They looked at Raja with a worried expression. "What is it? Have we done something wrong?"

"You haven't done anything wrong. I just want to inform you about something. It will only take a minute."

The twins agreed.

"Come up to my chamber," said Raja.

Following the Princess of Kazan, the twins started asking her all sorts of questions about her father. Raja tried to explain things in the best way that she could and said she would say more once they were seated in her chamber.

Finally, in Raja's chamber, the twins sat down and Raja stood in front of them ready to tell them the truth. "Your eyes are a blessing."

"What do you mean by that?" asked Isa.

"It means that because of your eyes, my father was able to identify you and we now know what happened to you as children. I know that this will be hard for you to hear, but your mother sold you as children because of you being twins and because of your eyes. Your mother's name is Harlyn Monique."

"But how is that a blessing?"

"Because now we know that your mother is my mother's half-sister."

The twins put their hands to their mouths. "Do you mean we are . . ." They couldn't finish their sentence.

Raja saw the girls were catching on. "Yes, that means you are of royal blood!"

The twins gasped. "Really!"

"Yes, you are my cousins. And your last name is Monique."

The twins looked at each other, wondering what this would all entail. "So does this mean we can marry royalty?" they asked at the same time.

"Yes, it does," said Raja.

"Perhaps Daxen?" asked Quinn, fluttering her eyelashes.

"No, I'll marry Daxen," said Isa, showing a pouty lip.

"No, I will," said Quinn, standing and putting her hands on her hips.

"No, I will," said Isa, pointing a finger at herself.

Raja looked between the two girls and smiled. "We'll see. Whoever you will marry, I'm sure you will be very happy."

Satisfied with that conclusion the two girls gave each other a hug.

"And one more thing, the tzarina wants you girls to go to Levap Castle. She says it would be good if the two of you could teach Cham some lady-like manners."

The girls accepted and discussed with Raja the future date for the move. The twins giggled and talked and couldn't stop bouncing around over the new plans. Raja thought they were amusing to watch, but in addition, they were such kind, considerate girls and pretty, too, with their eyes and freckles. Raja was sure they were the center of attention with their bubbly personalities and sometimes silliness.

In the days ahead, the tzar sat on his throne again next to the tzarina in Kazan Castle. The two made a perfect couple as they planned and worked together. They were a couple for everyone to take note of, displaying respect, consideration, and kindness to each other. The two of them completed the coat of arms for Zurkia, bearing two majestic eagles, an archangel, a crown, and the Zurkian flag in the center. The motto was inscribed as *Roboris Alas* meaning "wings of strength." It was placed on a large round shield and hung above the thrones.

Raja was very impressed with the royal arms. Before going back to the manor, she stayed for a good length of time at Kazan Castle to be with her father and mother. On different occasions she sat in a third throne chair and discussed important matters of the country, rulership, and the roles she and her parents had as royals.

Raja also had a chance to talk with Kuzma, refreshing some of the good memories from the past. He still thought about the dream he'd once had about the glowing spherical shape. Remembering the request of the monk, Kuzma wondered if he should still make the trip to the Montia region of Zurkia. He had been to Demarcus before as a merchant and thought being welcomed there would not be a problem. Perhaps he would do that sometime in the future, but for now, he would stay in Kazan for a while and continue to be a support for the tzar.

Eventually, the time would come for Raja to journey back to Victory Manor with Pavel, Jafar, and Kuzma. Everyone there would be happy to see Raja and hear the good news about her father. But for now, she would continue in joyous celebration in Kazan. It seemed the country could only become stronger with the new zeal of the tzar and tzarina.

Raja and Pavel sat side by side on the edge of the cliff by Kazan Castle that over looked the Volga River.

"Do you ever think of Hannah?" asked Pavel.

"Yes, quite often," said Raja.

"What do you think will become of her?"

"I am determined to free her."

"What about the slaves of the north?"

"I will fight to bring justice for all people."

Looking at the river, Pavel contemplated her statement and then said firmly, "And I am determined to help you."

Raja smiled. "Together, we can free Hannah and the slaves."

The two friends felt comfortable in each other's presence and continued talking for another short while.

Then Raja got that little twinkle in her eye.

"Race you to the castle!" she said.

"As you wish!"

The two of them ran up the path that led up to the castle. A white feather floating in the air stole Raja's attention. It floated right above her head and she caught it between her fingers. "A white-tailed eagle feather!"

Examining the feather together, they both ran their fingers along the soft curvature of the barb. “A gift from heaven,” she said, “and to be cherished.”

“Yes,” said Pavel. “The seemingly small things in life are often the most treasured.”

Raja looked above her just in time to see the magnificent spread of an eagle fold its wings and land on top of a nearby tree. “And surely a sign of strength.”

That’s exactly what Pavel liked about this princess. A measure of greatness was always seen in the small gifts of life. It’s what kept her spirits high.

Printed in Canada